YAD

# YAD[1]

Daniel Paweł Karpiński

Translated by Max Karpinski

---

1   The title refers to the Hebrew word "yad," which means "hand," and to a ritual
    pointer used to trace the words of the Torah.
    In Polish "jad" also means "venom."

 FriesenPress

Suite 300 - 990 Fort St
Victoria, BC, V8V 3K2
Canada

www.friesenpress.com

ISBN
978-1-5255-2368-7 (Hardcover)
978-1-5255-2369-4 (Paperback)
978-1-5255-2370-0 (eBook)

*1. FICTION*

Distributed to the trade by The Ingram Book Company

# *PROLOGUE*

‖‖‖‖‖‖‖‖‖‖‖‖‖‖‖‖‖‖‖‖‖‖‖‖‖‖‖‖‖‖‖‖‖‖‖‖‖‖‖‖‖‖‖‖‖‖‖‖‖‖‖‖‖‖‖‖‖‖‖‖‖‖‖‖‖‖‖‖‖‖‖‖‖‖‖‖‖‖‖‖‖‖‖‖‖‖‖‖‖‖‖‖‖‖‖‖‖‖

IN THE CITY WHERE WE LAY OUR SCENE, THE STREETS ARE NARROW and steep.[2] It is easy to stumble going down, and tiresome walking uphill. In the city where the plot unfolds, the houses are tall and thin. Pressed into tight rows forming ducts, they create chasms reachable by the noon sun when it shines almost vertically. The houses along the street are stacked in several levels, one above the other, connected by stairs like the rays of the sun at its zenith.

Every street is like fate, every house like faith. But this is a city, not a metaphor.

In the spring, when hot days bring the bullfighting season, canopies are hung between houses. White canvas sheets, rinsed by rain, dried by heat, like clouds drifting at the height of the top floors, they repeat the shape of the street to the birds.

Is that all?

---

2    Whose words are these and who spoke them? This is only an echo of the words
that in the original sounded like that:
"Two households, both alike in dignity,
In fair Verona, where we lay our scene,
From ancient grudge break to new mutiny,
Where civil blood makes civil hand unclean"
William Shakespeare, *Romeo and Juliet*.

In the evening, under the soaring canopies, lanterns are lit at dusk, turning the streets into tunnels of light, piercing the darkness. They are put out at bedtime. When the lights fade the canopies fill with the breath of the night breeze, sailing in search of the Golden Fleece or to Ithaca. In the night , late passersby with lights floating before them, look like deep sea fish mistaking the sails above for the Milky Way. Who will ever measure its length, or shake its stardust from their feet?

Is that it?

If you look up, you can read the prints of cat paws and bird feathers, you can see a skinny cat that lives on love and barley.[3]

Oh!

Straight from the open window jumps a barely clothed youth! A flight of triumph? Young like Icarus, but skillful like Daedalus, he balances a moment on the catwalk trampoline, then rushes in the direction of the cathedral. Barefoot, he leaps as though in seven-league boots. His every step is ascension, the moon kissing his sweaty breast through an open shirt. He rises like a balloon of the Montgolfier brothers, like the first plane of the Wright brothers. Flying is a brotherly thing. Jumping too. And further and further, like a cricket, like a grasshopper, like locusts…

Locusts? I should not have used that word. Suddenly, behind his jumping back another figure appears. He runs like an Andalusian dog, fully clothed, heavy boots, an overcoat. What's this? A sword of Toledo steel, cold and sharp like the moonlight. Stretched out just behind the youth's back:

"Turn around! You coward! You took my—"

A thrust! The sword pierces the back of the shirt and emerges in front. Blood from the youth's back repeated on his chest. Two stains.

The pursued does not fall. As if he does not notice the strike and the blood, he jumps ahead, leaping over the sagging sheets. Across the Milky Way he traces a new constellation composed only of red stars.

---

3    From a haiku by Matsuo Basho.

The pursuer, after delivering the blow, catches his foot in a seam. There is the sound of cloth ripping, the sheets tear in two throwing the offender into the abyss opened beneath his feet. He grabs an edge with one hand, grips his sword like a treasure with the other. The material slips from his grasp and he tumbles onto the lamp below, onto the rope, which he clutches, this time with both hands. The rope rips off from the wall flying like a pendulum. He slams into the opposing wall, then he falls limp into the street next to his humming sword.

Silence.

No one awoke, no one saw his fall. The sail above the street swayed to the rhythm of snores. The sky cried a lonely star that leaked into the grave[4]. An auburn shadow crawled from the alley, picked up the blade, which flashed in the darkness, and fled towards the Jewish quarter. And then another shadow and another… The second grabbed the purse and the jewels, and the third looked in the robbed man's face and began to howl:

"Help!!!"

---

4    Cyprian Norwid, "W Weronie": "In Verona" (trans. Max Karpinski)

I

Above the houses of Capulet and Montague,
Rinsed by rain, moved by thunder,
The gentle eye of the blue sky

II

It looks on the rubble of hostile castles
On broken garden gates
And drops a star from on high

III

The cypresses whisper, it is for Juliet,
For Romeo, that otherworldly tear
Falls…and leaks into the grave

IV

But people say, and say it knowingly
These are not tears, but stones
And nobody…waits for them!

On the ground, without feeling, lay Don Miguel de Juaclac, the public prosecutor of Toledo. Of the jumping youth, not a trace remained, if you don't count the red stars on the canvas sky.

Who he was and whose blood it is, nobody will know. Nobody except You and me. Only we know this leaping youth was named Narciso Tomé. This is his story. Keep it for yourself as a warning. I don't have anything to do with it. I'm just telling it.

I am this story.

Narciso is me.

# SUNSET

(Act I)

# Noche oscura del alma
## *San Juan de la Cruz (Juan de Yepes y Álvarez)*

En una noche oscura
con ansias en amores inflamada,
¡oh dichosa ventura!
salí sin ser notada,
estando ya mi casa sosegada.

A escuras, y segura,
por la secreta escala disfrazada,
¡oh dichosa ventura!
a escuras, y en celada,
estando ya mi casa sosegada.

En la noche dichosa
en secreto, que nadie me veía
ni yo miraba cosa,
sin otra luz y guía,
sino la que en el corazón ardía.

Aquesta me guiaba
más cierto que la luz del mediodía,
a donde me esperaba,
quien yo bien me sabía,
en parte donde nadie parecía.

¡Oh noche, que guiaste!
¡Oh noche amable más que el alborada!
¡Oh noche que juntaste
amado con amada,
amada en el amado trasformada!

En mi pecho florido,
que entero para él sólo se guardaba,
allí quedó dormido,
y yo le regalaba,
y el ventalle de cedros aire daba.

El aire de la almena,
cuando yo sus cabellos esparcía,
con su mano serena
en mi cuello hería,
y todos mis sentidos suspendía.

Quedéme, y olvidéme,
el rostro recliné sobre el amado,
cesó todo, y dejéme,
dejando mi cuidado
entre laz azucenas olvidado.[5]

---

5   The translated poem appears after the "Epilogue to Act I."

# THE TABLE

*(Toro, province of Zamora, ten years earlier. The entire family is
on the stage, summoned by Antonio Tomé, Narciso's father.)*

ON HOLY THURSDAY WE SHOULD NOT EAT, ESPECIALLY NOT SUPPER.
Not only because we are fasting. Who would dare compare a simple
supper with that other, the Last? I've gathered them today, however,
to predict their fate, to tell what awaits them. They have come obediently, like Isaac at his father's bidding. They sit, waiting in silence. They
stare with questions in their eyes at the fish on the table, which does
not seem to be food, but a sign, a hieroglyph. They think that its scales
conceal not only our Lord risen from the dead, not only the miraculous proliferation of food, but also the command to go to Nineveh.[6]

My Nineveh is Toledo.

Because of my work I wander the world, and now I will have my
place of rest. I am old and soon will die. My sons will finish my work,
my final job, for which I have prayed my entire life.

---

6   The Lord sent Jonah to Nineveh to persuade its inhabitants to repent and warn
    them of the coming end. But Jonah preferred to run away from the Lord's
    command to the sea, in a storm, in the belly of a great fish. Only there he under-
    stood that there is no fate besides the fate designated by the Lord.

My sons—arrows , and my quiver is full of them.[7] They will not be put to shame.

I look at them and I still cannot tell who they are, because even though I've lived with them for so many years, I do not know them. I can only tell that each one is different.

Andres is the same age as Christ on Calvary. Secretive, closed, impenetrable. Just see how he sits. Leaning over the table, he hides his face in his plate so that I won't see his embarrassed smile. The shield of the plate. White. Without a coat of arms.

How many times have I tried to get close to him? I've taught him my craft… The same as the other two. Only he follows the rules. Only he and I believe that the whole sculpture, the tower, the cathedral, must be hewn from the same rock. Each part of the sculpture must be in the same place it was in the rock. Andres and I know it is not right to put a stone at the top when it was found in the bottom of the rock. Everything has its place, as it was designated by nature. No, not nature—the Lord.

Did my teachings make him happier, a better sculptor than the others? Why then does he prefer painting to sculpting? The scaffolding obscures his wall as he transfers the figures from his imagination, figures he cannot see until the scaffolding is removed. Then, cocking his head, hour after hour, he stares and orders the construction of a new scaffolding behind which he disappears, only to come down after a few days and stare and construct again, and again, and again.

This method is called alfresco.

Andres's wife, Estefania, can endure the loneliness with her silent husband. She sings a lot. She bore me healthy, beautiful grandchildren, who are eager to help and dearer to me than to their parents.

Estefania… My three sons took wives whose names begin with the same letters: Estefania, Esperanza, and Esmeralda. But this is no coincidence. It is a plot against me. All three are so similar to me. Once in

---

7    Psalm 127.

my family I knew best—now they do. And they will not let themselves be convinced otherwise. My three self-righteous Graces.

Strange things, names. Where did we get the idea to name our child Narciso?

Six years we waited for him, until he came on Saint Anthony's day, whose name he should be given. Somebody told us about a Dominican father, a potter, almost a saint already, who had worked with the Natives across the sea in New Spain, and we gave our child his name so our child could be an artist and a saint and maybe he, too, would travel.

I once heard, even if it's probably complete nonsense, that the soul of the child, before it inhabits the body, seeks a place, family, destination, which will help it become better... Why did Narciso come to our family? He is not really a good fit for us. He was ill all through childhood, almost dying several times, and when he matured, he became greedy for life, overly ambitious, insatiable. He alone has fulfilled my dream—I am an ordinary mason, he is an architect.

However, he is the kind of architect that I wouldn't like to be. He is like a chameleon—today he designs in Herrera's style, tomorrow in Churriguera's.[8] When marble is too expensive for a client, he will make a saint's hands from alabaster, his robes from granite and, to make it cheaper, stand everything on sandstone. Horror! It's like sewing together a human from different parts: someone's heart, another's body, another's brain. Who would this person be?

What if Narciso is right? If you replace your heart, brain, and body and become a different person, but your face does not change, people couldn't tell the difference.

---

8    Juan de Herrera, who was born in 1622 in Seville, and died in 1685 in Madrid, was a court painter as well as Grand Surveyor. As an architect, he was the first in Spain to introduce the style of Francesco Borromini. His altar design in Santa Maria de Montserrat in Madrid inspired another architect and sculptor, José Benito Churriguera (1665-1725). Churrigueresque style is characterized by visual overload and excessive decorative detail.

Maybe only his wife, Esperanza, would be able to recognize him. Today she has brought a gift from them both: an Easter lily.

My youngest son, Diego, is a real Spaniard. Handsome and fragrant. He could be a toreador, but he follows my path. He lives with me, he carves like me. Not only can he carve the human figure, but he can prepare relief sculptures like no one else in our family.

What should I tell them?

That I did this for them? Rather, for the family. For myself, so that I can still enjoy them for a while, working together. All the great architects are too busy in Madrid. This was my chance—before the others could, I reached Astorga, the local cardinal, who might simply want to build himself a mausoleum. Anyways, who knows. Astorga told me:

"You see, Tomé, our cathedral is the most beautiful in all of Spain. There is none like this in the world. It is big... maybe even the biggest, and sometimes people lose their way, they forget where they are. In the back, in the ambulatory behind the main altar, where the Holy Sacrament sits in the wall, the youth arrange trysts, exchange illicit notes, hidden from the congregation. We must restore the sanctity of the space, remind the fools that although the people cannot see them, the Lord sees them. We must build an altar behind the main altar to mark this sacred space. There I will rest after death..."

\*

"I asked you to come here to celebrate with your mother and me in remembrance of the Last Supper. And look, there are thirteen of us! But I gathered you so that already today, before the Good Tidings of Easter, I can share with you my personal good news. I have a commission for a great altar in a great cathedral, in a big city that was once great. Once it was large enough to accommodate three religions, now it is too small for one—"

Before I finish, Esperanza asks, "Toledo?"

And when I add that once it was large enough to be the capital, and now it is still a provincial capital, they immediately erupt. One after another, like schoolboys, they start asking their stupid questions, bursting with jokes as if to relieve their earlier silence, our mutual awkwardness.

"One of you will go there after Easter. By the end of spring the design must be approved by the archbishop."

Andres throws up his hands, he will not go. Diego strokes Esmeralda's pregnant belly, neither will they.

"But Salamanca is still unfinished…" Narciso reminds me.

I know it will be him.

"Narciso, we will go. My family lived there once," Esperanza speaks up. "A distant relative of mine worked there as a translator."

Again they erupt with their old jokes. I quiet them and allow her to speak.

"This was a long time ago, maybe five hundred years. A translation school was founded in Toledo. First, they translated Christian texts, Jewish and Muslim texts as well, so that each religion could know the others. They believed, then, that there was one God in three religions. There was also a more secular purpose. Many texts that were previously unknown to our culture were made available through translation. They translated Ptolemy… But then they expelled the Jews and the Muslims from the city, or baptized them, or burned those who resisted. Toledo was the capital of the Inquisition."

"It still is."

"A hot place, huh?"

"And I'm supposed to go to this hellhole?" Narciso asks. Andres rushes to sway him:

"Forget about the Inquisition. For centuries they've forged the best swords there. Steel from Toledo conquered Europe and the East. First Hannibal, then the Roman legions, and later everybody who could afford it."

"If the sword doesn't appeal to you, Narciso," adds Diego, "the best marzipan comes from Toledo. Wait, wait, and that sheep cheese. What is it called again, Esmeralda?"

"Manchego."

I knew we would convince him. I imagine: "Tomé from Toro in Toledo." And I imagine that the three Ts are like the crosses on Calvary. The middle one for our Lord, the left one for me, and the third? The third...

I will build three crosses in Toledo.

Toledo is not Nineveh, it is Calvary.

This is my story.[9]

---

9   Then, still, I could not imagine that history would remember me as Antonio Tomé, who lived between 1664 and 1730, and who had three sons, Andres Tomé (1688-1761), Narciso Tomé (1694-1742), and Diego Tomé (1696-1732). History is silent about my daughters. Our family comes from Toro in the province of Zamora. We were first written about in Spain in 1715. We were recognized as the designers of the façade and main entrance to the University in Valladolid. History says, we were called to Toledo in 1720 to work in the thirteenth-century cathedral, on the altar t now known as "El Transparente."

## THE TABLE 2

*(Toledo, the province of La Mancha, some nine years later. We meet two women: one is the wealthy Doña Nora del Pulpo, whom nobody—besides You and me—will remember; the second is a poor shopkeeper's assistant named Maja. To this day, the whole world remembers Maja.)*

|||||||||||||||||||||||||||||||||||||||||||||||||||||||||||||||||||||||||||||||||||||||||||||||||||||||||||||||||||||||||||||||||||||||||||||||||||||||||||||||||||||||||||||||||||||||||

THE TABLE I'M SITTING AT STRETCHES THROUGH THE ENTIRE STORE and onto the street.

No, not quite.

My table ends on the street, in full sun, not covered by the canopy. Cheap castanets lie here along with lace and jabots, and a few linen fans. That end is for travelers who are looking for memories, cheap souvenirs, presents for a wife or lover. The sunlight helps them to choose quickly, make a hasty decision, fall for an object magnified by the borrowed light.

Here nobody steals, and even if somebody is tempted, the dark eye of the shop watches them. If you choose something from that end of the table and enter the cool interior, my assistant Maja will be happy to help you. If you are, in fact, looking for something else, something special, you can pass her and walk further, towards me, to find really unique wares. On the right—the real fans. On the left—unreal lace.

Usually, however, the customer doesn't walk past Maja.

I am staring through the window. It is small. I see the sloping city, the roofs of the Jewish quarter, the valley behind the walls, the rolling hills with trees growing at their peaks, as in old paintings. From where I sit, I cannot see the sky. Since I can remember, the view from the window has been the same. In this city, nothing changes.

I am sitting and thinking that beyond the roofs, the city, the countryside, beyond the horizon, there is another horizon. There is the sea, the waves marking the boundary between the dry grains spilling in the scalding heat of the beach and the cool line of the shore licked by water.

Beyond the sea is another beach. After the next horizon, there is no city like this one. There is not a single city. Beyond the sea, the sun has already scorched everything. Nothing to love.

I have two female cats. One is named Despair and the other Solitude. In public I call them Do and Sol. I joke that soon there will be eight of them. Do is fat. The second Do will be a thin cat living on love and barley... Anyway, maybe one day there will be twelve of them, not eight. That will be a "dodeCATphony"!

"Excuse me, Ma'am, can you serve me here?"

Somebody has slipped past my assistant. He appears foreign, not from Toledo, and yet I remember his face. He was here yesterday, he looked over some fans on the street and left empty-handed. Today he is back.

"Sir, I cannot serve you. I can assist you in making your choice. If you allow me, I will guess what you want. You are looking for a fan, a truly beautiful one. A fan for a gift, right? And although it will be an expensive gift, the kind you give to a sweetheart, you want to buy it as a gift for your beloved...granddaughter. What you looked over on the street yesterday, those were cheap flamenco fans. They are good fans, but you can buy similar ones all over Spain. You have seen, Sir, hundreds of fans like those. You have seen women spread them before their faces. You have seen that they are not for hiding anything, but for flirting, masking discreet glances, obscuring whispering lips, for furtive touching, for concealing caresses and drying tears. Their beauty is not in form, but in ornament.

"Inlays, carvings, precious stones, ostrich feathers, peacock feathers, even feathers from the birds of paradise in New Spain. Tassels attached to them, chains of gold with strings of pearls. All appear different, yet all are the same. To those still unimpressed, I show fans from China and East India. Foreign, strange, exotic. Fans like wheels of rice paper, hoops of parrot feathers, kites of fish scales, dragons shaped of snakeskin, elephants of ivory. Painted in foreign letters, symbols…

"If your love is real, choose something unreal. Something from Toledo. We invented the fan. Only we know what it really is.

"You think you know it too? A fan moves air, it cools. But this shop does not sell fans that serve for cooling. Even there, at the end of this table, on the street, those are fans for flamenco. The rest of them, up until here, are for flirting. Now, if you dare take one more step… I will show you the authentic fans from Toledo.

"A fan closes between two covers, which we call wings. The wings protect the fan like a guardian angel… Between them are the angelic flights. Each flight has a rigid, flat, bottom part, or a plateau, and a light, airy top, called the peak. The plateaus join at a point in the hinge of the fan, also known as the cave or head.

"A fan opens with its head up, spreading its wings, and then turns its head towards the ground to cover the body, like this, so that it reaches from the face to the heart. Never hold it like a glass. Never open it further than a semi-circle… If you can open it at all.

"Take one and close it, and then open it, please.

"Ha, ha, ha! Not so simple! The mechanism opens the fan, only for those in the know. You can't just use force to tear apart the wings. You must whisper a spell…

"The head of every fan from Toledo has a small opening, like a keyhole. But there is no key. It has a password, an incantation. Open sesame!

"The fan you are holding in your hand was crafted for a religious woman. She wanted an incantation like a prayer. For her, I chose 'Ave Maria.' Please, whisper it...

"It doesn't work? Put an emphasis on each syllable: "'A!-Ve!-Ma!-Ri!-Ia!' Or, simply, blow five times.

"Do you hear, after each blow, a quiet click in the head of the fan? It's a simple latch lock, and the key to it is a breeze—the essence of a fan.

"Why do we also call the head a 'cave'? Why do we use the word 'plateau'? You are probably thinking, Sir, that the sun has baked our brains and we are excited by erotic associations. The cave is an allusion to Plato's shadows. If reality is only a shadow of the ideal, then doesn't closing the fan remove the shadow and simultaneously reveal the ideal?

"You're laughing at me. You think that philosophers don't amuse themselves with fans. There, in the corner of the store is my small museum.

"The first, bland and grey. This fan was designed by Sir Isaac Newton from England. Pass me the lamp, please. In the head of this fan he fixed a crystal prism. When the light falls through the prism, a rainbow spreads across the flights of the fan. Look, isn't it a miracle?

"The second belonged to a lady from Salamanca. There—and here too—in certain circles you can watch nude women dance the flamenco. This lady, however, never exposed herself in front of her clients. She used this fan for her dance. It is made from ostrich feathers, stitched into salmon-coloured silk, very much like the lady's skin. The other side is made from black crepe, like the background of the stage. After the dance, the lady would open her fan and disappear. One day, she vanished forever.[10]

---

10 Of course, there is a different version of this story, which only I, doña Nora, can share with You. Well, one of the lady's clients claimed that she had just committed a sin. The lady responded that, as they were both unmarried, physical love is

"The next was a witness to a sad story. This fan is for correspondence. One plateau, one stanza. This one is about a fan itself:

> *En mi pecho florido,*
> *que entero para él sólo se guardaba,*
> *allí quedó dormido,*
> *y yo le regalaba,*
> *y el ventalle de cedros aire daba.*[11]

"Unfortunately, the husband of this lady, to read the poem, cut off the head of the fan, and then did the same with the head of his wife's friend, whom he accused of being the poem's author. An unschooled brute!

"Look at this one, red as the blood in which it is drenched.

"Pipin Lapa, the most famous toreador of our times, was once forced into the ring against his will. He had with him his sword, but not his muleta. Then, his lover, from the audience, threw him this fan, which Pipin used as his muleta. The incantation that opened the fan was Pipin's admission to his intimate relations with the girl who owned it, and it became his final judgment. It was the last fight of his life, which he lost soon after leaving the arena.

---

no sin. The client reported her to the Inquisition, who generously sentenced her only to learn the catechism. The lady was ordered to visit the Inquisitors weekly, until she could demonstrate her knowledge of the catechism. These weekly visits caused the poor lady to lose her health, so she removed herself from public life forever. (Doña Nora does not know that this same story has been preserved in the archives of the Inquisition.)

11  "My breast as a flower opens
Only for you, the One.
Stay, rest,
And for us
I will turn cedars to a fan."
St John of the Cross, "Dark Night of the Soul"

"This last fan has flights made of Toledo steel. It is made of a metal sheet, thin as lace. Once, at a meeting to which everyone had agreed not to bring weapons, a maid brought this fan to the wife of a certain gentleman, a gentleman who had lost his head in the embrace of another woman, a gentleman who was soon beheaded with this very fan…

"But you are looking for something for your granddaughter!"

*

He has bought something, he has left… And yet, why do I feel as if he visited my store for some other purpose?

When I finished showing him my fans, he said:

"Ma'am, even yesterday when I stood before your store, it looked the same as any other store in the city, which looks the same as any other provincial city. Thanks to you, I understand how wrong I was."

He immediately struck me as an arrogant Madrilenian (I recognized his origins from his outfit, I know what they wear in the capital), who came on business to the local curia (evidenced by the characteristic odour of the clergy that carried on him the scent of wax and incense-soaked pews).

"Oh no, you were not mistaken Sir, not a bit. But here, where life does not glisten at the surface, our treasures are hidden behind seven curtains."

"If you are the first, where in the city are the remaining six?"

"The second is at the bottom of this street, an entrance into a world of marzipan. Even further down, the cheese shops will prove to you, Sir, that Heaven begins in the mouth. There, whence comes that rhythmic sound, you will find that no love and no faith is as steadfast as steel from Toledo. In the south quarter of the city you can sip expensive wine from bottles shaped like Toledo women. And although at the border of the Jewish quarter you can taste delight with women from around the world, it is only with a Toledo woman that you can experience true passion. I know, I know, you are seeking something more spiritual… Once, in Toledo, there lived a Greek painter who left behind some disturbing paintings, wild, inhuman. If you would like to see this treasure, go to the church of St. Tomé…"

He interrupted me:

"Is this a local family?"

"Who? El Greco?"

"No, Tomé."

"This is not the Tomé family, it is St. Tomé…"

"But doesn't the Tomé family also live here?"

Then, still, I did not know that the Tomé family was the purpose of his visit. I did not know anybody of that name. In truth, some Tomé was working in the cathedral, but I did not know anything about him.

"Sir, the only Tomé in our city, who is not yet a saint, is building a tomb or an altar behind the main altar in the cathedral…"

"Narciso? Narciso Tomé?"

"I think so…"

This affected him. He perked up, began speaking quickly and more excitedly:

"My God, this must be the same Narciso with whom many years ago—we worked together, when he was learning the architect's craft! In the cathedral, you said, Ma'am? I don't have time, I don't have time. My coach arrives in a moment—I cannot stay for another day. If only I could exchange just one word with him. I haven't seen him in ages— Ma'am! May I ask you an immense favour?"

On the table he placed my store's little card, with which he had been fidgeting for some time. I always carry with me a few cards on which I've written out the name and address of my store. I urge my clients to take some with them and pass them around to their friends. In this manner, a few ladies from Madrid have learned about my fans. He took a pencil from his sleeve and wrote his address on the back of my card. What manners!

"Ma'am, I beg you! If ever you meet him at the cathedral, please give him my address in Madrid."

"Oh, Sir, I can send my assistant to him with this note immediately."

He turned and looked towards the bright entrance to the store. Maja stood there, sideways, like a black profile from a fashionable portrait. And how beautiful she was! A small head with smooth combed hair piled in a heavy knot. A long neck gently sloping to her shoulders. Her firm breasts, her belly and waist falling flat to the folds of her dress. The curve of her back mirroring her bust. Her youth made her a beauty to transcend the provinces.

He turned back to me and spoke under his breath:

"Ma'am, Narciso would never take a note from such a young girl... I should never have asked you. Please forgive my indiscretion, Ma'am. I was carried away when I heard that my friend is so close and I am unable to see him. Maybe I will come once more before he finishes his work... Forgive me, Ma'am, once more... This day will forever remain in my memory."

He bowed, took his purchase, which I had wrapped, and vanished. He walked past Maja without a glance in her direction. The note was left on the table.

"Maja?"

"Yes, Ma'am?"

"What do you think of him?"

"Of whom, Ma'am?"

"Of that client who has just left."

"Ah...of him. An old, Ma'am."

"Maja! He might only be a little older than me."

"Ma'am, that is something different. Honestly, I barely even noticed him. Maybe he was a ghost? Ha, ha, ha!"

"Maja, let's finish for today, huh? Nobody is coming anyways. You can go a little early after all. Have fun tonight, you are probably bored locked up all day here with me..."

Already she was gone.

Has nobody come all day? Was it only me? Telling anecdotes to myself and laughing at them alone. A madwoman in an empty shop.

I am standing in front of the mirror. How different I am from her.

A small head with combed hair piled in a knot. My neck sloping to the shoulders. I do not like how men stare at my breasts. I have narrower hips and a smaller bum than Maja. And I, unlike her, see ghosts, ha, ha! I speak to them! I can read their writing!

I might even be able to determine the purpose of this man's visit. I know what I can guess and what I can't.

My name is Doña Nora del Pulpo. This is also my story.

# DREAM

*(Toledo, soon after. On the stage, the wife of Narciso Tomé, doña Esperanza Tomé, who understands that although every dream has its key, no key has dreams!)*

||||||||||||||||||||||||||||||||||||||||||||||||||||||||||||||||||||||||||||||||||||||||||||||||||||||||||||||||||||||||||||||||||||||||||||||||||||||||||||||

IN THE NINTH YEAR OF OUR STAY IN TOLEDO, TWO DISTURBING things happened.

The key, with which I came to the city, opened a door. In other words, after nine years of searching, I found the lock for the key that supposedly came from the fifteenth century and that, since that time, had been kept in my family as a keepsake.

Since I can remember, we told a legend about someone who worked on translations in Toledo in the twelfth century. It's not known what the following generations were engaged in. However, what is known is that some branch of the family still lived in Toledo in the fifteenth century. During the expulsion of the Jews, many of the enlightened citizens left the city as a sign of protest. In this way, the city became an intellectual desert even before Philip II decided to move the capital to Madrid.

Because the Jews were not allowed to take their possessions with them, my ancestors left the city empty-handed in solidarity. What they took with them was the key to the gate of their home in which they had lived since the time of that ancestor whose work was translation.

Riding to Toledo with my key, I realized that finding the house and the gate that this key once opened would be practically impossible. I knew, of course, that after three hundred years many houses had burned down, had been demolished or rebuilt, had their entrance gates changed, or even just their ancient locks replaced with more contemporary ones.

After arriving in Toledo, I became further convinced that searching for the lock to this key was impossible. This city holds the stories of fleeing Jews who chose not to accept the true faith, and instead took their true treasures with them and locked the rest away in their homes. Believing that they would soon return, they also took their keys. As you can guess, the houses were soon plundered, their doors forced open. In other words, any search for a surviving lock from those days was a waste of time.

So I thought. Yet, from time to time, someone with an old key arrived in the city and tried to use it to break into certain homes. These few cases, which were punished in a manner I don't even wish to speak of, heightened the alertness not only of homeowners, but also of the public. Seeking a single keyhole by indiscriminately jamming an old and rather large key into every keyhole was pure madness.

At the same time, I could not resist the allure of family legend. When I walked the street, my gaze stayed always at the height of the keyholes, my mind registering houses with old locks. I stopped for things I had dropped in order to peer for a moment into the holes and see whether their shapes were similar to the shape of my key. Often the keyholes were covered with caps, tumblers, or bolts. I had to wait, return, check, stoop and swallow my disappointment.

Some three years ago I lost the desire to search. I lost the desire for everything. I remember, one day I was writing a letter, and I had the feeling that some dark presence was with me throughout, as if it were reading each word over my shoulder. And then it leaned down over me and kissed me. I felt its dark wings surround me completely and—I began to cry.

When I realized that I had been crying for an hour, I decided to do something. Anything, only to leave this darkness. I went to cover the children in their beds. It's a shame that we only have two children. Covering them helps, even though it takes so little time.

Yes, the children and my dog sweetened my days in those times.

The physicians named my suffering melancholy. Apparently, many women were suffering from it in this city. Some, alone, decided to end their suffering. For others, there was no help. Pain, an inexplicable pain of the soul, turned the day to night, one night to the next, and time ceased to exist.

Is it surprising that I lost interest in this absurd search for a lock, to fit the key from ancient times?

And then I found it.

I was returning from the market with heavy baskets and stopped, only for a moment, where they sell second-hand items. Sometimes I bought clothes and reworked them for myself, for the children, for him. Sometimes I bought something for the house. I would be proud of myself, proud that I was able, sometimes, to find lightly used things, for which elsewhere I would have to pay a fortune.

There was one stall with metal fittings, bars, padlocks—scraps collected from the ruins of the city. Among the scrap lay my lock. After all these years of searching, I was sure this was it.

The merchant pointed me to the house, under renovation for a year. When it was up for sale, we bought it. We live in it.

The first room in my new house was a hallway. Beautiful interior. Maybe it was its simplicity, the perfect purity of the two opposing walls. Two, because the third wall of the hallway was taken up entirely by the entrance gate, and the fourth—the same style of gate leading onto a small yard behind the house. Only two walls made up this room, and the floor was the same as the cobblestone of the street, pouring into the yard, and the ceiling was the floor of the first level.

Sometimes, when I would open both gates and stare through them at my open house, this space seemed to me to be an allegory of my life: the dark tunnel through which we are born, and the tunnel of light, which we supposedly see when we die. I opened the gates and I stared as the wind blew through the house, as it carried fallen leaves onto the street or swept trash from the city into our yard. It seemed to me, then, that we are also a gust of wind, never stopping anywhere, never resting in any place. This is the essence of wind. Not only does it fail to warm, but it blows cold.

Sometimes it seems to me that we live with somebody else. Somebody whom I don't see, but who leaves lamps lit in the night, goes imperceptibly but for the squeaking floors that indicate his presence, somebody whom I can almost feel watching us. Maybe there is already no space in the afterlife. Maybe here, already, some of us have found Hell, Heaven or Purgatory. We do not know that we ourselves choose this. When we find out, it's already too late to change.

*

In the ninth year of our stay in Toledo, I had a dream that I could not understand. Usually I explained dreams, my own and those of my relatives, my friends and neighbors. This time, not only could I not, but I also did not want to. This is
why I want to tell it, and maybe one of You can explain it to me.

I dreamed that I was in the cathedral on a Saturday evening, where, in the ambulatory that is in the space behind the main altar, my Narciso was building the altar-tomb, which also serves as a sign, a reminder, that the Blessed Sacrament is behind the wall.

I knew it was Saturday. Almost every Saturday evening my Narciso explained, to those parishioners who were eager to know, what had been done in the past week. He listened to suggestions and demonstrated his eloquence, with which he refuted the arguments of his critics. These evenings began after his father became ill and the curia broke off its contract with us without paying for our previously completed work, effectively bankrupting us. Indeed, Tomé Sr. stated then that Narciso would finish the job in his place, but the curia decreed that their agreement only pertained to Tomé Sr., and besides, the altar that we had made was disliked by the cardinal, by the members of the curia, and by the parishioners. Narciso grasped onto this argument, inviting everybody to a discussion on the construction site in the apse of the cathedral.

I do not know how he did it, but he convinced everybody that the family had created a unique work, and he managed to keep the commission. He was ordered only to replace a few sculptures, at his own cost, and to consult with any interested parishioners during the rebuilding process. We kept all the sculptures, believing that someday, in some other project, they would be of use. We hid them in the shop where Diego carved.

Since that first discussion, every week Narciso has his hour of glory, during which he shamelessly extolls his own talents and the talents of his brothers.

The altar was already almost finished. That evening's critique concentrated on the fact that the top half of the altar was hidden in the shadows throughout the day and night. Narciso argued:

"This altar pulses with inner light. It glows by itself and for this reason we do not have to illuminate it from the outside or expose it to additional light. You must remember, the altar lamp will hang before it.

"When I presented my project to Cardinal Astroga nine years ago, he agreed that this is the best possible composition dedicated to the Blessed Sacrament, the bread that becomes the Body of Christ, Christ himself. See how the light, its reflections and glares, will lead the eyes of the faithful through each successive level, through each successive significance on the path to the Lord.

"In the centre is the beam of light. It beats from the spot in the main aisle where the Sacrament is enclosed. It pierces the wall, pierces the darkness, here to us…"

He paused and took a torch, because the glow of the candles was too weak. He stepped back and pointed high to the altar:

"You see, the light flows down to us from Heaven, from the dark sky, as it is above Toledo. The highest ranked archangels guard this light. See how their symbols glow in the darkness— St. Rafael with the glittering fish, St. Michael with the glinting shield, St. Gabriel with the bouquet of golden lilies, and St. Ariel exuding the golden scent. And higher, do you see? It is Holy Thursday. In the dark upper hall, the apostles and the Lord at the Last Supper. The gloom of Easter flows from the sky.

"Look at the top, there where the Word becomes flesh. The adoration in the stable. This is Christmas Eve. There shines the star of hope, the Star of Bethlehem…"

He rapidly approached the altar and almost hit it with the torch. At the height of the heads gathered beside Mary with the Child, the bronze reliefs glowed with light like mirrors. On one of them, Ahimelech gives the sword of Goliath to David, a sword of Toledo steel like a beam of light.

In the depths of the crowd, the flash of the sword reflected like hunger in someone's eyes.

And then an extraordinary thing happened. I, doña Esperanza Tomé, who is telling this story, looked through those eyes. I looked at my Narciso as I had never yet stared at him. I stared not at Narciso, my husband, the architect, the person—but at a stranger, an unknown man. I stared at his arched calves and his buttocks in his tight-fitting pants as he raised the torch. I stared at the front of his pants, below his belt, and his shoulders, open, at his gesticulating arms and his hands, holding the torch, hands that were perceptibly warm and soft, and I swayed to the rhythm of his voice, not caring what he pointed to on the wall, but what showed under his jacket, in his pants, in his eyes. And I thought: "Now there's something to look at…"

And I felt that I was someone else, not myself, and some vanishing remnant of doña Esperanza begged me to wake up and I even wanted to scream to wake myself up, ignoring the scandal that would come of a scream during a meeting in a church. I felt myself imprisoned in someone else's body and I could not understand who I was, and then he lifted the light higher and I saw my reflection in a window of the ambulatory.

I had a small head with combed hair tied on top in a knot, with a comb in the shape of a fan stuck in it from which flowed a dark veil covering my neck, shoulders, and breasts. I saw my face, a dark Arabian face or the face of a Jewish woman from the south. And like a sick person who knows that something is wrong, but does not yet know what, I began to examine my body…

The horror! I gasped, I breathed quickly, and my breasts—completely different from mine—squeezed by a soft corset, one I have never owned, rippled to the rhythm of my breath, tense. My stiff nipples seemed to pierce through my underwear, my corset, my silken dress, delicate and light, seemed to pierce through my veil.

And in my stomach, I felt a locked cage in which moths and silk-worms fluttered.

I was not examining my body; I knew that I was not myself, I could feel that my feet were smaller and my shoes were flatter, and never before had I worn my stockings to my knees, and my underwear had never been so loose, as if it wasn't there.

And I, doña Esperanza, felt the remnant of my past shame, felt that I was about to die, drop dead, burn up with shame, though it is an unbelievable thing to burn up in a church, but with a cry I was unable to return myself to a different reality—I felt that I was burning and melting at the same time.

Along the inside of my thigh a drop slowly rolling. Down, down, until it reached the edge of my stocking rolled up below my knee. My body opened like lips, desiring.

I was dying of shame, not daring to move, but the meeting ended and only a few remaining parishioners and priests were patting Narciso on the back. I walked up to him as in a dream. I was dreaming, after all. And so that everyone could see my pure intentions, I gave him a note, speaking loud and clear:

"Sir, your friend greatly regrets that he could not meet you today. And I will add from myself, he should also regret that he could not hear you, Sir…"

This was unbearable! My heart beat like a sculptor's hammer, forging a path out of the boulders of sleep back to my own reality.

Beside me slept my Narciso. He was smiling in his sleep. I don't know when he came to bed, when he fell asleep. Through the open doors of our room I saw the stairs below, the lamp light on the floor above, as though someone had lit it for us. I heard the calm breaths of the children from the next room. The light night breeze gently tugged at the canopy above the street.

I did not need to know, I felt it. An anxiety that something had invaded my life through my sleep. A feeling that I would no longer be happy.

Yes, until now I had been. I loved Narciso and I was loved by him. Our daily life could be meager and depressing, but our love gave it meaning. What we shared was unique, after all… This is what I thought in those times about which I write.

A chill came the next day, and the nights were not as hot as before.

# DREAM 2

*(Shortly after the previous scene, doña Esperanza
Tomé is disturbed by another dream.)*

|||||||||||||||||||||||||||||||||||||||||||||||||||||||||||||||||||||||||||||||||||||||||||||||||||||||||||||||||||||||||||||||||||||||||||||||||||||||||||||||||

SOON, I HAD ANOTHER DREAM.

Maybe because—I thought— I worried so much about the first one. Day after day I analyzed image after image, I searched for symbols, I tried to understand why I had become somebody else in my dream to lust after my Narciso. We had been together a long time. Maybe our love was not burning as strong as it was once, but it was love that united us, after all.

Love, yes, love.

Do not think that beyond running the household and raising our children I did nothing. Like many educated women in Toledo, I gave the city the benefits of my education, sometimes translating, sometimes teaching, and sometimes guiding visitors through the cathedral.

Melancholy does not interfere with these activities.

The same way—I thought—that it did not interfere with our love. Although, for that matter, my passion—but not my feelings for Narciso!—suffered. At the urging of physicians, I drank infusions, which soothed the pain of my soul, but which left me feeling numb. Something new slipped between my skin and myself, a veil woven from snowflakes. Not only did I not respond to Narciso's touch, but I myself did not want to touch him.

These troubles usually come in pairs. In our case, there was a whole herd of troubles. My illness came at the same time as Tomé Sr.'s illness, the troubles with the curia (which was withholding pay), a lack of money (although we bought the house I had found) and finally, Narciso's strange affliction.

Narciso, especially in the evening after dinner, became red in the face. His eyes bulged, he breathed shallowly, and he said he could hear bells in his temples. This last symptom coincided often with the real tolling of the bells, whose frequency confounded Narciso.

This condition interfered with his work, because neither in the studio nor in the quarries could he lower his head without blood flooding his eyes. Sometimes the blood appeared as broken blood vessels in his red eyes.

Of course, the physicians have a name for everything. The more difficult it is to give an opinion on the patient's symptoms, the more intricate that name. Usually, despite the complicated diagnosis, the treatment is simple—leeches.

In the house there appeared a jar of yellowish liquid with black, oblong worms similar to larvae, floating like drops of shade in a golden sunbeam. The jar stood first on the kitchen table. It didn't belong in the kitchen. It contained something disgusting, even dirty. I was disgusted more than glad that the shoal in the jar might save my Narciso. It was difficult for me to imagine how their bodies would fill with Narciso's blood, how they would swell as though they were about to deliver, to give birth to something made of his blood.

We moved the jar to the window. There, beside the compotes and fermenting vegetables, it became even more defiant, flagrant. I heard the leeches almost as a flock of bloated drunks, shamelessly bleating to the whole world: "It is us who suck your Narciso."

A screen, a bowl, a veil was the only solution not to look at the abomination. I covered the jar and stopped thinking about it.

Before I could forget it, the maid knocked it off the window sill. It fell into the yard and shattered. From the kitchen window the dark stain appeared alive, the leeches trembling as they baked in the sun. I ordered them all gathered and returned to the market.

If the leeches couldn't reduce the excess blood in Narciso, any physician could bleed him instead. Any physician could, if not for my husband's fear of foreign objects penetrating his body. He could not imagine a scalpel slitting his vein, and especially not if the scalpel was real. Narciso explained to us that he once befriended a Portuguese Jesuit who was adept at drawing blood, and into whose hands he would willingly submit, but the man had died shortly before our arrival in Toledo.[12]

My husband was prescribed a powder ground to dust. Narciso joked that it was precisely the dust from which we came and to which we will return. A bad joke. Indeed, under the influence of this powder, he became quieter, paler, more peaceful. He became gloomy. He said he felt colder. A chill lived within him. A chill that could be felt on the skin and a deeper cold hidden beneath his eyes.

After some time on the medication, Narciso also began to complain of a loss of virility. I do not want to dwell on that. You must know, however, that one of the features of my husband that I most valued was his vitality. Joy and hunger for life, the readiness to approach me, desire me, my body. It all raised my spirits, kept me alive, before the melancholy made me indifferent to Narciso and his advances. Although even then I felt a pleasure flowing from his desires, from the power of love he had in himself and he felt for me. Not even for a moment did I imagine that my Narciso could be an ordinary womanizer, adulterer, or sex addict.

Even if he had once been, he—it seemed to me—had ceased.

---

12  I, doña Esperanza, had no idea that this physician was Bartolomeu Lourenço de Gusmão, who appears in the chapter titled "Exultation" in the Third Part.

Every morning his nightgown, once bloated like a sail before a full wind, hung limp and empty.

Of course, we were together from time to time. In the night, as he pressed himself against me, I felt his manhood tense. He urged me with whispers and caresses, and sometimes he was able to achieve his goal. He loved me long and attentively, bringing me to the edge of pleasure and fulfillment. But even this became sporadic. Slowly we began to resemble a medieval couple that had vowed chastity.

Maybe that's why I understood my strange dream as a blessing. Since, while awake, I was unable to, in the dream I took the form of someone else to desire my Narciso. I wanted him as much as ever since the days of our youth— even stronger still. Much stronger.

I'm not promiscuous, but the desire I felt in my first dream was doubly sweet: I wanted him, and at the same time I was happy I could feel my own desires.

Was I happy that I had this dream?

Do not think that I only occupied myself with dreams. The house consumed me to the same degree. I wondered what I could learn about the lives of its previous tenants. To what extent could I know them by knowing our house?

Our house stood on an irregular plot. The walls of certain rooms converged at odd angles. Others concealed walled-up recesses. I did not delude myself about the possibility of hidden treasures, maybe some souvenirs. Like the lock, they would be waiting to reveal not only their existence, but would allow me to understand that they were a part of the history of our family, that they once belonged to my ancestors.

I did not delude myself because the renovation had been thorough. There were many changes and improvements to the layout of each floor. The space felt as though someone had spent many hours inventing a new character for the house, trying to breathe new life into the old walls. For example, contractors eliminated the wide staircase leading from the top floor to the small, covered terrace on the roof.

Without the stairs, the top floor was larger and more functional, but to me it felt as though this change was an attempt to erase the house's ability to use the terrace on the roof to celebrate sukkot, the Feast of the Tabernacles.

The kitchen was my favourite room. No, not because I liked to cook. I would say, rather, that I liked to cook sometimes. The kitchen was unusual, triangular, domed, with a hole instead of a keystone at the peak of the dome, an opening like a chimney, which eliminated any cooking odours and any sense of stuffiness, and instead granted contact with something above—maybe the blue sky, or maybe celestial Heaven.

Although the house was not located in the traditional Jewish quarter of the city, I immediately felt a hunch that somebody, whoever designed this house, had wanted to say more than he could.[13] For example, on the final beam above the main entrance gate, a symbol was carved in the shape of a braid or loop:

$$[\textbf{IXX})\textbf{O}(\textbf{XXI}]$$

What did I see in this pattern?
Two symmetrical halves composed of a Roman numeral:

$$CXXI$$

So, in Arabic script, 121.
You're probably thinking it's nothing important. The house number, its location on the street, right? No, no street in Toledo has 121 houses. No house could have this number.

---

13  I also knew (because the official propaganda told me) that in 1492 in Toledo the Jewish ghetto, or "Aljama" as the Arabs called it, had only forty houses. The Jews were already not part of the wealthy class. The Inquisition did not occupy itself with the poor.

"121" refers to David's psalm 121. A fragment of this psalm was inscribed on two columns that once stood before the synagogue in Toledo. The synagogue was converted into a church. The columns were lost. This fragment appears above many entrances in Toledo:

*"The Lord will guard your going out and coming in from this time forth and forever."*

This psalm stayed with me like a mantra when I left my skin and slipped into someone else's in my dream.

I, doña Esperanza Tomé, who is telling this story, dreamed that again I was in the cathedral on a Saturday evening where my Narciso was explaining to his audience why the altar and the figure of the Blessed Virgin was flanked by two bronze reliefs. The one on the left side of the altar depicts David receiving Goliath's sword from the hands of the priest. On the right, David receives a tribute from Abigail, who is kneeling before him. On one, the priest gives a sword to David, on the other, Abigail pays tribute to David.

Previously, these reliefs shone like a beacon, guiding my husband's argumentation. Now they scattered golden light on his hair and dress. My husband was much calmer, his voice deeper and more seductive.

I heard little of what he said, and of what I heard I understood even less. I stared at his face and lips, at his cheeks and ears, at his hair, and I felt like a young woman in love again for the first time. This time for real. I felt a delightful warmth in my breast, a warmth that flowed from the rest of my body, leaving a flutter in my limbs. I felt a cooling drop after drop; I was unable to dry the sweat gathering on my chest and in my armpits, above my upper lip and in the lines of my hands, falling like a mist to my feet. And only on my back did this alarming sweat turn into a thrill, ascending upwards towards the base of my skull against all logic.

As before, I examined my body. I was strangely pleased to see that I was not panting, that my heart was not pounding like a hammer, that I was not swaying with his voice. I felt an inner satisfaction that my body and hair were freshly bathed, rubbed with oil and spotted with perfume. My dress, corset, and underwear held me so firmly, giving me both freedom and shape. I knew that I was modestly dressed. Modestly, but cunningly—my breasts were completely naked! They were covered only by black lace, so delicate and dense, almost opaque, and thus even more enticing.

Today I was not alone. A young girl was with me, perhaps a maid. A chaperone.

When Narciso finished, I stayed, waiting. I knew that soon I would approach the pews to kneel and pray. I stood prolonging the moment, staring at his face. Someone was still asking about something, pulling him by the hand, pointing to the altar, but Narciso ended it quickly and kindly. He turned and walked straight to me.

He stood before me and spoke only to me. It was sweet and pleasant, but it stunned me. I was deaf. My ears closed and I could only raise my head from time to time and nod, even though I did not know what he was saying. And then I bowed, and the body which I inhabited in my sleep whispered some pleas for forgiveness. I took my girl by the arm to move towards the pews.

When I was turning, I found myself nearer to him than I had been during our conversation, if you can call my embarrassment a conversation. He bowed to someone and leaned in even closer to me. And in this bow his lips found themselves right next to my ear and whispered something. A word that sounded like a number, not at all a secret, or something to be hidden from others.

His breath touched my ear and felt even deeper. Like the small pebble that causes an avalanche, his breath grew within me. The brush of his breath invaded me like a tsunami, a wave that throws onto the shore sailboats and sea monsters greater than ships. A spell that would open Toledan locks tore me apart like a fan. Before I reached the pew, I lost consciousness.

For the first time in my life, I fainted with delight. I fainted, of course, in the dream.

Narciso lay beside me in bed and slept deeply. I don't know when he came, when he slipped between the covers, or when he fell asleep. The whole house was quiet. All in my home was at rest.

And then I was overcome by a strange feeling. Something I had never felt before. There was anger and resentment inside me. At first I thought my dream had ended abruptly and prematurely.

I wanted badly to return to my dream and finish it. Finish it! Yes, somewhere in my subconscious I knew there was still supposed to be more of this dream in which nobody revives me, nobody lifts me from the cold floor or asks, "Ma'am, are you okay?" but something completely different happens.

I knew, and I did not know how, that that evening I had come to the cathedral to propose a job to Narciso— a design of a summer residence for me and my husband. I planned the next meeting, or maybe the next dream, in which I wanted to meet with him, but not in the cathedral, not in public, but alone, maybe one on one in the quiet of my home. Not this house, in which I lived with Narciso, but in the home of the person whose body I was using in my dreams.

Using?

I understood, suddenly, that the person whose body I was using in the dream was not letting me use her body, but was using me, forcing me to take part in something against my will.

I tried in vain to return to the lost path of the previous dream. I wanted to believe that I would fall asleep and wake in the same place where I had fainted, before I had fallen to the cold stone floor of the cathedral. I was terrified that my dream was living its own life, somewhere beside mine. I would never be able to catch it, never be able to control my second life in the dream. I struggled for a moment and when I gave up I fell asleep.

The next day, the southern winds brought rain and storms, and it turned cold. Very cold.

# DREAM 3

*(Some weeks or maybe even months later,
doña Eśperanza Tomé continues to dream.)*

|||||||||||||||||||||||||||||||||||||||||||||||||||||||||||||||||||||||||||||||||||||||||||||||||||||||||||||||||||||||||||||||||||||||||||||||||||||||||||||||||||||||||||||||||||||||||

FOR MANY NIGHTS I WAITED FOR THE DREAM TO RETURN. IT DID not. A new one did not come. I would catch myself trying some sort of magic to recall it. I would put on the nightgown in which I had the last dream or position myself in bed as I had been that night. I even tried to repeat from memory what I had done the day before my dream, what I ate and drank, to whom I had spoken.

Nothing worked. I finally forgot and abandoned my attempts. In those days I immediately fell into a deep, heavy, dreamless sleep. I was very, very tired, as we were continuing renovations to the house. This time I was carrying out the changes.

Narciso was furious. We fought when he was in the house, we fought when he ran away, we fought when he returned. We fought not only because we did not have the money for the renovation, but because of the unbelievable mess inside the house. The chaos stemmed from my ambitions which fuelled me. First, I occupied myself with the stairs. The main ones, at the front of the house facing the street, and the servants' stairs, at the back.

The first stairs were not a problem. It was rather easy to reconstruct the connection between the top floor and the terrace on the roof, and even though the terrace wasn't finished, breakfast on the roof in the morning breeze and supper by sunset were the great rewards for all the inconvenience during the renovation. The second stairs, however, became a real Pandora's Box, a bottomless pit—call it what you will. For us, they were primarily a hassle.

When we moved in, those stairs formed an absurd link between the basement and the attic. The doors to the other floors had been walled up. A senselessly tall and thin corkscrew pierced the entire house. Our troubles really began when we broke through the walls from the landings on each floor.

Our house—like I said—stands on an irregular plot. Every floor has a very complicated layout. I was unable to figure out where exactly the new doors would appear. We had to hammer from within the staircase to the rooms outside. Sometimes only a shelf would fall from the walls, but often it was much worse.

The cellar in the basement was unsuitable for use after we broke open a second door. The kitchen had to be extensively rebuilt, and in the bedroom, we had to move the fireplace which was installed during the first renovation. Worse still, when we broke through to the attic, we accidentally pierced the roof's truss, almost causing not only the roof, but also the entire house beneath it, to collapse.

Until now, Narciso drove me wild with his criticism of the renovations. After the incident with the roof, he exploded. He could have warned me to be careful with my design—he's the architect, after all, not me. I blamed him. Anyways, he employed many workers at his altar in the cathedral. I had to lead my renovation myself, with only the help of the girl from the kitchen and our errand boy. We had a few accidents, but we also made a discovery.

The stairs in the basement did not end at the floor but wound beneath its cold surface. And yet there was nothing else there, no basement beneath the basement, no second bottom. Maybe only Hell.

We began to dig. Under the slabs was loose sand, the kind that fills hourglasses and covers graves. Dirt. Dust which turned thick and pungent in the throat. We dug and carried it out, threw it away and continued to dig. The whole house became coated with the dust from the basement. The whole house filled with the unbearable smell of musty earth, the smell of the cemetery. It was impossible to live…

So we poured water on the sand and carried mud out. We lacked strength. We had to stop. One day, when the basement was dry once more, to air out the stench, we decided to open the doors at the top of the stairs in the attic. In the blink of an eye, a draft swept through, sucked the sand from the basement, vacuumed the house, and… covered half the city in ash. Toledo went gray.

Our basement, the low-vaulted hole, in which the arches of the ceiling touched the floor, became instead a spacious square hall, something like an alchemist's laboratory, with a hitherto hidden basalt floor studded with mica gleaming like good intentions, with which our Hell was paved. Through the open door at the top of the stairs and through the window in the attic, through the entire staircase a ray of sunlight wound itself and filled the basement with brightness. I had never seen anything like this in my life. And in the glow, we noticed something else.

In the wall, next to the unearthed stairs, was a small doorway. I recognized the lock at once. The same lock, the same key, which once fit the front gate of my house. We brought candles and a torch, said a prayer, just in case, and turned the key.

(It's getting late. I'll tell you what happened next some other time. Now I still need to add a couple of words about Narciso's illness and maybe I'll have enough courage to describe my third dream.)

Narciso refused treatment from traditional physicians. I preferred not to think about what might happen if one day my husband would suffer a stroke and be unable to work. With his father's illness and without Narciso, one of the brothers—Andres or Diego—would maybe finish the work on the altar, but my children and I would be at the mercy and grace of other people. I had begun to worry seriously about his health when one of his friends put him in contact with a doctor of alternative medicine.

In Toledo there were once many doctors like this. They lived here beside Christians, Jews, and Muslims, and they had their own culture, as well as their own medical traditions. Thanks to the Inquisition, they all vanished from the city. There were, of course, those brought to the Church by force or threat, who disowned their faith and culture either of their own volition or to maintain their position. Many of those who managed to survive in someone else's skin continued to cultivate their practice in secret. Did the Holy Office know about them? Everybody knew, but for years the Inquisitors occupied themselves only with rich infidels. The poor were safer.

Blessed be the poor, for they will be left alone.

Narciso was given some herbs and told to boil and drink them. The smell of the drug, heavy, muggy, intoxicating, hung for many hours in the house. One day, tired from the work in the basement and dazed by the scent of the herbs, I fell asleep. I, doña Esperanza Tomé, who is telling this story, dreamed that I was waiting for Narciso in an inn somewhere outside the city. This wasn't an ordinary inn. I recognized it at once. It was the most expensive inn between Madrid and Toledo, the "Palacio de Galiana."[14]

---

14   Long ago, Galiana, the most beautiful daughter of King Galfara, a Moor, lived here. She was given away to the king of Guadalajara. She did not love her forced fiancé, Charles, Duke of France, who won her in a duel at the local court and took her with him to France. Charles became "Great," but news of Galiana faded away. The palace remained. After the Reconquista, it became the property of the Christian kings, who changed its name to "La Huerta del Rey." Here, in the thirteenth century, Alphonso X built a scrumptious nest in the Arabian style for his Jewish lover Rachel, who was known as "The Quail." The defenders of racial purity smothered the Quail in the kitchen and served her to Alphonso for dinner... For three hundred years the palace has been in the hands of the Guzman family, who are trying to squeeze everything they can from its erotic past.

I was sitting in the women's lounge with a girl, the same girl as the last time in the cathedral. I, doña Esperanza, felt what the woman who was lending me her body felt. How she was thrilled with herself, and terrified! I felt that she had mustered the courage to do something like this for the first time in her life. I remembered that earlier she had picked out a pair of stockings that gently held her legs and that did not need garters, that she had picked out her best skirt, that she had spent a fortune to rent a room in this inn, that she was happy with herself and excited, unimaginably excited, about what was to come. She felt a lightness in her feet and the warmth of her body. Only her nipples suffered, pressed in her corset and underwear. She waited. And when he came, embarrassed, shy and apprehensive, she took him with her, she showed the way to the room. She did not care whether someone was staring at us, whether the girl was following us. She was with him and she was only with him.

The girl stayed in the hallway, and the body given to me locked us in the bedroom. Suffering the same embarrassment as he, she overcame it with her desire:

"Oh look, Sir, a bath and some wine has been prepared for you."

It was dark. Earlier she had ordered the shades drawn because the twilight had yet to come. One candle inside did not dissipate the darkness.

He stood, uneasy, in the middle of the bedroom. And then her mouth—it's not mine, after all! —said:

"I'll teach you, Sir, the art of seduction."

While the hands poured the wine and lifted the shaking glass to his lips, I, doña Esperanza, combed the memories of her body like the sand in the basement, in order to understand what she said. And when we drank, I discovered some memories, some pictures, scenes with my Narciso in his shop at the building site. Together, first speaking, then joking, his hands trying to reach after this body and a firm refusal again and again, until she threatens to leave. His whisper and her submission. No, nothing happened. A touch. A kiss. A hand sliding under a shirt, into the pants, to feel his desire.

Nothing happened. Narciso felt regret; he had not won her. Maybe it was he who had been seduced.

I, doña Esperanza, felt rage. Not towards Narciso—I was with him, after all. But I felt rage that I had missed this previous memory or dream before. My exhaustion from digging in the basement, my overwhelming melancholy, had prevented me from having this dream and stopping the body that was exploiting me now, as its witness, in the seduction of my husband in my dream.

Meanwhile, she leaned at his feet and ignored his protests that it was improper for women in his culture, and so on, to remove his shoes, stockings, trousers, shirt. My heart was jumping in my throat, and my temples throbbed. My lungs were bursting, my breaths short, and under my fingers I felt the heat of a man's body, not my old Narciso, who usually threw off his clothes and quietly crawled into bed, but someone new, someone I had never seen. As though looking through another's eyes gave me a new perspective. She let him stay in his underwear, lacking the courage to remove them (I knew my husband's shame, since the illness, at his flaccid manhood), and then led him to the bath.

Oh, what joy to have in her hands Narciso's submissive body! She washed him, ignoring the fact that she was ruining her best skirt which she would probably never wear again. She laughed with joy, drying him and laying him in the bed, rubbing him with an odorless oil, which she had picked so that his wife—me! —would not discern a foreign smell on my Narciso. It amused him. Lying on his stomach, he removed his underwear so I could anoint his buttocks.

"And now, Ma'am, allow me to do the same."

Narciso wanted to undress her! I felt a panic in my borrowed body, I wanted to flee. No!

"Oh no, Sir. I will undress myself. And allow me to put out the candle… I am ashamed of my body."

Ashamed? How absurd! We had been together so many times, not only as husband and wife, but in a completely normal, natural way. My body was never shameful for me. Now, when I was lent another body, it—not me—felt shame. I felt shame through my borrowed body, shame as in the Garden.

It became dark. She tore the dress, corset, petticoat, and shirt from herself. She kicked off her underwear, rolled it up, and threw it away to hide its dampness. Covering her breasts and belly, she knelt on the bed:

"Forgive me, Sir, may I stay in my stockings? I have ugly legs and I don't want to ruin your mood with their sight."

He held and kissed her. In his arms she was a little calmer, but further humiliated by her body. Her drooping breasts and round belly, thin hips and short hair…

I felt this, but I, Esperanza, examining the body granted to me, must admit that I had a different impression. The breasts were much smaller than mine, but the nipples were unusually hard and large. The stomach was quite flat and meaty compared to mine. I felt good in this new body. I felt good under Narciso's new touch. His hands, accustomed to larger breasts, abdomen, thighs, arms—learned new shapes. His caress of my belly and hips calmed me. I heard my voice, however, speaking:

"Forgive, Sir, my stomach."

But already his hands moved across her stomach and wandered past her hips to the back where he held her buttocks, of which she was proud because they were small and strong—and her hand slid down and took…

In my dream Narciso had nothing to be ashamed of. I felt a wave of happiness, devotion, and excitement, like a fist kneading my stomach. Like a strike that forces you to curl up. Moisture between my thighs. Moisture, already dripping on the sheets. I wanted him, wanted him in me as fully as possible, as deeply as possible, as much as possible.

Instead, she said:

"Sir, can I put on you a condom?"

For a moment I did not know what I was saying. I realized only after an instant that this was a new device that men would place on their penis to prevent pregnancy. I was astonished because I knew this cost a fortune, and besides…how could a woman get "that" in Toledo?![15]

The body turned to the edge of the bed to reach for something it had hidden earlier. I fell into a panic, because I had never, never until now put something like that on, had never used…a condom.

The hands pulled something from a bundle, something wet and elastic, something that entirely resembled, no…something that was a fish bladder.

To my surprise, she raised it to her lips and bit through the wider end. It did not smell like fish. The air had still not completely escaped from it, and already she had placed it on Narciso. The bladder stuck to his penis, becoming almost undetectable.

Before I could even think with horror that something like this would be inside me, Narciso knelt, grabbed me by the hips, pulled me to him across the bed until my buttocks touched his knees, and craning my legs up, plunged himself into me violently, deeply, and completely.

\*

Oh, forgive me, you who have never experienced this! Who do not know of that which I am telling. Even though you do not understand the language I speak—do not lose hope.

---

15   I knew, of course I knew, that the syphilis epidemic in Europe in the sixteenth century inaugurated the widespread use of primitive condoms. The word "condum" was first used in some poem in 1704. Apparently it came from the name of the physician of Charles II. I also knew that Gabriele Falloppio constructed the first condom as a canvas hood, which was tied with ribbons across the lower back. In my time, condoms made from animal intestines were already appearing.

But you, pioneers of pleasure, who have dared to give yourselves over to the senses, who contrary to the principles of faith, morality, social norms, and all other regulations, have allowed yourselves to be carried away by lust, who have believed that the rapture can lift you above all else, above the peak of the sweet mountain up there, where orgasm and revelation live on the same cloud—you are able to understand me. When under your feet opens the abyss of condemnation, Hell, eternal reproach—in this one and only moment of a fall dwell together a crime and a sweet reward. For a moment, punishment hangs in the air. In that instant you are an angel, a soap bubble, pure happiness. Oh moment, be eternal!

\*

Before he joined with me, my body opened to receive him. Before he filled me, it was filled to the brim with anticipation. Before my body closed itself on him, I possessed him.

Never before had I felt him like this. Maybe this new body joined with his differently. Maybe he was somebody else. Leaning above me, he loved me with passion. And when he lost his breath, the sweat from his brow dropped on me like rain. I turned him on his back and galloped on him like a horse, asking:

"Is this good for you?"

He laughed under me, trying to catch his breath. When I lost my strength, he leaned up to me, wiped his wet face on my breasts and did not stop.

We fell apart from each other. I tried to use my hands, but he complained that my fingers were too dry, and again he was above me, and I received him, incomparably softer than my hands.

Hour after hour passed, and I whispered:

"Why did you never love me like this?"

He did not know it was me.

Until finally time stopped. We found ourselves outside reality. Outside the window, the wind tore at the shutters and the rain slashed walls. Somewhere in the city the bells measured the lives of others, and we were suspended in my infinite amazement that not too long ago Narciso had complained of impotence and cursed his condition, and now he loved without pause for yet another hour. And maybe we would live in this state forever if I had not asked:

"Sir, shouldn't you have come already?"

Then he ripped away what I had put on him at the very beginning, and I felt as he, without warning, filled my hands with liquid.

Bestowed with an unexpected gift, I heard myself speaking:

"Oh, this would make a wonderful hand oil … but that's probably…"

I wanted to add that that was probably "the end of it," but he read my mind and made himself come yet again. The surge, suddenly abundant, washed my stomach and breasts. As if nothing had happened a moment ago.

Once, when we were young, our nights were filled with love. We fell asleep and we awoke and we began again and again and again. Narciso always rested after love. Now it was different. This was not my Narciso.

We fell asleep… Maybe only she fell asleep, maybe it only seemed that way to me, or maybe Narciso thought that she fell asleep. She lay on her back with her legs spread, as if she were cooling her thighs. Through her half-closed eyes I saw his head somewhere near the hips of her body. I felt his fingers on the hips, moving under the thighs like a pianist grasping an octave above the tops of the stockings, the delicate fingers peeling, rolling the stockings lower and lower. I saw how this happened through his eyes, saw what emerged from the lace stockings.

First a glow, a sickly light like the reflection of the wings of a butterfly, glistening skin—no! —rather a scale, a rainbow iridescent, like the crests of fish, nimble lizards, mermaids. The bedroom filled with the multi-coloured glare of the rainbow. From beneath the stockings, the scaly thighs, knees, and calves glowed with an inner light.

The legs in the dream were covered in fish scales.

He sat terrified, stunned, confused, and in my borrowed body there was only shame:

"Sir, I did not want to reveal them…They are disgusting, aren't they?"

"But, Ma'am, no! They are beautiful…I was just not expecting… somebody could have scales…I mean, have skin like this. How did it happen?"

He pretended to be calm. And then I began to speak of something about which I, Esperanza, had no idea:

"My great-grandmother was a witch who lived on the fringes of society. Supposedly her home was an old willow near the Forgotten Crossing on the Tagus, which has since been named the Sulphurous Swamp. Sometimes she helped travelers, but few passed that way, and for this reason she often dipped her legs in the water. The silkworms slept through winter in her hair, the birds laid eggs between her breasts, and the fish nibbled on the soles of her feet. Nobody knows what happened. Maybe Aquarius fell in love with her, maybe she fell in love with a lizard… What a curse that in our family we are born with fish legs… Now, Sir, you don't want to see me again!"

Angry with him, that he had invaded her privacy and discovered her secret, she pulled up her stockings.

He held this body and took it more gently than before. We made love like fish, rubbing our bellies against each other. And when we were resting again, nestled together, and he stood to go behind the curtain, where there was a bucket instead of a toilet, these lips— because, after all, it isn't me, Esperanza—said:

"Sir, do not leave! Don't take yourself from me. You may urinate on me…"

He was leaving. To stop him, she added:

"…just not on my lips."

He stopped. This statement did not fit within his reality. Mine neither. It fit within the reality of the body, in which I loved my husband. The body in this dream, in which I betrayed him with him, and he betrayed me with me…

I awoke in my own bed near noon. First, I examined my legs. They were mine. I lay in bed and I could not come to terms with the knowledge that a lizard dwelled in my dreams. And although until now it had seemed to me that in the dreams I inhabited a body, a body that was granted to me, now I saw clearly that I was embodied in someone else. Yes, I was embodied without my permission and without the ability to refuse to participate in my own dreams.

Maybe these dreams weren't mine? Maybe they weren't dreams?

I ordered a fire in the fireplace. Never before in Toledo had autumn been so cold.

# DREAM 4

*(A few weeks later, doña Esperanza Tomé discovers a shape from another reality in the basement and finds delight in a dream).*

||||||||||||||||||||||||||||||||||||||||||||||||||||||||||||||||||||||||||||||||||||||||||||||||||||||||||||||||||||||||||||||||||||||||||||||||||||||||||||||

I WAS SUPPOSED TO TELL YOU WHAT HAPPENED WHEN WE OPENED the small doors beside the stairs in the basement. As I wrote, I recognized the lock in these doors immediately. The same lock, the same key, which once fit the main gate of my house. I had this key, I kept it on me, it was my key of the office of St. Peter. I like to believe that everything means something. If the key once opened my Heaven, could it now be a sign of my banishment? Is this how my unhappy life ended, a life that for many people might appear very happy?

We brought candles and a torch, said a prayer—just in case—and turned the key. Nothing happened. We stood and waited. My errand boy, my new kitchen help, Petra, whom I hired after firing that slob who smashed the jar of leeches, and I—we knew that something must happen. Otherwise I wouldn't be writing about it.

Not even for an instant did the thought come into our heads that the doors, which had been closed for many years, might have rusted shut, grown old, become stuck and would not open themselves. Come to think of it, what kind of doors open themselves?

These were different—they creaked and slowly began to give. From between the doors and the frames, like an hourglass, sand poured. And as the sand heaped at our feet, and the doors leaned open a little further, we heard it.

It was like a sigh, like the stretching of stiff joints, like a dragging. There was something behind the doors. Something like a being, which we had awoken.

The errand boy fled. He had been standing closest to the stairs. I didn't blame him. I would have done the same, but between me and the doors—opening further still—stood Petra, who did not know what to do, or who was so afraid that she was unable to move. I pitied her, because I had barely hired her, and already here I was about to allow some monster to devour her.

Yes, this is exactly what I thought: "devour her." Is it because I expect danger behind every door? Do I think negatively? Not at all. I have a very sunny disposition and I look at the world optimistically, even if others do not think this way of me. I knew, after all, that the same key does not open the gates to Heaven and Hell. I must have understood that behind these doors of evenly carved and tightly packed strips of oak, nailed with steel ingots to the hinges, there cannot sit a beast, an evil being, a werewolf, a goblin. Nothing that has a mouth and that devours could sleep under our house and wait for this day without sustenance. If we had a bloodthirsty neighbour, we would have noticed the traces of his meals.

Who thinks soberly in the face of the sinister unknown?

We threw ourselves together on the doors, trying to brace them. We held them up with our backs, our asses, trying to bolt them, and our feet were slipping on the sand pouring through the opening door. Feet like on ice, on scatting ring of our childhood. The doors were small—we found ourselves shoulder to shoulder, hand in hand between her and my thigh. Close. Of course, we could feel that something was pushing against the doors, pushing against us, not something like an inert heap of sand, but like living muscles, springy, meeting our opposition, something that we felt could, after some time, overpower us slowly but decidedly.

Despite the danger, the unknown threat, the person inside me who gave her body to me in my dreams—because who else?—glanced sideways at Petra, and saw her not as a maid, but as a woman. We were so similar. The same skin tone, hair, even eyes. We were the same height, similar proportions. Maybe my belly and breasts had become larger after the births of my children, my figure more rounded, but otherwise we were like sisters. We were separated by some twenty years.

"Petra, run! Save your young life!"

"Oh no, Ma'am."

She was gasping with her lips half open, red-faced, glistening with sweat. Her breasts heaved. I once had breasts like that. Breasts like that, and that flat stomach.

"I order you!"

"Ma'am, please let me stay."

When I thought about her stomach, I realized how near my stomach was to the edge of the doors, how exposed to a potential paw, talon or claw that might extend from within and tear out my guts. Without thinking, and still pressing against the doors with my body, I rolled onto my stomach: my thigh on Petra's thigh, my breath and her breath, and my hand searching for a spot on the doors and landing on her right breast. I once had breasts like that.

I did not know what was scuffling with us from behind the doors. On our side of the doors, Petra's breast gave itself up to my hand, and I gasped:

"Go!"

"Oh no, I'm not going to leave you now… Ma'am."

"For the third time, please, listen to me."

"For the third time—no!"

"Petra, don't pretend to be St. Peter, just get help!"

And then everything happened in an instant. Pulling Petra by the breast and ripping the material of her dress, releasing her youthful breasts, I tore her away from the doors, and as she was running in the direction of the stairs, she must have seen, in the yawning gap, the thing with which we had been fighting, and she cried:

"Och!"

And then she fled. This "Och!" terrified me, and maybe I did not have the strength or reason to defend myself against the thing that was behind the doors. I jumped, stepped back, and could not believe my eyes. Now too, I cannot believe that everything that had happened had happened in the blink of an eye, as if without time or outside of time. And even though it was outside of time, it did not bother me to think such nonsense, and just remembering it makes me blush and I still cannot believe that I am telling it.

Well, feeling no resistance, the doors opened with a crash, and into the basement through the opening a shape began to crawl…a shape of monstrous size, which might resemble a snake or eel. Its skin was bright and dry, not slimy, and quite frankly my first thought was…a condom. A condom placed on something so big that it had difficulty fitting through the open doors. The shape slid in my direction, so I stepped back— I had barely made a single step on my shaking legs, and I stumbled upon an uneven floor and tumbled on my back. Precisely in that moment, the shape arrived at the spot where I had just fallen and…it dove into my upturned dress and starched petticoats as if it wanted to violate me.

"Stop!!!"

Everything stopped, although it was not me screaming. At the foot of the stairs stood Narciso, furious and red in the face. He was screaming something, something I could not understand, shocked and embarrassed by my position and the shape between my legs. My legs were bent, and I could stop myself to squeeze the shape. It felt elastic, as if empty instead.

Narciso picked me up and took me to the kitchen. He forbade me to talk to anyone about what I had seen. He stayed alone in the basement.

When he returned to the kitchen, where I sat with the errand boy and with Petra, whose breasts were hidden again in a new dress, he was smiling and hid his embarrassment with his easy demeanour. At the same time, he tried to make his voice strict and serious:

"I am very sorry that such a thing has happened…The mechanism that you saw in the basement must remain a secret until we can use it at the site. Yes, it is a construction mechanism, for… for raising heavy weight—stones or bricks, for example. I didn't invent it, but its developer trusted me and entrusted this mechanism to me and that is why you must swear that nobody will ever know about it before…before we can show it to everyone. Swear it to me!"

I swore like he ordered, even though I could feel that he was lying, or that he wasn't telling the whole truth. I did not know this side of him. This day I understood that Narciso was a skillful liar.

By that evening, I had changed my mind.

By that evening, I was sure that Narciso was just a liar.

When I saw him at the foot of the stairs, he was amazed, but not by the shape— by something else. He must have known what had burst into our home. He had to know this shape or have seen it earlier. Bah, he probably had buried the shape himself near our house, not even knowing about the existence of our basement behind the wall, not knowing about the secret, submerged doors. He did not know that we might discover something while working on the other side of the walls, something that was supposed to have been hidden from us.

By chance, we discovered the unknown shape.

I knew that this wasn't any machine for construction, because, after all, we had kept it shut behind the doors together, Petra and I, two "weak" women. Besides, the springy nothingness within the shape, when I pressed it with my knees, made me uneasy. I had seen similar shapes once at an exhibition, an exhibition that had come from New Spain. The Natives there had used similar contraptions for their tents and boats—leather stretched across emptiness, like a body without a soul, a vessel, which is easy to carry from place to place without much effort. A nomadic shape.

The one from the basement was this, must have been this, something always on the move. Maybe it was an earthly bug, an earthworm, which does not crawl underground, but which folds the earth around it, moves present time into the past. I imagined a sort of vehicle that penetrates the depths as a rhizome, which might emerge here or there, which wanders independent of any roads. So precisely did I imagine this new way of travelling that I slowly began to believe that the shape in the basement was a machine for transporting people, a tool for carrying individuals into spaces unseen. We would just need to burrow at the foot of the house, dig past the molehills and emerge somewhere, somewhere where no one expected us.

Unfortunately, in my head I got stuck on the word "dig," and immediately came other associations: burrowing not only under, but also within the ground, a wild snout, the snout of a boar rooting among trash, drinking swill, or finding a truffle, a truffle that takes other shapes, shapes similar to the one in the basement. These thoughts filled me with disgust, and in turn with fear and anger at Narciso that he was guilty of something, that he was hiding it from me.

Maybe, when you read my story, having such a worm that travels underground will be nothing unusual, and maybe each one of You will have such a vehicle or maybe even a few of them. In my times, at the beginning of the eighteenth century, every rational person would consider this vehicle the creation of Satan or the result of his persuasions. Given that the majority of these rational people were in the Holy Office, this vehicle would take us straight to the stake…

Narciso swore on all that is good and holy that he had already has removed the shape from the house, and that the shape would be hidden, so that no unauthorized person would ever see it again. He was losing himself in his lies, and, pressed, he admitted that the shape was given to him by a monk, who he had met just after his first trip to Toledo. This monk dealt mostly with the treatment of certain male disfunctions, and the shape was his research tool for the study of some bodily mechanisms.

I flew into a rage that some degenerate monk's artificial penis wanted to violate me in the basement, (even though I truly thought it would have torn me in half) and that for something like that, all of us could be imprisoned, condemned, burned. I got so worked up that in my fury I threw all Narciso's clothes down the stairs and told him to get out of the house. I don't know how this scene would have ended if not for a tiny box falling out of one of Narciso's coats. I exploded:

"And what's this!? A condom to help you with your research?"

Although he was amazed at my use of the word, he knelt before me and unwrapped it:

"Honey, this is a gift for you from my client."

He opened the small, decorated packet, which housed some small figures made of marzipan: a little pink piglet lying between four marzipan truffles. I love marzipan, and Toledan truffles leave a heavenly flavour on the palate. I immediately ate two. But the piglet and the remaining two truffles at each side reminded me of the shape and infuriated me even more:

"You pig! You're sure that this is a gift for me from your client, and not a gift for you from a lover?"

He apologized and assured me. I forgave him and told him to clean up his clothes so the children wouldn't see the mess when they got up. I don't know why his clothes angered me, even though I leave mine strewn about. They littered the bedroom, pouring out of cabinets and off shelves on the walls, lying all around, so that if I wanted to lie down I would often have to dig up my wardrobe to find my bed. Eventually I decided that the bed would have a high headboard, maybe even some poles, so that in this way, at least, they would tower over the piles of clothes. Unfortunately, this didn't do much good, because the headboard and the columns soon became hangers and camouflaged the bed. Sometimes I was so tired and melancholy that I didn't even have the strength to search for the bed, and, without undressing, I would fall asleep where I stood, or where I fell on the soft river of clothes and flowed, flowed somewhere, somewhere far away…

My bedroom, which in fact was our master bedroom, had an irregular pentagonal shape. I mean, when we moved in it was a normal, rectangular bedroom. It had two big windows facing the doors, and on the wall between the doors and windows, a space for our bed. Behind the wall opposite our bed was our closet, which we incorporated into the room by tearing down its wall. On the new wall, previously hidden, we discovered the remains of an old fresco. What it depicted—it's hard to say. You would say, perhaps, that it was an abstract mural. Vertical lines, like bars over a tangle of yellowed green stems, like immense blades of grass, from the floor to the ceiling. Here and there, trapped rhizomes timidly extended a stem, as if suggesting that the bars did not separate our bedroom from the painted lushness, but vice versa. Sometimes, while lying on the bed I tried to put together the fragments of the mural into a cohesive whole.

I would fall asleep before I was able to see anything.

In those times, I slept a lot. I felt very alone and abandoned. I would bury myself in bed, sewn into my bedroom, and sleep. One afternoon, I had a dream.

I, doña Esperanza Tomé, who is telling this story, dreamt that I was in an inn, but a different one than in the previous dream. This one was in the city, near the Iglesia de Santo Tomé, where to this day, "El entierro del conde de Orgáz" by El Greco hangs in the vestibule. The inn was cheaper, but not cheap. She had been here earlier and had prepared a meal for us in the room. She had placed many candles as well, although I sensed that she wasn't romantic on a daily basis (Narciso isn't either, but the body lending itself to me in the dream thought that he was). When she was finished, she went out into the common hall. He wasn't in sight, only the female chaperone:

"He is waiting there in the corner, Ma'am. Should I fetch him?"

"I'll do it myself, myself!"

She ran through the hall, as confidently as if she were meeting her cousin, someone from her family. I was internally angered, upset, nervous all at once. I mean me, doña Esperanza, deeply hidden from everybody. That concealment, a safe haven, allowed me to make certain observations about the body that was lending itself to me. First of all, I knew that when we made love, I would probably remove the stockings that hid my ugly scales (ugly, of course, for her, not for me, or for Narciso). Besides this, I clearly felt that I was expecting something else. Something closing in, at which we would inevitably arrive, which might cause something terrible to happen, something far worse than my serpent legs. I, doña Esperanza Tomé, did not know what it was, but I discovered that in some way I could enter the consciousness, maybe the memory of the person whose body I was wearing in the dream.

No, not wearing, and not using—I was staying in it, although I did not quite know on what terms. We all have a soul that inhabits our body. So we think, because those who control reality think it and teach it. They—men. Seeing the world through the prism of dualisms: night and day, the moon and the sun, dark—light, women and men, body and soul. Good and evil.

And yet, when the nightingale, not the lark, speaks, when the body of Narciso joins with mine and our breath is a shared breath—love is the one, the only thing, and the whole, divided world of these old scholars vanishes and we are alone but together at the same time, together and fully fulfilled.

Is this what I thought about when I ran to him? Oh no, I didn't have to think, I always knew it. I thought I had the key to this woman's interior, this woman in whose body I was. Somewhere in the depths of her thoughts I was able to fish out some information that I had never had before. Among other things, I discovered that my name was Nora, even though I was almost certain that Narciso addressed the body in which I was as "Ma'am," never by name.

Suddenly, as I was running through the inn, I stopped and I understood that I was able to control Nora … for a moment. And then again she was chasing her lust like a cur, taking me with her, in her, burnt with the embers of desire, which only he could extinguish now. She had to have him. Her moment. Her second of freedom and triumph …

Triumph? Over whom?

I did not know. Nora's interior, like a dark pool, was filled with some liquid shadow, like water over mossy stones. From beneath her, from beneath the surface, shone a different body, the body of one loved and hated simultaneously, an abandoned image of a husband.

Nora, like my Narciso, was married.

I was shocked that neither of them was bothered not living together, and to make matters worse, they were sinning in my dream. Of course, I was shocked only to a certain extent, because I still thought I was taking on the body of Nora for the quite pious reason of communing with Narciso in my dreams, since our love had grown tepid while we were awake. Naturally, I was afraid, because since I was taking on the body of some Nora, then maybe my Narciso was also only a vehicle for someone else, who fraudulently, or at least without my knowledge, haunted my dream and slept with me. Ha! He didn't sleep and he didn't allow me to sleep, and yet everything was happening in a dream …

Was it that somewhere there in the universe there was some soul, the second half of my own, which found its way to me?

This last question drove me to begin reading about Platonic dualism, about finding the second half of one essence, the issue of perfect fullness. Regardless, whatever I was doing and whatever I was reading, I was only seeking confirmation that Narciso had always been my missing half.

When they arrived at the bedroom and locked themselves within, leaving the girl in the hallway, when Nora poured the wine and offered the previously prepared meal, when she was ready to throw herself on

my Narciso and possess him, I, doña Esperanza Tomé, who is telling
this story, decided to put an end to her desire, to stop her:

"Sir, I feel that I must tell you how much I love my husband and
that he will always be the most important to me. But do you know that
in my heart there is a different, strong feeling, a feeling for you?"

"Yes…?" He was embarrassed, as if he did not want to have
this conversation.

"And can you, Sir, say the same thing?"

"Ma'am, you know that I have a family that I will not leave. You
know that I am drawn to you by your beauty. I want your body, but I
don't desire your love."

"Oh, Narciso! How can you separate making love from love? I
make love to you because I love you."

"Are we not, therefore, lovers?"

"I think not. *Einmal ist Keinmal…*"

"What?"

"Once is not enough, but if we go to bed tonight, then I think we
will be. If we go to bed… Narciso, do you not feel remorse that you are
cheating on your wife, that you are not honest with her?"

I felt that Nora had not asked that question, but that it was I, doña
Esperanza Tomé. He was impatient, and he was not hiding it:

"Oh, Ma'am. Are we doing something wrong? I am not here with
you so that someone else cannot be with me. I do not want to harm
or hurt anybody else, I am not with you against anybody else. I do not
need to take revenge on my wife for anything. I'm here out of pure
selfishness. I do not feel remorse, because satisfying my lust gives me
joy, a feeling of lightness. Beyond this I remember: 'Ye shall know
them by their fruits.'"

"Narciso, you say this because you think nobody sees you. Nobody
knows your other life. Nobody except Him."

I whisked myself away from his hand, which was outstretched for
Nora. He was gorged, and now he wanted to gorge himself on her body.
I wanted to revive him, to awaken his conscience. Because although I

did not doubt it for a moment that this whole scene was playing out within my dream, one of the main actors was my Narciso after all. My Narciso, impeccable, sparkling, loving only me, Esperanza. And I wanted for him to remain that way even in the dream. I felt that I was controlling the situation, that I could control it the same way I could control Nora.

And everything would have gone on the way I desired, if not for the gap above the door to our room. In that gap, dark and deep, two pupils smouldered. Nora's girl, her chaperone. She was spying on us.

And strangely, what moved me, Esperanza, and touched me to the point that I could not maintain a conversation with Narciso—made Nora laugh. She made some sort of gesture towards the indiscreet eyes, a gesture like a wave of coldness, like ice, and behind the doors there came the dull crash of a body on the floor.

Nora was laughing.

For a moment it seemed to me that I (or maybe the person in whom I was imprisoned) had the supernatural ability to move objects at a distance. A moment later I knew that it was not me, but her. Because Nora was already sitting on Narciso's lap, talking rapidly:

"Oh, finally, finally! As if something came over me, I talked like a fool, cha, cha, cha. Oh yes, yes, Narciso, whisper in my ear…"

Me and her, right?

Esperanza and Nora?

Well, not quite. When Narciso was panting in my ear, I, doña Esperanza, I felt wave after wave flow down my—not my body, opening me like spring buds. I felt his arrogant hands caressing my breasts, pulling down my shirt—Oh!—sinking down the waist, between my thighs, already parted by his whispers—Ah!—his hands like a mole digging through my dress, petticoat, and underwear and touching my belly—Oh!—his hand on my bosom and breath in my ear and his tongue following inside and his teeth nibbling my earlobe, and there his fingers slipping between the petals of my body, the other ear and—Oh-ho-ho!!!—this anteater tongue and lemur fingers running to meet together within me somewhere, somewhere where my heart beats: Boom, boom, boom!—like a bell, like two bells, which he shook while also holding—the way only he knew how— both my nipples in the fingers of his one hand.

Oh pleasure, you who spread yourself so deliciously before you begin! Oh wonderful instant, running through the body like lightning, which predicts the coming rain and storm. Fall on me with the rain, the breaking of the clouds, because you are heaven, and your thunder swells like a candle.

"Of course you don't have condoms?" – I asked, not in my own voice, and the body immediately responded: "It does not matter. Today you can use me instead of the condom."

He snorted at the vulgarity, and looked me differently in the eye, unable to believe that someone could deny herself to that degree, only to give herself fully to him, only to him, my Narciso. And already they were tearing the clothes from themselves and kissing laughter on their lips, when he, without any further caresses, entered me violently and loved me without respite, until his body became rain that fell on me and cleansed my skin so that I could rise from his waves and gallop on him as on Triton through the seas of our desires, with lips just above the surface gasping for air:

"Does-this-please-you-Nar-ci-so?"

And he clutched my breasts, as if afraid that he would drown.

\*

When I became my husband's lover in my dream, I stopped being ashamed— not only of the body I was borrowing while asleep, but also of voyeurs. I, doña Esperanza Tomé, wondered only how the woman who was lending me her body did not fear that her girl would report her to the Holy Office.[16]

And I was no longer bothered by the wide eyes above the door-frame, the eyes that could not believe that this was what love looked like between two people twice as old as her, the one who looks. And when I was dying from pleasure, and Narciso was dying on me, it seemed to me that those eyes glazed over with the pain of emptiness.

They lay next to each other, panting, when she pulled from the scattered clothes a card with a forbidden poem:

"You know, Narciso, I was thinking that today, before we love each other, I would ask you to read this poem. Look..."

She gave him the paper with the poem, which she had transcribed earlier, and he spread it above him and read a few lines:

> *En una noche oscura*
> *con ansias en amores inflamada,*
> *¡oh dichosa ventura!*
> *salí sin ser notada,*
> *estando ya mi casa sosegada.*

"I think it's about me..." he said, still holding the paper above him, caressing the body in which I was. He spread the liquid that flowed from him to me, saying:

"Poetry like this requires special interpretation."

He pasted the page to my stomach, text to body, and still he caressed me, this time through the poem and through the page, which

---

16  Here is an example of how I was intimidated by the Inquisition. Of course, I knew that bigamy was not their main enemy, because in a country where divorces were outlawed, the Church saw bigamy as a potential alternative to accepting the failure of marriage. This is also a reason why bigamy occupied only five percent of the Inquisition's courts in our country. From the mid-sixteenth century, the relatively light sentence of five years in the galleys became the standard punishment for male bigamists.

stretched from below my breasts to my belly button. When he peeled the paper away, a mirrored reflection of the text remained on the skin. He took a mirror from the wall and gave it to me to hold so that I could see the poem on my belly and him, leaning over me, licking me, pure poetry. I saw Narciso reciting the poem once more, letter A!-fter letter, verse A!-fter verse, image A!-fter image, careful-YES! and accurate-YES!

When he recited the last dot above the "i"—I died of pleasure.

# DREAM 5

*(A few weeks later, doña Esperanza Tomé dreams of an
orgasm, which brings a new Ice Age to the world.)*

MY PREVIOUS DISCOVERY IN THE BASEMENT MADE ME THINK ABOUT
the reality in which I lived. No, I did not share my observations with
anybody, knowing that the only reaction to my thoughts would be the
label "old madwoman." So, if you get bored with my musings, I suggest
you move on to my next dream, which surprised even me.

Let's get back to reality. It began with an inkling of doubt. What if
the appearance of this shape in the basement was some catastrophe of
reality? Catastrophe in what sense, You ask? It is true that without any
objection we accept our everyday reality as built on a set of binaries:
here and there, now and then, me and You, and so on and so forth. I
lived every day "here and now," in my house, I saw the "there" through
the window, and the "then" I remembered or dreamed. And suddenly,
from "there and then," that object broke into our reality, suggesting
that "there and then" can force itself into our lives without our permission, knowledge, or ability to cope. Catastrophe.

I performed several experiments. I left my here and now and went
there and then, if only to convince myself that no matter where I am,
I am here and now.

I began to doubt that "there" exists at all. No, I did not think I was being lied to, or that, for example, New Spain did not exist, even though it was "there" and not "here." I knew perfectly well that Cristóbal Colón, also known as Christopher Columbus, began his first voyage exactly two days before the scheduled date for all Jews to leave Spain, not in order to "discover" new countries, but to hide the Jews, the converts, who constituted the majority of his crew and whose wealth financed the expedition.[17] I thought, if "there" is a place used to conceal, then maybe it itself does not exist, is unseen. How do you hide something that exists in something else that also exists? After all, this would merely be masking, covering one figure with another.

So how do objects from there arrive here? How do we come to such catastrophes?

Boring? I told you, go to my next dream.

Good. Now that we're alone, I need to ask You to be discreet. One day, I got it in my head that it is the confusion in our lives that introduces us to language. In truth and faith, we say: "There is one God." And the same God on Sinai says: "Thou shalt have no other Gods before me," as if acknowledging that there are many Gods. Only God can do that. My ancestor here in Toledo translated texts from many cultures, and he came to the conclusion that there is one God, but in many religions. If, then, He manifests himself in various ways, then maybe the worlds He has created are various, parallel, complementary, fulfilling each other, coexisting together, and only sometimes meshing, connecting, overlapping, and intersecting. That "sometimes," or that moment when the worlds of different Gods collide, I call catastrophe. Catastrophe, for example, was when the shape broke

---

17   Of course, converso sailors were not as well known as converso physicians, who were eagerly employed by the court. Among the biggest names were Francisco López de Villalobos, a physician of Ferdinand and Charles V, as well as Dr. Andrés Laguna, a physician and botanist, one of the most enlightened minds of these dark times. Many names will probably survive for centuries more, thanks to the sentences of the registers of the Inquisition…

into the basement and between my thighs. You can probably guess that soon after, I learned that this object was from a different reality, a reality that I had no idea existed. It appeared unreal and disappeared, returned to its reality. Through its disappearance, it made me realize one more feature of those other worlds, those parallel realities. Specifically, it made me realize that those "other" worlds are continuous, parallel also in time. Even if they do not manifest themselves in our world, they accompany us beyond an invisible border. Time passes there the same as here. Or, almost the same. Parallel realities aren't exactly parallel.

My dreams convinced me of this. Somewhere there, in my subconscious, some romance was unfolding. I entered a different body and was the lover of my husband, whose body might be the same, but who was capable of so much more than when awake.

Forgive me, this is not what I wanted...I was supposed to write about how catastrophe happens, how different worlds collide.

I don't know. I have no idea. I would like to know. Or, more precisely, I had wanted to know, but now I have no need for this knowledge and I would gladly not know it.

I began to explore our house. Right, it seems completely logical: since something entered our house from another reality, then maybe our house is exactly the place where this intersection can be understood.

I wrote earlier that our house stood on a misshapen plot, and because of this its interior was also misshapen. The shape of the interior spaces was a reflection of the plan of the exterior walls, not a translation. Inside, however, you didn't feel this. At first glance, the majority of the rooms were quite geometric, and it was only the placement of our old things that revealed their lack of right angles, or maybe only the inadequacy of our furniture. Sometimes the wardrobe did not fit the corner, or the bed would not sit against the wall.

I started to measure our house, to watch it carefully.

Surely you remember the sight of a straight road stretching along the horizon. The two lines vanish on the horizon where sky replaces earth, and the road disappears. Yes, everybody has seen it and knows it from her own experience. The road ends on the horizon, ends in that vanishing point, where everything disappears. Each of us has gone there, to check, to see if this is really how it is. And the vanishing point ran before us, the horizon hid itself beyond the horizon, and the road ended in infinity.

Perspective, an illusion we have all accepted. Not only accepted, but we use it every day there where two parallel lines run to meet at the horizon. We know what they do not know. The horizon does not exist, it becomes "down the road," though it never comes, and it cannot be. We can never meet it.

Really?

If we apply this same knowledge to parallel worlds, then these worlds should never meet, and if they do meet, it is only because they are not parallel. Or the horizon has stopped hiding behind the horizon.

My house was telling me something else, although not right away. I had to toil, measure each room's width, length, and height. And then I had to measure again because I could not believe what I found.

No wall was parallel to its opposite, just as the ceilings were not parallel to the floors. The windows in the rooms also differed significantly from each other. The doors were crooked, not warped. Even each individual step was different.

You will probably think that they built so poorly in Toledo. Oh no! After arduous study, I understood that it is quite the opposite. The builders of my house used perspective, optical illusions and geometrical manipulations. They used them in order to create the impression of shape where there was formlessness, harmony where there was chaos, proportion where there was none.

I lived in an artificially created space whose perfection and order was a sophisticated optical illusion. I became used to it. Sometimes, when I left the house, reality offended me with its primitive literalism.

Which is why I slept so much.

There were dream-filled nights without dreams, restful insomnia. I woke from them sleepily and fell asleep anew, to dream. One night, I, doña Esperanza Tomé, who is telling this story, dreamed that I was in an inn, the same one from the previous dream. I was with Narciso.

As usual, desire denied the body conversation, caresses and touches, and the body quickly threw off its clothes to be closer to him, closer to his body, breathing his breath, feeling his whole being, having him inside and being one, one, one… I was not embarrassed by my body; on the contrary, I was embarrassed by my clothes before I took them off. I did not mind the light and the chaperone shamelessly spying on us from outside the door. I did not mind that throughout the inn, everybody could hear our violent union. No, not because of my cries of pleasure. The body that was lending itself to me might have been dying of pleasure, but in silence. The bed, on the other hand, was not. Not silent, that is. I did not care whether some reality beyond our senses might exist, or whether the creaking bothered everybody else.

The bodies were together, held, beside themselves with desire, and the desire became a creek, a stream, a river of love. I held him like a sparrow in my hand, and he rose above me like a falcon on the roof, he carried me higher and higher, or pecked at my liver—and when it was getting so incredibly hollow in my stomach, then he filled this body to the brim, to the horizon.

Only this time, it was different than usual. Much different.

Of course, there was the bath in the big tub and the wine, fatty olives, sweet figs, and juicy grapes. This time, Nora had commissioned a musical ensemble. No, they did not play in the bedroom, but behind a wall. Maja, who was spying anyways, was supposed to give them a signal when we had stopped making love. When they began to play, Narciso was astonished. Not by the surprise, but by the fact that we were so openly announcing to the world that we were together.

We?

Them, rather. I, doña Esperanza Tomé, who is telling this story, I could not hold my fury, my rage at Narciso, who so shamelessly betrayed me. But the body that was lending itself to me in the dream turned my fury into dance. Instead of roaring in pain like a wounded lynx, I wanted to dance until the dawn.

I cried:

"I'm in Heaven! Dancing naked for a lover, is there any greater bliss?"

What happened later convinced me that there is.

Narciso, tired from our earlier lovemaking as well as an excess of wine and dance, was lying on the bed watching my dance with excitement. She celebrated him as an object of worship. And, finally, she could not resist. She sat on him.

And then the rhythm of the dancing body focused there, on him, on Narciso. Like a leaping horse, the body opened on him and closed, calling on and on, higher and higher. The leaping horse, not walking or even trotting, and more than galloping.

While the rest of the body was relatively static, the vibrating abdomen behaved like an independent being in ecstasy.

Perhaps one can only dream about something like this, but I was a part of this dream and although I could observe myself and him, terrified by my greed and lack of self-control, I also felt that the soul of Nora (so far as Nora had one) was afraid of something that was coming, something that was coming closer, almost there.

I said earlier that there were a few times, when I was dressed in Nora's body, that I died of delight. This was not a figure of speech, a euphemism for the word "orgasm" or something equally poetic. I died, I lost consciousness from pleasure, before the body that was lending itself to me in the dream could achieve it. And now I was only a step... from orgasm.

Perhaps I could have remained in this ecstasy forever. And perhaps we could have galloped, connected like a steed and rider, across the Tatra Mountains through time, from Ulan Bator not only to Legnica and Vienna, but all the way here, to Toledo, if Narciso had not flipped her underneath him and, trying to speed up—leaped all of time.

Before he yanked himself out, they were already beyond that peak that the body of Nora had so feared. I felt that the fire in her abdomen, and the flame between her thighs, was focussed in a spark, which contained all the flames, blazes, and ten thousand suns. And then the spark imploded on itself, somewhere beyond the border of eternal ice, and became a single crystal, a ball of hail, a snowflake.

Implosion. This was the peak. Nora's body absorbed into itself the heat of the world. The room shivered in icy breath.

The bedroom which was just a moment ago filled with steam from the bath, from the dance, and from love—it froze, turned into blocks of ice. From within the body, across the bed, across the room, the inn, Toledo, the world, spread a wave of glaciation. Hoarfrost covered hair, bodies froze together, flowers of frost grew on glasses and windows, and outside waves of hail and snowstorms raged for the first time in the history of the city. The bedroom had become a crystal hall.

And no one would ever learn about this, because how can you tell the story when you are frozen like a couple of crabs, locked for eternity in a crystal or amber?

When our bodies thawed out, steaming, he approached the tub pressing melted footsteps into the frosted floor. The water in the bathtub was still frozen! The swelling ice slid above the edge, so that she, lying in bed and shivering with cold, could see it.

I awoke in my own bed. I was alone. Beyond the window a snowstorm raged, the same as in the dream. The first snowstorm in the history of Toledo.

Since that night, just in case, I locked the gate to our house with a key, which I then hid. I slept peacefully, believing that Narciso could not escape from the house and into my dream.

# DREAM 6

*(A few weeks later doña Esperanza Tomé, while awake, meets
the figure from her dreams, and in a dream, she forges the
sword that has already appeared in the "Prologue.")*

||||||||||||||||||||||||||||||||||||||||||||||||||||||||||||||||||||||||||||||||||||||||||||||||||||||||||||||||||||||||||||||||||||||

DIFFICULT TIMES CAME. MY ILLNESS DEEPENED AND I SUFFERED,
without any support from Narciso; indeed, I suffered by him.
Financial problems made him acerbic and sensitive, so that not a week
passed without a fight or an argument. Still, I loved him. Our love was
my life, it was pure, unique.

I fought with him in the name of this love. I demanded everything,
full devotion, a complete merging of our souls. The lout, he could not
stand it. He would have probably been happier with a submissive and
completely yielding partner.

I was difficult and demanding.

"No, I will not get out bed today, and you can shove it! What have
you prepared for me today? Nothing! Give me some peace and quiet
and go to Hell."

He would throw on some clothes and run out to the marzipan
shop for some French croissants. They were made of delicate petals
of dough, light as a feather. Then he would bring breakfast to bed and
fawn over me.

He was able to appease me for a while. Food calmed me, soothed my pain as long as I was kept unaware of his treachery. After finishing breakfast, I threw the tray at him, screaming:

"You pig! You want to fatten me with these pastries? Don't bring them ever again! I can see your plan! You have woven yourself a comfortable nest and you think you will become a great architect, you will barge into history on our backs, but you are just a miserable creature who uses anybody he can."

I suffered greatly.

Relief came only once, for a brief moment, when the bank where we had our debts was forced to close. Across from the bank, on the wall of the cathedral, an inscription was engraved encouraging repentance:

"Jesus saves repentant sinners."

On our bank, a similar phrase appeared:

"Jesus saves."

Within a week, thanks to the Holy Office, the four owners of the bank lost a fortune as punishment for their blasphemy. Savings were requisitioned, and the bank ceased to exist. We were worried about the fate of the bankers, but at the same time we were happy that our debts were forgotten, along with their bank. Soon we would realize that everything disappears but debts. To make matters worse, we were given a higher interest rate on our loan.

I worked more so we could survive. My most frequent business was giving guided tours of the cathedral. One of these times, a catastrophe occurred.

That day, I had a normal group. A few people from Madrid, several locals, someone with an aunt from the provinces. I was taking them through the sacristy, where the majority of the modern paintings are located. We were stopped in front of "El caballero de la mano

en el pecho," by El Greco, when one woman spoke out with undeni-
able astonishment:

"But he looks just like master Narciso Tomé!"

I admit, I have stood before this canvas many times, but I had never
noticed the similarity between the painting and my husband. There in
the frame, on a deep, black background, El Greco had placed together
three stains: the head, the hand, and the handle of a Toledan sword.
The head was proportionately smaller than Narciso's, but it was similarly elongated, with a strong nose and heavy eyelids. Above his high
forehead, nearly as high as my husband's, the figure in the painting
had almost black hair, which, together with the strong growth of hair
along his lip and jaw looked nothing like Narciso. On the other hand,
the protruding ears did liken the model to the "master."

What was in that picture? Some secret, a quiet, not to be guessed.
The portrait delighted me. Until the voice behind my back asked:

"Is he a Jew?"

I shuddered. The question shocked me. To ask if my husband
was a Jew was to offer madness to a madman, to tempt fate, to invite
some scum to denounce Narciso on suspicion of concealing his
Jewish ancestry.

After a moment, the thought calmed me that perhaps the question
referred to the painting, not to my husband:

"No, he is not. This portrait was painted at the request of the
Spanish hidalgo. Once, 'El caballero de la mano en el pecho' had a
name. But accusations of Jewishness forced the painting to be hidden
for many years, and to have its title changed. Can anybody from the
group guess what gave rise to these accusations?"

I always tried to draw my listeners into conversation, to make them
work and think. This allowed me to control them.

Somebody said:

"It's the hand on his chest, right?"

The face staring at us from the portrait was calm and closed.
Focussed. Maybe a bit too focussed, as if it wanted at all costs to

hypnotize the viewer, to draw him away from the remainder of the portrait, including the hand.

An older gentleman began to speak. "Actually, wasn't El Greco Jewish himself? He lived, after all, in the Jewish quarter, right? I had the pleasure of helping a bit in our Holy Office of—"

"The Inquisition."

"Yes, the Inquisition. There I became acquainted with certain Jewish gestures. There is a blessing that involves a similar spacing of the fingers. This painting might be some kind of crypto-Jewish secret. Do you, Ma'am, have a different interpretation?"

I began to defend El Greco, even though I knew that he did not need any defending.

"I believe, Sir, that you are thinking of the birkat kohanim, which began from the word: 'Peace,' that is 'Shalom.' The first letter was the letter Shin, which resembles the arrangement of the knight's fingers in this portrait. Only that, in this blessing, you joined the pointer finger with the middle finger, and the ring finger with the pinky. Not quite what is shown in the painting."

"You know a lot about Jews, Ma'am…" the man grumbled.

Someone spoke up in my defense:

"Oh, every other stone in every Jewish cemetery has this symbol, the one she is speaking of."

The lady who had brought her provincial relative joined in:

"In Madrid, I came across the 'Exercitia spiritualia' of Saint Ignatius of Loyola. He advises that we lay our hand like so on our chest when we feel sorrow for our sins, when we confess them to God."

The relative interrupted, not wanting to be left behind:

"Ignatius of Loyola didn't play with his fingers, cousin. Loyola does not suggest we spread the fingers in any way…"

"Well then, where does this finger arrangement come from?"

I began to speak. Always, when I explain something to others, I feel calmer. I know I can decipher each puzzle with the aid of interpretation. I looked at the portrait and I explained:

"There are many paintings in which hands are arranged similarly. For example, it might be the hand that feeds, a woman's hand, it seems. But only a woman's hand? Right there, on the gable wall of our sacristy hangs another painting by El Greco, a gift to the cathedral. He chose a moment that is appropriate for the sacristy, where the celebrants assume their vestments, 'El Expolio.' In a moment, Christ will be raised on the cross. Before they nail Him down, they will tear His clothes from Him and gamble amongst themselves with them. Christ gives Himself up, He accepts this, He lays His hand on His breast in the same gesture as the knight."

They noticed the similarity and whispered their approval and amazement. I went on:

"Grace flows from the heart of Jesus, and so Christ's gesture might be a gift, a symbol of sustenance. However, in the case of the knight, it must mean something else, right? Maybe it is simply the secrets hidden in the heart of the knight, a feeling for someone whose image is almost entirely obscured under the robe. Maybe the fingers of his hand are arranged in a story. The thumb, bent upwards towards the head of the knight. Addressing the entire gesture. 'I.' The second figure pointed towards his heart. 'Love.' Further, the middle finger joined with the ring finger. And, finally, the little finger pointing towards his sword. We can read this as: 'My love is so, that only the sword (or death) can separate my lover from me.' Or maybe: 'My secrets are safely hidden in my heart, and who wishes to discover them will face my sword.'"

"Whom does he love, this knight who resembles our master Tomé?"

The same woman who had started the entire discussion asked this question. And then I looked at her for the first time. She stood beside the gentleman who boasted of his contacts in the Inquisition. Maybe this is why I had not noticed her, as this gentleman was huge, hulking, his face crooked and hidden behind a beard and moustache. He dominated this group.

The woman was short. She had a small head with combed hair piled in a knot, into which she had clipped a comb shaped like a fan, and from beneath it flowed a dark veil covering her neck, shoulders, and breasts. Her face, the olive face of an Arab or a southern Jew, was familiar. I had seen her often in mirrors during my dreams about Narciso.

It was I!

It was her, Nora. At least, that is what I believed, then.

I was not dreaming. My legs were shaking and I felt the sweat on my upper lip, but I continued coldly:

"Many people believe that this painting is a self-portrait. Hence, hidden in the paint among the folds of his coat—right here, at the height of his belt—there would be a likeness of his wife, doña Jerómina de las Cuevas—"

"Or the knight's mistress?" Again the same voice, giggling quietly.

"Or the unrequited love of the artist. There is a story that El Greco loved and corresponded with Rachel, the beautiful daughter of the rabbi Saul, who left Toledo for Poland. To know for sure, it would be enough to reveal the top layer of the painting, the folds covering the small portrait. Or maybe the portrait is of Vázquez de Coronado, who conquered Granada, and whose saying, 'So instructs the heart' has been so artfully reproduced here."

I showed them a few other paintings and returned to my house. I felt cramped in the dress I had chosen for today. My blue dress, which clasped my chest tightly, flattening my bust.

Days like this I hate my life. Anger bursts my body from head to toe. In the kitchen, Petra was cooking a meal for us. I gave her the dress I had been wearing.

In the evening we tried to make some alterations so that Petra's new dress fit her flawlessly. Then a strange thing happened. I did not notice that Petra had removed her old dress and was standing before me in only her underwear, audaciously beautiful, the perky peaks of her girlish breasts, narrow hips, heavy braided hair. Then, when I pinned the bosom of the dress to her breasts, Petra clung to me, panting.

I should have understood her needs. She was, after all, a lonely girl from the province in a big city, without her family, without any relatives, without friends. Maybe I was going to let her have this moment, but when I felt her hands on my back, my loins, my buttocks—I could not stand it.

I hit her in the face and Petra fell to her knees.

I had not hit her hard. She fell to her knees and to my surprise she took my hand and raised it to her lips:

"Kill me, Ma'am, but do not send me away."

I let her stay, her head on my lap, her hands on my calves. It was sweet. Petra did not need to say anything. I understood everything wordlessly. I had become accustomed to passion only in dreams, and coldness in waking, and I needed time to understand that somebody loved me, desired me, felt passion for me. And at the same time, I was quite indifferent to the fact that she would have her moment of satisfaction in the caress of my yielding body. And it was the caress she desired, not me.

And after, as if nothing had happened, we stood before the mirror, me behind her back, behind her body. It seemed that she was I, and I was Nora, a disembodied figure manifesting herself only in dreams. Petra, even though she was twenty years younger than me, was very similar to me, especially in this dress.

That night I fell asleep hard, heavy, and fitful. I escaped into the dream. Not into an ordinary dream, but into that particular dream, of Narciso. I escaped into the dream not only because the day had been difficult, but also because I wanted to see if I, Nora, had been in the cathedral, if I had guided myself today.

Did I answer this question?

When I am with Narciso, I, doña Esperanza Tomé, who is telling this story, and I, Nora, in whose body I am—I do not think, we do not think.

They had stopped loving each other and lay, trying to thaw the mountains of snow on the bed. I grabbed a knife and thrust it against

Narciso's neck. I dug it into the Adam's apple on my husband's neck, my lover's neck, snarling in his face:

"I will kill you if you betray me with another!"

He swore his faithfulness.

Now that I think about it, it seems to me that he did not know who he was promising it to.

And then she took him, sat and galloped forwards and backwards, pulling him inside her. Had somebody poured five hundred pearls on our bed, she would have pulled them inside her one after the other. His ecstasy and her trance, the dance on Narciso's stomach lasted until my husband, my lover, lost consciousness. And maybe even a bit longer, because, blinded by her desire, she had not noticed the moment in which he began to fall.

She revived him and, afraid for his health, wanted to take him home.

He was so weak that he agreed.

Yes, I was furious, that I, in a stranger's skin, was betraying a stranger's husband with my own husband. At the same time, I felt a sweetness flowing from the sky, with nightfall, curling once about us like a cat.

They walked close together through the dusk, along the edge of the Jewish quarter, holding hands like lovers. Her body moved with pleasure, every muscle sore and stretched, smooth and happy. Even her crotch bitten like a dog was happy. Especially happy. And when she understood that until now nobody had made her this happy, she pulled him to the side, into an alley, and kissed him. He staggered, leaning, and then rolled against the wall, so that she noticed something familiar behind him.

The blacksmith's shop.

"Come, I'll show you something."

It was very loud. The others in the workshop had not heard them when they entered. At several stations, blades were being forged, inserted into embers until glowing red, and then placed on an anvil and hammered again and again.

I had lived for so many years in Toledo, and I had never seen how they forged rapiers and swords. My body moved easily past the furnaces and anvils in order to arrive at the end of the workshop.

There, at the last station, a red-haired youth worked, naked to his waist. His body shone fiercely, defining every muscle, every sinew. He was beautiful and shy and wanted to cover himself with a shirt, but she told him not to put one on. I felt Nora's domination of him was a show for Narciso, a demonstration of how she could have this youth, and yet she wanted only him, her architect.

"This is my architect, Narciso Tomé," I said. "And this is my blacksmith, Italo Calvino, making the most expensive sword in the city for my husband. Show us your work."

Italo obediently pulled the blade from the embers and dipped it into a vat where the water surged. He wiped it with a thick cloth and laid it on the anvil before us.

"Nothing special, right? Do you know, Sir, you are looking at the best blade in the world? You are probably thinking that I am prideful, that I should be more modest… In Toledo, the local blacksmiths have worked for centuries, but it was my great-grandfather, an immigrant, who perfected today's methods. Do you know how, Sir? Listen, please, it is not a long story…"[18]

---

18 A story about the poet who revolutionized the production of swords in Toledo.

My great-grandfather's name was the same as mine, Italo, and he came from Italy. He was a free thinker and—as it was called in those days—a religious dissident. He was not a Roman Catholic, but a Calvinist. Most importantly, however, he was a poet and revolutionary. When the Jesuits in Vilnius murdered his friend Francis de Franco, my great-grandfather immediately set out for Poland to murder the Jesuit who did it. This Jesuit was named Skarga, Piotr Skarga, and not only did he survive my great-grandfather's visit, but it was precisely my great-grandfather who saved Skarga from the Jesuit henchmen who wanted to try him for treason. A complicated country, this Poland.

In Poland, Italo met my great-grandmother, the beautiful Helena, with whom he ran away to Spain, here to Toledo. Helena became a model for El Greco, and my great-grandfather, who went lame along the way, became a blacksmith. Initially,

"Touch, Sir, the metal. You cannot feel any tension in it. There is only a deadly calm and lethal cold. This blade, Sir, could be used by a surgeon to operate, or as a battering ram to crumble the walls of a city. It does not leave wounds, because it does not hesitate or tremble when it strikes. It is a part of the cosmos, like a bolt of lightning created by nature, not by a blacksmith who sat the whole time at the anvil and polished his fingernails."

"Do you know, Sir, that we blacksmiths from Toledo believe that every blade has his master, who it will be unable to kill? You must only add a hair, a drop of blood, or a piece of the owner's skin, and the blade will not turn against him… The lady's husband has refused. He does not believe in superstitions. He also does not like that the basket, the handle, is copied from El Greco's 'El caballero de la mano en el pecho.' This is the very sword from El Greco's painting, ha, ha, ha!"

"Ma'am, Sir, please wait, I will bring the key to our chest and I will show you a wonder. They delivered it today."

The red-haired blacksmith placed the blade in the bucket of water and walked away, leaving the couple, covered by their cloaks, at the end of the workshop. Their cloaks shook to the rhythm of the hammering behind their backs. Their faces were lit by the fire, and they felt the rumbling, grinding, and hissing of the forge:

---

he hammered and shaped steel like French dough for a "croissant," because this is the local secret for the production of blades. You need to hammer and wrap the steel a specific number of times, and only then is it strongest. Unfortunately, if you make a mistake, the steel vibrates and becomes brittle, like French pastry. Italo, who played the lute, introduced a new chord, from a different metal, to the swords and blades. He increased the blades' internal tension in the same manner as the strings of the lute, or, the same manner as a story's unexpected turns.

Of course, it's simple to fold a blade over and to hammer along the length, but to fold over the long edge and hammer along the width—that was a real art! It is my great-grandfather who taught this art to the blacksmiths of Toledo.

first
    once together
        the anvil and hammer,
then pressed to
    the heat
        and straight to the water,

and steam to the sky!

and again on the anvil,
    the heat,
        the fire
            the water,
and with bellows
    propel it
        and sparks to the stars!
bang! boom! swish! Oh, oh…

Her hand crept from under the cloak into his pants where it rose and fell with the rhythm of the forge, until suddenly she yanked his penis from his clothes and directed his spurts towards the bucket. White drops fell on the metal and ran softly down to the water's surface, slipped beneath it and continued sliding along the blade to the bottom in the darkness and tremor.

The redhead returned with a great key, opened a chest chained to a post, and removed an elaborate gold hilt. For a moment, he laid it in Nora's hands, and then took the blade from the water, wiped it, and gave it to Narciso. Guiding their hands, he slid the end of the blade into the hilt, turned the two parts together and pulled Narciso away. On Nora's open hands lay this fantastic weapon. Perfectly balanced, it hovered horizontally in the air. Immaterial. When Italo pushed Nora's elbow towards the post, the sword softly entered the wood and stayed there, motionless, in the same position as a moment ago, on the hand of Nora, this time hanging in the vibrating air of the forge.

"The sword serves well for thrusts, but it is also similar to its brother—the rapier, which stabs, cuts, and parries. The secret to their difference lies here..." He pointed to the handle of the sword. "The handle is the basket, which is made up of the grip and the ricasso. Both parts are separated by the hilt—this is the transverse element, which in every sword and rapier looks like a cross. The part above protects the hand and is called the guard, and this, the parts below the handle, are the sweepings..."

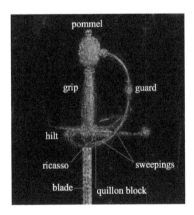

"Blacksmith, what use do we have for this knowledge?" Nora asked.

And then a strange thing happened. The blacksmith continued to speak, but the voice seemed to come not from his lips, but from the sword:

"This is not just knowledge, but the key to your story, Ma'am. The thought is simple: a man meets a woman. This meeting is represented by the intersection of the hilt with the blade. The sweepings represent the complexities of history, its tangled events, intrigues, sudden turns. The guard suggests a solution, the climax."

"It seems as though this story is going to break away from the meeting of man and woman and soar into the sky…" Nora said.

"Just as well, the whole story will go to the man's head."

"Or hit him in the head…" Narciso added.

"Maybe everything is simply happening in somebody's head, Narciso."

"So why, then, do you forge a sword for a hand, and not for a head?"

"You are mistaken, Sir, because this weapon begins with the head and ends with a hilt, and along the way it winds its way into a horseshoe, a horseshoe for asses that do not understand the essence of the sword or the meaning of their lives."

"Is the essence of the sword not killing?"

"Is the end of every life not death? And yet, death is not the meaning."

"Blacksmith, if you dream that you are a philosopher and not an accessory to murder, it is time to wake up."

"But Sir! Rather, I should repent for satisfying the vanity of my clients. For them, my creations are confirmations of their masculinity. For them, I am like a caveman producing clubs, and the best club will always confuse the enemy as to the size of its owner's manhood… Forgive me, Ma'am."

The group laughed. Nora pointed to something on the post:

"And this, what are these strange symbols?"

"Yesterday some blacksmiths arrived from Nippon, in order to learn how to forge swords for their nobles, who are called Samu-rai, like 'ray,' because they live in the light. One of the blacksmiths wrote a poem with these 'hieroglyphs,'[19] and here is his interpretation in Castilian.

---

19   麦めしに　やつる〻恋か　猫の妻

Mugimeshi ni yatsururu koi ka neko no tsuma

Girl cat, so thin on love and barley (trans. Lucien Stryk)

This is a haiku written by the Japanese poet Matsuo Basho (松尾芭蕉) in the seventeenth century. Basho urged poets of haiku to liberate themselves from

Girl cat, so
thin on love
and barley.

"Wait a minute, wait a minute," the blacksmith said to himself: "Something isn't right. They told me that the poem must have only seventeen syllables. Five—seven—five. I think it should be translated like this:

Thin is the she-cat,
When all she has to live on
Is love and barley.

"Wouldn't it sound better like this?" Nora asked and recited:

So that the she-cat
Remains skinny, she must live
On love and barley.

Cutting through Nora's voice, I gave my own version: "And what would you say about this:

To keep herself thin,
They betray his wife. Barley
And lust, fill her life.

They laughed and waited for Narciso's version. He struggled, and finally blurted out:

---

an attachment to surface reality with the help of "karumi" (lightness). The typical "detachment" from reality that accompanies artistic expression in Zen Buddhism grows out of a deep reflection on the fate of humanity.

Skinny, the she-cat's
Barley is her daily bread.
And for dessert, love.

\*

"Wouldn't this world be paradise if blacksmiths forged literature, not swords?" Nora asked after they left the shop.

"I do not know if the world would be beautiful if everything they created in the forge was literature, Ma'am. This hammering does not always strengthen its object. I am weak like... a cat without barley..."

"Then let's eat something in the Jewish quarter, Narciso!"

But Narciso was not to be persuaded. He left me at the edge of the Jewish quarter and its smells, open taverns, inviting music, bubbling wine. It was only midnight. Life in the Jewish quarter was beginning in earnest.

She covered her face with her veil and scurried to a familiar place. Above the entrance hung a stuffed and inflated spiny fish, whose meat is a delicacy (when skillfully prepared) or poison (when the cook is inexperienced). Beyond the creaking doors, rows of animals were standing, hanging, or resting on shelves, so that the shop resembled Noah's ark, congealed into eternity before settling on Ararat. Noah, the owner, looked stuffed himself:

"Oh, it's you, Ma'am... What do you need today?"

"Advice, as usual."

"I've got a stuffed donkey on which a certain young lady with an illegitimate child fled to Egypt. Maybe it is time for you, Ma'am, to do the same..."

"Have an illegitimate child?! Don't be ridiculous... My love is cooling, old man. Give me something, please."

Noah brightened, and with a slow step went to the corner where a wardrobe consisting of a thousand drawers took up the whole wall.

Like a blind man, he pulled out drawers of surprising length, reached a hand into them, and then returned to the fireplace without closing any. He laid something on the edge of the hearth. After a few breaths, the embers made visible the small body of a beetle lying there. It was thick and long like a thumb and had a greenish sheen. It was dead. Noah crushed the beetle and rubbed it in the ash, and then poured the powder into a small wooden box. He gave it to Nora without a word.

"How much?"

"The same as for the donkey."

"What?!" Nora, after a moment of silence, reached into her purse and counted the money: "Poured into food? Mixed with wine?"

"Some medications must pass through the entire organism in order to work. From mouth to end. But this one works just at the end… It will be enough to rub it in, pardon my language, Ma'am, on the anus."

"I paid that much for this bullshit?"

"I assure you, Ma'am, that a tiny bit of this powder on the tail of any of my stuffed menagerie would resurrect my shop into an orgy."

"What have I bought?"

"Spanish fly." He hesitated, as if to say something else, and then added: "But before you decide to use this powder, Ma'am, please accept my advice. God gave men two heads, but only enough blood for one. If you cut off the blood flow to the one above, then the one below will come alive… Place a noose, Ma'am, around the neck of your partner and tighten it, when you are together. Of course, do not strangle him to the end… If this does not please you, use the fly."

Before I awoke, I heard Nora, through my dreams, speaking senselessly:

"A fly, a fly, to get me high…"

I still did not know the relationship between Nora, whom I had guided through the sacristy, and Nora, into whom I was transported in my dreams.

# DREAM 7

*(Two weeks later, doña Esperanza Tomé no longer talks about so-called reality, and only escapes into dreams, where she chooses to die from pleasure.)*

MAYBE THIS TIME I WANTED TOO MUCH TO FLEE, BECAUSE I IMMEDI-ately found myself in Narciso's arms. My dream began in the middle of the action, in the middle of the fear that a new ice age was coming, maybe already the second this evening. The room was like a battlefield. The table overturned, spilled wine, broken glass. Among the broken plates, liver and oysters. The sheets drenched in red wine like blood.

The drunken eyes of the chaperone in the crack above the door every so often changed into another's, a stranger's, the eyes of male voyeurs, to whom Maja sold admission to the intimate moments of her lady.

Narciso loved me still another hour. He was exhausted. Between his ribs throbbed balloons—as if his heart was trying to burst from him. His sweat poured on me in streams, biting my eyes and mixing with my tears. She cried and felt the sweetness that comes before death. Narciso was approaching that singular spot in the depths of her body, sensitive to the point of unconsciousness, killing her. She was dying not only from pleasure, but also physically. This second death was not a metaphor. She felt it coming:

"Narciso, I'm dying…"

"Oh yes!" he gasped: "We will die together. Now! What future for us? Only in death can we be together. Let us love each other until the end."

He terrified me, because I knew that he was not joking. His eyes bulged from his skull, blood rushed to his face. He terrified me so that I began to plead from Nora's lips:

"No, please let me survive this day! We will die tomorrow. You will visit me. We can die at my place."

I don't know if he heard. In this dream it was like I was in a dream. It seemed as though I was standing beside Maja behind the doors, listening to the scuffling in our room and counting the pay of another voyeur, whom I allowed to take my place, to stand on my chair. I saw how he crawled up, stood, put his eyes to the crack and grabbed his crotch. I waited a moment still, until he began to pant and kicked the stool out from under him.

I was able to guide Maja from a distance? I could be her!

Immediately I was filled with rage at Maja's disobedience—after all, she was supposed to have prepared my husband for his trip today. My husband, meaning Nora's. I found I had access to Nora's thoughts and these strange abilities. When Narciso fell off me for a moment, I grabbed a glass and threw it at the doors. It shattered. I howled from the bed:

"You bitch, you were supposed to prepare your master's luggage!"

A strange feeling—as if I, doña Esperanza Tomé, who is telling this story, uttered with my own words what Nora wanted to say. And when Narciso caressed me and licked away the sweat that mingled in the cavity along my spine, I wanted him again, yet I hurried after drunken Maja, for the first time went to my home, to Nora's home, where I watched over Maja's shoulder as she packed a bag for Miguel.

My husband, Nora's husband, is named Miguel.

I saw him for the first time, I, doña Esperanza Tomé, who is telling this story. He was stocky, square, heavy like an Andalusian. He was wearing a heavy coat and riding boots. He was silent.

I, Nora, in my dream, in the dream of doña Esperanza Tomé, could pierce the souls of Nora and Maja. But Miguel's soul was like a stone, basalt. Black, impenetrable, hard, cold.

Suddenly he growled like a dog.

"The lady is where?"

"…Petting, no…she is praying. She is in religious ecstasy." I was inside Maja. I felt that I could make her say whatever I wanted:

"Sir, do not worry, for I will always hold the doors for you, in order that you will not catch on them…catch on them with…"

"With what?"

"…with those cuckold horns you are wearing," said Maja, and I could not believe my own ears in the dream. "The bitch is cheating on me!" Nora was being betrayed at the same time that she was betraying Miguel.

He hit her in the face, hit me in Maja's face. Maja fell on the bags, and I giggled drunkenly from inside her:

"Do you know, Sir, what dandruff is?"

"Of course—when skin peels from the head."

"Yeah? And I thought that it was powdered horns!"

He stared at her, at me, as she rambled:

"Sir, just make sure that you leave out the key to the lady's cha-ha-hastity belt, so that she does not ha-ha-have to use a pick! Ha-ha-ha! Because sometimes, even a pick can turn into a dick!!!"

Before he kicked her, I began to run from her body so as not to feel it. He kicked her again. I thought about the bruises. Before he kicked her a third time, he asked:

"When?"

"Tomorrow, here—Aj!" she cried, when Miguel's boot landed on her temple.

"This is for your loyalty to your lady," he said, spitting on her. And then, tossing her his purse, he said: "And this is for your loyalty to me."

He left.

It had happened. Miguel knew. He would leave and give her, Nora, time to prepare for his return. He would give me, doña Esperanza Tomé, satisfaction for what his wife had been doing with my husband in my dream…

Is any sort of satisfaction still possible?

I flew back to the body of Nora in the inn. My husband was dying. His pale body lay stretched on the red sheets, as if all the blood had leaked from him. Nora sat astride him, tightening the noose on his neck.

I was terrified that I was losing my husband, but when I found myself in Nora's body and I began to feel—I could not do anything but lean back with her and pull the scarf that was choking Narciso. Narciso's manhood was bursting inside me. And when he gasped and died with the convulsions of a hanged man, and already there was no saving him, a spasm threw her body forward, and the noose on his neck loosened so that the blood from his body, submerged in mine, surged violently, hitting his head like a stroke.

*

I awoke around noon. Narciso was gone. Petra too. For a long time, I called weakly, until I fell into a rage, which gave me energy, and gave my voice strength.

Petra came and reassured me that Narciso was at the cathedral. She did not look me in the eyes.

I told her to bring me something to eat and I fell asleep for the rest of the day and night, which must have inevitably come. The last image I remember before sleep was of "alfileritos," small needles, which grew to the size of swords piercing my heart.[20] If I, too, had been able to keep myself from sleep, would all of this, everything that I had dreamed, not have happened?

---

20  Not far from Plaza de Zocodover, at the end of Calle San Vicente, is the figure of Mary, at whose feet women pray for protection by placing needles. Apparently, a certain Toledan woman prayed here for many days and nights for the safe return of her husband from war. To keep her from sleep, her caregiver, her dueña, pierced her skin with needles, which she then laid at the feet of statue.

# EPILOGUE TO ACT I

IF NARCISO LAYS STRANGLED, OR IF HE HAS SUFFERED A STROKE AT the inn, should we not lower the curtain? I think it's time. Let the actors and the stuntmen rest, because what awaits in the second act will require much of them. Very much...

So, here ends our tragedy about love and desire, betrayal and loyalty, about dreams and reality. Wait a minute! Didn't we forget about something? Shouldn't we, even just for a moment, give our main character a chance to speak?

"Narciso! This is your story, after all, don't you want to add something from yourself?"

"..."

"No? This is not your story, just a story about you?"

"..."

"You think that somebody wants to appropriate your story. Well, defend yourself Narciso! Say something! Tell us the whole truth."

"..."

"There is no 'truth'? You don't have anything to say? Absolutely nothing?! What is this? A poem? That's it? I'm supposed to quote some poem instead of listen to your words? Well, if that's what you want, so be it."

# The Dark Night of the Soul
## *St John of the Cross*

*On a dark night*
*Burning with my love's flame*
*! Oh, happy adventure!*
*I am secretly running away.*
*Silence in my home's doorway.*

*Under the wings of darkness,*
*And through a secret gate.*
*! Oh, happy adventure!*
*In disguise, I am running away.*
*Silence in my home's doorway.*

*On this happy night,*
*Secretly, unnoticed,*
*And being seen by no one,*
*Without a guide or a lantern,*
*I was led by my love's light.*

*My love showed me the way,*
*Much clearer than the sun at noon,*
*Where someone was waiting for me.*
*Someone I will see so soon,*
*Far from here, further than the moon.*

*!Oh, night that leads!*
*!Oh, night fairer than dawn, morning!*
*! oh, night when*
*Beloved is a lover,*
*And lovers become beloved!*

*My breast as a flower opens*
*To you, my only one.*
*Stay, rest,*
*And for us*
*I will turn the cedars into fans.*

*Wind high above us,*
*My fingers in your hair,*
*Your hand*
*Embraces my neck*
*And takes my senses away.*

*I stayed, all was forgotten,*
*My face on the beloved's breast.*
*The whole world was suddenly steadfast,*
*worries among lilies could rest,*
*And I was free at last.*

# NIGHT

(Act II)

## PROLOGUE TO THE SECOND PART

IS IT THE END OF THE BREAK ALREADY? ARE WE SUPPOSED TO RAISE the curtain and begin the next act? No, not yet. Let's leave the actors behind the curtain, and when the audience quiets down, we'll be able to listen to them…

Yes, quite clearly you can hear two voices: one is female, and the second male.

"…*how blue these welts on your neck, Narciso! Forgive me, Sir, forgive me… Has anybody noticed them?*"

"Nobody else has seen them… We live beyond the time of other people. Today I wore a high collar. This does not matter anymore…"

Silence, in which you can hear only the rustle of clothes, steps, and then:

"Will you not be afraid today?"

"*Ach, let whatever happens happen… After all, there is no help for us. We are damned, and only death awaits us, contempt for life, murder or the stake, which is also murder, and then burning in the fire for all eternity…*"

"Just one of your orgasms will quench the fires of Hell…"

"*… as long as we are seated together.*"

"I would rather they stand us…"

"*Speaking of standing, look Narciso, what I have for us today.*"

"What is it?"

"*A spur for your stallion and a whip, so that you can beat the horse into a gallop. A whip twisted from Spanish flies. An aphrodisiac.*"

"From Africa?"

"*No, from the Jewish quarter... I bought it some two weeks ago. Allow me, Sir, to rub it here, between your buttocks...*"

"Auuu! It burns!"

"*It burns at the back, but look, look what it does in the front...*"

"Oooo... Opposite a fly in the ointment must be a fly in my ass! Is it only for men?"

"*Oh, no. It's even better for women...*"

"Then allow me, Ma'am, to put it now between your buttocks..."

At this moment, the duet transforms into a trio, because <u>a third voice</u> includes itself with these two previous, a male voice, resounding, assisted by the whistles of a sword cutting the air.

Third voice:

"<u>And this between your ribs!</u>"

"*Miguel!?! You missed!*"

"<u>You slept with her!</u>"

A swish and the patter of feet.

"I assure you, Sir, I didn't sleep a wink!"

"*Miguel, you were watching us?*"

"<u>You lay with my wife!</u>"

Another swish.

"I had no idea, Sir, that you were married!"

"*You had us followed?*"

"<u>Draw your sword!</u>"

The dull thud of falling furniture.

"Sir, I did not yet sheath it, how would I draw it?"

"*I knew it, that bitch turned us in!*"

"<u>You took what was most precious to me!</u>"

Swish.

"Sir, you see I can hide nothing from you, even if I wanted to. If this fly belonged to you, then I will gladly return it..."

"*Majaaa!!! I curse you! To the end of the world you will be young, you will want and you will be wanted, but you will never know fulfillment, you will want it forever as I want it in this moment!!!*"

"Aaaaa!!!"

A series of swishes and the rapid patter of feet towards the audience.

# 8. NIGHT OF THE SOLSTICE

*(Later that night, doña Esperanza learns the truth about her past dreams and dreams a few others on the topic of the future. She has not yet found out that the Inquisition has, just now, decided to eliminate the future.)*

THE DREAM WOKE ME, THE PATTER OF SHOES RUNNING TOWARDS the window. A clash of arms, the sound of the military marching over cobblestones, shouted commands. Someone had wanted to jump into the room through the drawn blinds. No, I did not think of war; rather, I felt anxious, as though something was burning. I was lying on my back, and the ceiling reflected the glaring light of torches, a light falling through the blinds, the curtains, the canopies under the window. I heard the slam of windows opening, first on the left and then on the right, the houses of doña Estefania and doña Westefania. The former was always playing dumb, and the latter—she was well informed. I heard:

"What's happening?"

"The public prosecutor is dead..."

My first naïve thought was that now, fewer would go to the stake.

"What do you mean, dead?"

"He fell from the canopies..."

It was one of the first nights of the spring, when the canopies return. In our city, the canopies were like migratory birds. They came back after winter.

"What was he doing there?"

"He was chasing his wife's lover…"

I felt something coming, some unstoppable terrible moment and I pulled the sheets close.

"The public prosecutor had a wife?"

"Of course…"

My legs wouldn't listen to me, my head was spinning as I crawled to the window and heard:

"Who was his wife?"

"Doña Nora de…"

My heart pounding in my temples, I did not catch the full name, but I knew of whom they were speaking. They were speaking of me, of Nora, in the body in which I was betraying my Narciso by sleeping with my own husband, and in this way betraying Nora's husband—the public prosecutor. I leaned on the windowsill and pushed open the shutters, which crashed against the walls of the house. I stuck out my head. Below me, beneath the surface of the canopy under the window, as though in the depths of the Milky Way, lights passed. The street was filled to the brim with light. I would never have guessed that there were this many soldiers and police in the city.

My neighbors fell silent, scared by my sudden appearance. I looked at one, then at the other, and asked:

"Are you sure that this isn't a dream?"

Doña Estefania laughed nervously, slid inside and closed the shutters behind her. Doña Westefania laughed scornfully and said:

"No, this is not a dream!" And then she added, giggling hysterically: "Finally something is happening in this hole! Apparently, the lover of the public prosecutor's wife is injured and the police are searching the entire city for him."

I went back to bed. Shadows and lights moved across the ceiling. I did not wonder where Narciso was. I knew that my two worlds had collided, and that it was I who had brought the anger and vengeance of Miguel upon Narciso and Nora. I knew that my Narciso was hiding somewhere, bleeding, and that the lifeless body of Miguel had been exposed to the public's view.

I stared at the wall, at the crumbling, yellowed fresco that had accompanied me for so many nights. I saw it. I saw the outline of a woman, quite clearly, freeing herself from the blades of grass and the shoots of tangled vines, a woman, who was pointing the way. Was this the way to freedom, or was it, rather, pointing in the direction of the stairs?

I had to calm down. I thought about my house, I thought about each floor plan, in my head I fit room over room and suddenly, like a flash, I saw another chamber, a room, hidden inside. Just under the roof, on the landing at the top of the stairs, there should be another interior space, probably octagonal, connected to the attic. A moment ago I had been tired, but now I rose quickly and ran to the stairs. On the landing I felt a different surface with my hand, a different material, a painted wooden panel. I rubbed at it, pushed at it with all my strength.

A few months ago, with Petra, we struggled to close the doors in the basement, we were afraid of the unknown behind them—now, without fear, I wanted answers, I wanted to know what my house was hiding, to know its soul…

The panel gave way and let me inside—I squeezed through a thin gap and lost my breath. Before me was a miniature replica of the interior of the Dome of the Rock. A golden dome closed the octagonal interior, reflecting a warm light that filled the room. As in Jerusalem, a great stone occupied the centre of the room. Only, in our house, there was a vessel, red-hot and filled with yellow embers, on the centre of the stone. It was like a sacrificial altar. For a moment I thought, with horror, that our house was hiding the chapel of some unknown cult, especially because on the other side of this altar I saw a priest lying on the floor.

He was blowing on the embers.

When he looked up at me and raised himself on his elbows, not only did I notice that the sacrifice must have already been made—the priest was covered with blood—I also noticed that he had the face of Narciso.

Before I could scream, he looked me in the eyes, and said:

"I destroyed our marriage. You may do what you will…"

I turned and went back to bed. Before I fell asleep, I stared at the frieze, at the woman, who I saw so clearly for the first time, saw her bursting from the dark forest, towards the light, towards a new life…

# BEING AFTER BETRAYAL I.

TRUST ME, DEAR READER, AND DON'T TRY TO FIND IT OUT FOR yourself. The moment when you discover that you have been betrayed brings shock, but also euphoria. Shock, because you feel that the reality in which you have been living is a fiction, is a lie, a deception. At the same time, however, you know that the betrayal belongs to the past— it has happened, and now there will be no more lies. The moment when you find out that you have been betrayed leaves a lot of confusion. First of all, you don't know what to do.

That night, Tomé Sr. called us to him. He was dying.

With Petra, I dressed Narciso as well as I could and we brought him to his father. By some miracle the police did not stop us on the street—I don't know. The whole time we were repeating, Tomé Sr. is dying.

It was, however, a night of lies—Tomé Sr. welcomed us in the best of health, smiling and happy. He knew about everything. He knew that Narciso was injured, that they were searching for him, that the public prosecutor was dead. Tomé Sr. quickly explained to us that we, too, were a dead family. If the public prosecutor's colleagues could prove that the whole family knew about Narciso's affair—and, after all, the Inquisition was capable of proving even the impossible to prove— the whole family would need to repent for Narciso's sins. I began to scream and demanded an explanation for why the elder Tomé had not told me that my husband was having an affair. He claimed that there was no time for explanations and that we had to act. His plan was simple: Narciso must disappear from the city, disguised as Tomé Sr. Since everybody knew that Tomé Sr. was dying, Narciso would take his place tonight, and the "body" would be carried out of the town, giving Narciso the opportunity to escape. At the same time, Tomé Sr. would replace him at the cathedral.

When the police broke into the shop by the cathedral, where Tomé Sr. had lived since the beginning of the project—Narciso, disguised as his father, was just then in the process of leaving this world. He was dying, surrounded by his family. Not everybody knew what had happened. The children, especially, were kept in the dark. Tomé Sr. confided the plan only to his confessor, who pretended to give the last rites.

Throughout the ceremony, Tomé Sr., leaning on my shoulder, poured tears, though to this day I do not know if he was pretending to cry, or if he was crying from laughter and joy at the fact that he had managed to pull off such a fantastic joke at the expense of the police.

What my children felt, and what I felt—nobody cared.

The next day, Narciso left the city in his father's coffin, snuck out of it in the cemetery chapel, and then we lowered his empty coffin into the spring earth in a small cemetery outside the city.

He did not speak to anyone. I bid him farewell without a word. I could not pull myself together after yesterday, after what had suddenly become clear. Narciso left for the city of Jaca, in Catalonia, where they had hidden the chalice known as the Grail in the old cathedral. Living as a mute, he worked as a gardener at the monastery, where he apparently made his living. I never saw him again.

Did they find the public prosecutor's wife's lover that night?

Yes and no. Because many separate groups carried out the search, each wanting to prove themselves before the new public prosecutor, a number of lovers were found. Some admitted their guilt by pulling their swords and dying on the spot, others could not withstand the torture, carried out simultaneously in many of the city's districts, and others still quietly let themselves be cuffed and brought before the slowly dying public prosecutor.

Yes—Miguel did not die that night. His fall broke his back and crushed the bones in his face. But he lived. He was paralyzed, but he could move his left hand and his right eye. He babbled.

Of course, before he began to babble, his terrible howls of pain filled the city. When the best surgeons relieved the pain in his body—he began to forgive. He forgave the potential lovers that had been brought before him in large groups by the eager police. He even forgave his wife.

Miguel's family locked Nora up with paralyzed Miguel in the old tower by the river. People say that Nora took care of him until his death, washing, feeding, tending, and suffering his furious moods for many, many years. Once a week, as though they were prisoners, food was brought to them.

Was this supposed to be a punishment for Nora?

What punishment is adequate for the crime committed?

A few days after the whole incident, Tomé Sr., disguised as Narciso, faked a fall from the scaffolding in order to explain the new way he moved. Tomé Sr. was much older than Narciso. After the accident, he moved into the same hut by the cathedral, in which he had previously lived. He never stayed with us to pretend to be my husband. He allowed me to sell the house, take the children, and return to my family in Barcelona.

# BEING AFTER BETRAYAL 2.

I AWOKE AND THOUGHT THAT IT HADN'T BEEN SUCH A BAD DREAM, it was a nice scenario, but I was terribly sad that Narciso was disappearing from my life forever.

Forever.

The word "forever" carries such terrible judgment.

I dragged myself out of bed and went upstairs.

He lay there, still, bleeding and blowing into the embers.

"And you, what do you want, Narciso?"

"Me? I finally understood that I want to be with you. With you, with the children. I want my family back... Only, there is no way back. I must flee. Otherwise, I put you in mortal danger."

I went back to bed.

I closed my eyes. Again I heard my neighbours. Their voices flew above the street like carrier pigeons.

When the first shock passes, you begin to feel sorry for the person who betrayed you. You worry about someone, who only a few days, a few hours ago, was not thinking about you at all, about your family, your life, your children, about all that you had built together through all these years. He was thinking only about himself, about his pleasure...

Despite this, I felt sorry for him. I wanted to help him.

Outside the window, the footsteps, the shouts, and the bustle of the woken city slowly subsided. It became eerily quiet, as though everyone in the city, everyone, who a moment ago had gossiped from open bedroom windows, filled their mouths with water. As though the city had sunk in some shipwreck. Toledo had become Atlantis.

One by one, quietly, like the fluttering of butterflies, the beating of moths against glass, the flutter of birds—from lips to lips, from window to window, the message repeated until street after street learned what had happened.

I did not have to participate in the gossiping. I knew. Besides, even if I did not know, the city was so quiet that I would have heard what was happening.

There, where they had carried the body of Miguel, in his home, a miracle happened. The public prosecutor came to life. This was not some unexpected miracle, because the public prosecutor was a hardy man, and the fall from the second story, softened by the canopy and his crash into the wall, robbed him of his consciousness, but not his life. When his senses returned, he expressed shock at the news of the slaughter of the alleged lovers of his wife and ordered the search ended. Unable to find his sword, he took the first rapier he found and went into the street. And then…

You do not need especially sensitive hearing to recognize the steps of a broken man, stumbling along a bumpy road and looking up, where the blood of my husband marked an escape route along the canopies. I listened with the entire city as Miguel turned and headed towards the cathedral. He walked slowly and steadily. Without a shade of doubt, he knew what he was doing. He walked to the construction site. And then, after a moment that seemed to last an eternity, I heard the familiar creak of the doors to the shop where Narciso usually worked the stones. Now, there should have been nobody there.

The doors were open. Miguel went inside and closed them behind him. The whole city held its breath. In the stillness I heard "to the dirt!" spoken with a typical Andalusian accent, and then—the horror!—the sound of a blade piercing flesh, grating against bone, and last, the ripping of a throat, a short breath.

I knew whom Miguel was seeking, and I knew that Narciso could not have suddenly transported himself from our attic to the shop at the cathedral. I did not have to wonder long, because after Miguel's words, instead of the dull thud of a body against the clay earth, I heard first the scrape of iron against stone, as though someone had lifted a sculptor's chisel, and then the sound of a body shuffling, as though someone had turned quickly, saying: "You first."

I knew that voice—it belonged to Tomé Sr.

Then I heard two dull thuds against the earth, quick steps, the creak of the gates, and cries, the voice of someone else who had been in the shop, a voice like the voice of Tomé Sr.'s confessor, explaining that Tomé Sr. had just killed the public prosecutor in self-defence.

In this way, the public prosecutor of Toledo died twice in the same night.

Of course, the city began to roar like a hive. I knew this was not the end. To the souls that had flown off for judgment that night, the souls of the public prosecutor and Tomé Sr., the souls of those murdered, alleged lovers of doña Nora, she, herself, added her own. Before the tragedy in the shop at the cathedral, Nora took her own life with the help of an overdose of some other aphrodisiac, different than the Spanish fly.

As I lay and listened to the melody of our city, played on the lowest note, above my head, halfway to Heaven, my husband bled out. He bled out, and then he fell into the embers he had prepared earlier, without knowing why. Incinerated, nothing of him remained.

It was the same with our family.

Before we buried Tomé Sr. and Narciso, letters arrived from the curia and the Inquisition. The altar was taken away from us, we were not paid a cent for the work already performed, and, at the same time, they confiscated our house, evicting us in the course of a single day.

That same day, Andres and Diego duelled and died, stabbed in a dark alley. Four widows and some children remained.

Grandmother Tomé sent us all back to our homes, to our families. She alone wanted to remain in Toledo, because her husband was buried here. Our husbands were all buried here too, but it seemed to her that it would be better for us to leave. I could not pay for my trip. In one day, we had been reduced to the depths of misery.

Did we not blame ourselves? In this state, were we not indebted to Narciso?

I do not know. I prayed for him, so that the good Lord would accept him, at least, to Purgatory, where maybe I would be able to meet him someday. I prayed, asking for help. And help came.

When we carried our meagre belongings out of our confiscated home, which the Inquisition had not taken for themselves, but had immediately placed on the market, suddenly, from out of nowhere, there appeared a young girl. She had a small head with smoothly combed hair piled on top in a heavy knot, a long neck gently sloping to her shoulders. Her breasts, pinned by her corset, were firm and her belly and waist fell flat to the folds of her dress. Her youth made of her a beauty transcending the provinces. If I had not been so dejected, I would have immediately recognized her as Nora's chaperone, who had so often accompanied us on our escapades around town with Narciso. Maja, because that was her name, brought me a bundle of money and a letter. Apparently the package, with our address, was found near Nora's body.

The letter was to my husband. My husband was dead. The seal was poor. The paper, exquisite. The script, hurried. The content, unacceptable.

"Dearest Narciso, My Lord!

If I must never see You again, let them poke out my eyes. If I must never touch You again, let them cut off my hands. If I must never again hear the beating of Your heart, let mine cease beating too.

Lord! Miguel has gone to kill You, but I know that it will not come to that, that he will stop this insanity and forgive You, oh My Lord, and everything will return to normal. Please do not tell your wife of our love. Do not destroy Your happiness. She does not need to learn of anything. You may live as though nothing happened.

Lord, I want to tell You how grateful I am to You for the happiness that You have carried into my life. It doesn't matter that we could not love each other like a man and a woman, it doesn't matter, that our love remained pure to the end, because You have given me more than any man who has ever entered me…"

I threw the letter in the mud, returned the money to Maja, screaming and spitting on her.

We were poor as church mice. The only person who helped us was my maid, the kitchen help, Petra. She invited us to the country, to her family, where we would be able to stay for some time, maybe even make enough during the harvest to return to our family home.

Harvest. I knew the parable of Ruth and I did not want to go to the country. I only felt well in the city. I agreed, however, because of the children.

I say this because Petra's village lies north of Toledo. To get there, we had to pass through the Jewish quarter. Just before leaving the city, before the gate and the guards, something strange happened.

Petra walked ahead, the children behind her, and I at the rear, with food and water for the road. I stopped only for a second, to readjust my pack. Without thinking, I glanced to the side, into a shaded hallway. On a hot day, even the sight of shade cools. At the very end of the hall, in complete darkness, an eye flashed. Maybe this made me look again, wait until my eyes accustomed to the darkness, and see that there, in the deep dark, someone was standing, someone who was motioning to me. This person beckoned to me with his hand. I did not know him, I had no idea who he was, but as I approached him I saw that he had only one eye (the second was covered by a black band), that he had only one arm (the other was hanging in a sling), and that he was covered in scars and bruises. When I was an arm's length from him, I saw also that his hair was dyed black. If he had red hair he would resemble... bah!... he might even be the blacksmith who had forged Miguel's sword in my dream.

From the corner, he pulled a gnarled shepherd's staff and handed it to me, saying:

"This is for the road."

And then he turned the staff upside down, and a sword slid from within:

"This sword belongs to your husband... and it will never kill him."

"Sir, how do you know who I am, and yet do not know that my husband is dead."

He laughed:

"The Lord will guide you with staff and cane..."

And he vanished.

We left the city without being stopped by anybody. I was sure that the man who gave me this staff wanted to rid himself of the evidence of his theft.

The blade in the wood was simple and bare. It was without any expensive handle or guard and had probably been broken into pieces and sold. It was only when we sat down to rest in a green pasture, next to calm water, when I was breaking the bread for our group and thinking that the Lord, indeed, was guiding us, and that happiness and grace would follow me everywhere, and I already knew where I was meant to go, yes, to be able to live in the House of the Lord for years to come, only then did the suspicion begin to rise in me.

After all, what the boy told me as he handed me the staff did not necessarily have to mean that the sword could not kill my husband, since he was already a cold corpse. Rather, the sword could kill anybody, just not my husband.

My husband lives.

The realization struck me. After all, no one had seen him incinerated in the attic. The body was half burned... And maybe it was not his body, but the body of the errand boy who vanished that same night on which Narciso was devoured.

Suddenly, I realized that I was holding the answer to the riddle in my hand. If the sword would not kill Narciso—is was not clear, that every man who died by this sword could not be my husband.

I would find Narciso by simple elimination.

I was smiling, immersed in my thoughts. Petra did not return my smile. On the contrary, she looked into my face with horror.

# BEING AFTER BETRAYAL 3.

||||||||||||||||||||||||||||||||||||||||||||||||||||||||||||||||||||||||||||||||||||||||||||||||||||||||||||||||||||||||||||||||||||||||||||||||

I AWOKE AND THOUGHT THAT IT HAD BEEN A TERRIBLE DREAM. Terrible, although there was something to it. The desire for revenge. When the first shock, and the desire to help the person who has hurt you, passes—you begin to think differently. You begin to feel something else. This new feeling is usually pain.

He sat there still, only he seemed to be bleeding less. I bandaged his wound as best I could. It looked as though someone had pierced him through. A wound on his breast, a wound on his back. Little blood. No fever, no weakness. I always envied his vitality.

"This was supposed to be your revenge on me, yeah? For what? For what, you pig? I gave you my best years. I fed your children and ran your house! I washed your dirty underwear and treated your wounds. My ass wasn't enough for you? You had to find yourself someone younger, someone without children? Why did you do this to me?"

"Please, understand, I did not do this to hurt you…"

"Always, you've always denied everything! You coward! You were never able to admit anything. Why can't you say, 'Yes, I wanted to take revenge on you, because I pity myself!'"

"Can I finish just one sentence?"

"No! Because you have nothing to say! This slut destroyed my life and the life of my children. Because she had to have a married man. Let her keep you! You think you're special? I hope you die, you scum!"

Yes, I was outraged. I was mad as a dog. No, not like a dog, like a bull in the arena. I felt like I was dying of anger. I went back to bed. I fell asleep. Because when I am not asleep, life goes on the same, without control, without order.

Falling asleep, I heard his heavy steps going down, down. I did not care. If he wanted to give himself over to the Inquisition, he deserved it.

I worried about the children. They should have a quiet and safe place. I woke Petra and the children and we fled to Estefania, the wife of Andres. Unfortunately, my closest family, the brother of my husband, did not allow me into his home. I begged him to have pity on his nephews. He was unrelenting. He did not know us, already we did not belong to the family. The same message awaited us at the home of Esmeralda, Diego's wife. Even Tomé Sr. pretended not to hear the pounding on his door and our voices behind it.

They were afraid. They had left us to fend for ourselves. Just a little while ago, I had trusted this fate.

Instead of begging for accommodation, we bought a room in an inn near the Jewish and Arab quarters. I had never seen this inn before. Its entrance was so near the church that the beggars leaned their pans to both sides, towards the faithful and the transient. The inn was modest, but sufficient for us.

The next day I sent Petra and the children to Barcelona, where my family lived. Sending the children on such a journey was very difficult, but I knew that it was the only way out of this situation. Admittedly, by the morning, the fevered search for Nora's lovers had passed, and everything seemed to be returning to normal, but I wanted to know what was happening with Narciso. I wanted to talk to him, I wanted to talk to his family. I stayed in Toledo, promising my children that we would meet again in a week.

When I returned to the inn, all the money had vanished, along with anything of any value. The innkeeper, who also operated the bar on the ground floor, did not believe my story, and immediately demanded money for my stay. Our discussion became an argument so aggressive that the innkeeper threatened to send for the town militia. I begged him to let me work off my debt for the room. He calmed down and took me to the back of the tavern. There were stairs leading down to the basement.

Below the tavern stood rows of caged women. Some were dressed as ladies, and others were completely naked. Women from different parts of the world of all ages.

The innkeeper spread his arms and said:

"They too did not have a means to pay, and now they are saving up to buy their way out of their misery. From time to time, I put something into their purse, myself, he, he, he! Now, let us check yours…"

The innkeeper lunged at me and we tumbled beneath one of the cages. Women rushed to the bars, screaming in different languages, extending their legs and fists through the cracks, threatening the innkeeper, or me, I couldn't tell. Suddenly the basement appeared as the familiar frieze from my bedroom. Colourful dresses, legs and hands, rising like stems from between the cracks. Only the nearest cage was dark. From within the gloom, dark eyes stared at us. The innkeeper began to tear the dress from my breasts, to rip my petticoat. When his head strayed near the crack of the cage, two black hands reached from within. One grasped the innkeeper by the hair and yanked his face up, and the second plunged two fingers into his eyes, up to the knuckles. He cried out, some warm liquid gushed over me, and he convulsed. Meanwhile, the hand that killed him searched his clothes until it found his ring of keys. Then the first hand dropped the innkeeper's heavy head, and now both hands opened the cage. A black, thin, young woman stepped out. Her hair was tied in a leather sash and stood upright. Her breasts were pointed and erect. The only ornaments she wore were metal hoops and bracelets, if you did not count the thin leather bands on her hips.

The black woman tore the clothes from the dead man and put them on, and then opened the rest of the cages and fled to the floor below. I did not wait to see what would happen. I ran after her. It was clear that the space one floor down might have once been a flamenco hall, maybe even a club for naked flamenco. It had been turned into an exotic dance club. Now it was an ethnic brothel.[21]

In the city we stole two horses and galloped south. When we paused, we became friends wordlessly. My black saviour had the gift of hypnosis. She was able to look through the eyes and into the thoughts of a person, command him, read his thoughts, bah—even make him speak. Hypnosis was very tiring. Often we lay together, in each other's arms, and Uhuru, because that was her name, read my memories and cried for my fate, read the books that I remembered, giving me in return her ability to heal, her herbal medicine. It was a form of unmediated learning. We shared our knowledge through her talent. I was afraid that we would become the same person.

Our separation was approaching. I wanted to return to the city to heal, and she wanted to ride to the Sierra Madre and lead the revolution. One night, I'm sure it was the night from Friday to Saturday, we arrived at the ruins of a village. Uhuru felt that someone had left this place very recently. We began to search, but there was no trace of a living being.

---

21 Across Spain, brothels had already been recognized municipally for two hundred years, and they turned their greatest profits on religious holidays. Who benefitted from those profits, I need not say. The beautiful women of these houses convinced priests that extramarital love was not a sin. Sometimes, the clergy engaged in "Franciscan" absolution. This name was adopted after a judgment in Guissona, in Catalonia, in the year 1581. A Franciscan confessor, as penance, ordered a thrashing for the beautiful Margarita, and then pulled up her skirts and, with his own hand, made atonement on her bare bottom. In 1608, a pastor in Benigànim was convicted of extorting twenty-nine women, forcing them to commit "dirty and immoral" acts for their own absolution.

After some time, we stumbled across a hidden synagogue. The small room had to have been abandoned in a panic, because they had managed to hide only the Torah, and the pointer for reading from the Torah remained on the floor, discarded: it was thick as a baton, with a hand at the tip, a single finger pointing. Uhuru took it, and we fled the village.

I did not know what someone who could not read would want with a tool for reading. Soon I would find out what Uhuru wanted to use it for. With the help of a few leather straps, we affixed the pointer to Uhuru's abdomen, in such a way that she could manipulate it into a state of "erection" by pulling the right strap. This was the final piece of her male disguise.

"Why do you need this phallus?" I asked, as Uhuru gave herself erections on demand.

"To dominate others."

"But you are able to dominate with your mind, hypnosis… Everyone will submit to you."

"I will rape only men." The metal fist with its index finger pointing to the sky protruded from her pants: "Maybe we should break that finger off of my phallus?"

As we worked on the fist, Uhuru asked what name she should take as a robber. I suggested "Ernani," because it came to mind, and then she gave me a new name: "Ahara." I never understood its meaning.

When my name changed, I changed my life. I returned to the city and lived in the Jewish quarter. I treated the sick, collected herbs from the slopes on the other side of the Tagus, where sheep grazed. I had many sick clients…

I never learned what happened to Narciso that night. Our family—Tomé Sr., the brothers and their wives, vanished, nobody heard of them or wanted to speak of them. In the cathedral, somebody continued to work on Narciso's altar, someone whose name and position was: "Narciso Tomé—Maestro of the Cathedral in Toledo."

This was not my husband. I did not know him. This was somebody completely different.

# BEING AFTER BETRAYAL 4.

I AWOKE AND THOUGHT THAT THIS WAS A TERRIBLE STORY. However, it was lacking in pain or any feelings of guilt. I sat on the bed and let my legs down. The floor was cool and soothed my tired feet. I felt that Narciso had left while I slept. I had to check. I dragged myself upstairs.

He was still in the room, which I had come to call the "Chapel of Departure," struggling with strings, which he was hanging in the corners.

"Here, Narciso. This key opens the doors in the basement. You'll escape beyond the walls."

"In this state? With my strength I wouldn't be able to get beyond the river. Please, leave me here. Save yourself. Take the children and flee. I'll go by air, and you by land..."

I thought he had a fever, he spoke deliriously...

"Narciso, before you run away, tell me, why did you do it?"

"I don't know, I don't know, I feel like I don't understand anything. And I definitely don't know 'why.'"

"I don't care that you took some whore for yourself, slept in another bed with her, but that you broke the promises you made me... We made vows, not only before the altar, but during our love. Did those words mean nothing to you? You say nothing... Think, what will happen to your children? They will burn, they will be orphans, they will live on the street. Was satisfying your lust worth their lives? Was it more important than my life? Your lust will kill us... Would that I had never met you, that my children had never been born... How you must have hated me, that you felt you must commit such a terrible crime!"

It was as if the air had left me. I had to lie down again. Organize my thoughts. Calm my breath. Take it easy. Shhh... Spend just another moment in leisure before they came. Still enjoy the sleepy breath of the children before I heard it no more. Still a second without fear... A moment of trust in my fate.

The next day I learned that during the night the paralyzed public prosecutor had somehow ordered the search to be abandoned. The pursuit ended as abruptly as it began. There was no trace of Narciso, and nobody asked where he was. I searched for him everywhere. To no avail. The bedridden public prosecutor was replaced by another, a kinder one, it seemed. Everything returned to normal.

And Nora? Nora vanished from her store, which was boarded up.

As for us, the curia ordered us to leave the city without completing the altar. The days were filled with bustle, we sold our houses, our possessions, we sent the children to Toro, and so on. I spoke to no one. Locked in my bedroom, I wanted to wait, I wanted not to look into anybody's face, to speak to no one, to explain nothing. I wanted to die. Yes, I pitied the children, but the pain of a broken heart and a torn soul was greater than I could bear.

I wanted to die. And still I lived. I lived in humiliation and shame, without respect or honour. I lived in the bedroom. Even from the bedroom, one can make decisions. I fired Petra, sent the children and the rest of the women away, offered suggestions as to the sale of our belongings. I got rid of everything. The new owner of the house was to have it in two weeks. I had time to grow accustomed to the pain.

The pain overpowered me. I stopped eating. I drank only wine. I stared at the fresco, its tangled stems and bars. An image depicting a life frozen and static. For whole days I studied the old fresco and I could see nothing in it. I saw only herbs, mustard, deadly nightshade, the opium poppy dripping white, cannabis, the peyote cactus of New Spain…

I wanted them, I needed something to dull the pain. And then I remembered the shop from my dream. I dragged myself from the bed and in the light of the dying day went to the Jewish quarter, to Noah's shop. It was closed. Store hours mean nothing for someone for whom time has stopped. I banged until the doors opened.

Noah looked at me and knew what I came for. From his drawers he pulled herbs, already in powdered form, ready for consumption, and from the corner he pulled a stack of prints, cruel, terrifying, which he showed me after each herb. I could choose for myself, not only death, but the pain before it. A pain that would kill my pain along with me.

For Noah, pain did not have to be overcome by a different pain, a greater, more powerful pain. Just as death does not need to have anything to do with pain. According to Noah, death was a condition, a consent to a lack of life. Everyone carried it with them, delaying this agreement as long as they could.

We talked long into the night, until the conversation soothed me. I fell asleep by the table. The next day, Noah suggested that I stay and work for him. I would have, on hand, as much poison as I desired. And the decision, the delayed decision to accept any of them, would depend only on me.

I stayed.

Sometimes I served customers, but mainly I worked in the back, preparing medicines, herbs, packing, and cleaning. One afternoon, I overheard a conversation between Noah and one of the customers in the store. A woman wanted to buy a chastity belt from Noah. She had a maid, whom she did not trust, and she was afraid that the maid would seduce her lover.

"Well, Ma'am, do not give him any more of that Spanish fly…"

My heart sank when I understood who this client was.

I followed Nora when she left the store.

They lived on the edge of the Jewish quarter. It was easy to squeeze through the gate and into their yard. I listened to their conversation, from which I learned that they had rid themselves of Miguel's body, and that Narciso had taken his place. I heard also that Narciso did not want Maja to be shackled in a chastity belt. Nora threatened to report him to the Inquisition. Furious, she left the house and stumbled upon me. Narciso, disguised in casts, could not move. I did not realize how strong I was. When Nora fell, unconscious, I rushed into the house and beat Narciso. I locked him into Nora's newly purchased chastity belt. I ruined the lock, so that it would never open. I set fire to their home.

I do not know if it is just my bad luck, or if grace saved me from guilt. Nora and Narciso saved themselves from the fire. They say the two of them escaped the city towards the Sierra Madre, Narciso dressed as a woman, and Nora as his coachman. They died there, soon, at the hands of thieves.

# BEING AFTER BETRAYAL 5.

I OPENED MY EYES. UPSTAIRS, NARCISO NO LONGER TIED STRINGS to the corners of the room, but was now attaching them to a basket, with the fire at its centre.

"Now what?" I asked.

"I need to flee. If they find me here, I'll lose everybody."

"You should understand, you've already lost all of us. How do you expect to flee?"

He pointed upwards and did not speak.

"Yes!" I cried: "You should hang yourself! You should have hanged yourself before you brought this nightmare upon us! Tell me, how did this all start? When did you sleep with her for the first time? You… you pig!"

"I cannot speak now…"

"Then when will you tell me?! You're fleeing, after all, and here they will burn us all alive! In Heaven you'll tell me, or in Hell? Or maybe you will write us a letter from New Spain. Only, we will already be gone!!!"

I hit him as hard as I could, so that he would die, bleed out, and I ran downstairs.

I feared for the children. They would be here any second and they would arrest us. I needed to close the gate, lock it. Should I prepare for the siege, or rather commit mass suicide, burn the house and give them nobody?

I felt terror that I could do this. The pain drew me to the kitchen, the sharp knives, the children's bedroom so near… No…!!!

Rather, I could kill myself, leave the orphans. They cannot be condemned, after all, for the sins of their father.

On the bed, as far as possible from the kitchen, my head in the sheets, to die, to suffocate myself, to sleep, if only to keep myself from going mad with anger, with fury, which floods the eyes with blood. If only not to add my own madness to his…

I fell asleep, half strangled by the sheets.

Before the banging on the doors awakened me, I dragged myself from bed, gathered all my precious belongings, all those that had worth to me, and especially the key to my house, to which I would return someday, and I woke the children. Without a word or a question about their father, they followed me to the basement, where I turned the key once more in the lock and opened the doors wide. From the opening to the basement, sand began to pour, dirt, stones rolled past us and all the way to the opposite wall, filling the basement. Until finally, everything sank and the dust settled.

Behind the underground doors, a black abyss opened like a tunnel onto a star-filled sky and freedom. I brushed the earth from the doors and remembered to lock them behind me.

By Ávila and Salamanca, in a week we arrived in Toro, and then after another week, travelling through Santiago de Compostela, we gained entry aboard a ship to New Spain.

Life in New Spain was very difficult, so I decided to take all my things once more and go with the children to New France, where the weather and the land was unbelievably harsh, but life was easier. Through the first few years I was a midwife and I treated the children that I had helped to enter this world. I founded a school, which my daughter Hannah ran after me, dividing her time between teaching and her farm. My son Max finished university at Montréal, where he taught afterwards.

For some time, I was a subject of Napoleon Bonaparte, who, before leaving New France in that same year (1801), helped me to reclaim my house in Toledo. I returned to Toledo as a French subject. Spain, under French occupation, was waging the "Guerra de las Naranjas."[22] The local French cacique was very gracious to me. Thanks to him, one day I ordered the tunnel excavated, the tunnel through which I once escaped with my children. I used my key and stood again, after almost seventy years, in my basement. The house was abandoned, but it was our house. The same tools, floor, colours on the walls, curtains.

I walked upstairs very slowly, because when you are my age you don't walk quickly anymore, if you walk at all. I climbed to the very top. I was not interested in our bedroom, or the children's room, or the kitchen. I wanted to get there, where I had seen him last… I was so close, I was squeezing through the gap between the stairs and the chapel…

And then I awoke with the key in my hand, in the basement, seventy years earlier. I did not know anything. Not what had happened, not where I was, not when I was. For a moment I thought I was with Petra in the basement and we must open the doors, behind which there would be the underground passage. I thought nothing had happened yet, that everything could still be saved.

Startled by the cold of the basement I ran, breathless and gasping, upstairs to the children's bedroom, to make sure nothing had happened to them.

---

22  In April 1801, the French army entered Portugal, and on the 20th of May the Spanish army, under the command of Manuel de Godoy, joined them. In a battle that devastated the Portuguese, Godoy occupied the city of Olivenza on the Spanish border. After the battle, he gathered oranges and sent them to the Queen of Spain, with the message that he was advancing on Lisbon. From that moment, the conflict became known as the Guerra de las Naranjas.

The children slept. I calmed down only when I touched each of them. Warm cheeks, calm breath. Their world had not yet collapsed. They could still sleep calmly. For how long?

I did not know.

I returned to the chapel upstairs.

# BEING AFTER BETRAYAL 6.

|||||||||||||||||||||||||||||||||||||||||||||||||||||||||||||||||||||||||||||||||||||||||||||||||||||||||||||||||||||||||||||||||||||

HE SAT THERE, STILL. THIS TIME IN THE BASKET ABOVE THE GROUND. From the basket, strings extended upwards and downwards. Between his legs was burning fire.

"Why didn't you come to me and tell me that someone is trying to seduce you or that you are trying to seduce someone? Anything… You could have told me that you wanted to sleep with someone… Anything, anything would have been better than hiding this from me, from the children, from your family! How could you look us in the eyes when you were coming home after rolling in your lust? How could you kiss our children with those lips, which licked her? How could you touch me and go with me to bed as though nothing had happened? How? How!"

He did not speak. His shoulders slumped and he sat, sobbing.

I ran out of that graveyard chapel. I ran to a room I had previously arranged as a library. I wanted to be near something that could help me. I wanted to touch books, which suffered as I did, which were shredded by the Inquisition, their bodies ripped apart by the censors, written by those frightened, gagged, trembling.[23] I reached for the books, when suddenly they poured from the shelves in a stream, covering me like earth in the grave. I quieted. I calmed down.

When I dug myself out from under the piles of books, before me stood two figures. Both were similarly dressed in Arab garb, completely mismatched to the present.

"Who are you and what do you want?" I asked, surprised with myself for not demanding: "How did you get here?"

"In Hebrew my name is Moshe ben Maimon, in Arabic Mussa bin Maimun ibn Abdallah al-Kurtubi al-Israili, and in Greek Moses Maimonides. Often they call me Rambam.[24] And this is my friend, Averroes.[25] We came to correct two errors that your distant relative committed in this city many years ago."

"This is not the time for such things. My husband is in the process of leaving me, and meanwhile the entire local Inquisition is searching for him. What am I supposed to do with my life, how am I supposed to save my children?! I don't know!!!"

---

23 Of my favourite authors, the Inquisition censors twice interrogated Góngora in 1627 and 1632. Cervantes had to answer for *Don Quijote*, Francisco de Osuna and Antonio de Guevara in the year 1612 found themselves on the index, Florián de Ocampo in 1632. The index tracked even the dead, as in the case of Lope de Vega.

24 Maimonides was born in Córdoba in the year 1135. He studied the Torah under the watch of his father, Maimon, a disciple of the Rabbi Joseph ibn Migash. In the year 1148, Córdoba was conquered by the Almohads, who graciously offered the Jews of Córdoba a choice between conversion to Islam, exile, or death. Maimonides's family chose exile. Living initially in the south of Spain, the family eventually moved to Morocco, where Maimonides attended the University of Fez. Near the end of his life he settled in Fustat in Egypt, where he was the physician of the Great Sage Alfadhila, and possibly even the Sultan Saladin himself. While in Egypt, Maimonides wrote his most important works. He died on the 13th of December in the year 1204, in Fustat, and was buried in Tiberias.

25 Averroes was born in Córdoba in the year 1126. He died in Marrakesh, in Morocco, on the 10th of December in the year 1198. He was a philosopher and a physician.

"Very good," said Maimonides: "When you know how to say 'I don't know,' only then can you finish what you have started."

"What is there to finish if I cannot make any sort of decision?"

"The risk of a bad decision is better than the terror of a lack of decision."

"I don't need your wisdom, especially when I don't know whether you are a product of my sick brain, a mirage, a ghost, or an undigested piece of dinner."

"You must accept the truth, regardless of its source."

"Exactly," the one who was introduced as Averroes interjected. "It is not true that I could not find the referents for words such as 'tragedy' or 'comedy.' The proper translation does not exist, and the boundaries of my language are not the boundaries of my reality."

"Yes, definitely not..." I said, looking at them carefully, because if they were philosophers, how could they have entered my house in the night?

"That's the influence of my 'negative theology.' And that is the second correction that we wish to make."

"And the first?" I asked.

"Haven't I told you yet? The inadequacy of the non-reality of language to represent our unnameable unreality. I howl and I express that I feel pain, but I howl because I do not have, in my language, an expression that can express this pain verbally and physically. I am not seeking impossible words like 'tragedy' or 'comedy,' I just cry or laugh. My whole life I did not write or speak in a language other than Arabic, and nobody else wrote or spoke in a language other than Arabic, not only in Spain, not only in Africa, and not only in the East. And nobody understood me!"

"Exactly," Maimonides added. "Was it not your ancestor, Jacob Anatoli, who wrongly translated into Hebrew, from Arabic, my colleague's commentary on Aristotle, and then was it also not him who translated my "Guide for the Perplexed"?"

"I've never heard anything about my ancestor Jacob..."

"Exactly. I wrote that there should not be any contradictions between the truths revealed by God and those that the human mind discovers. However, to describe God, we should not say: 'there is one God.' To gain and to express knowledge of God, we should describe not what God is, but what God is not."

"Describe God in negative terms?"

"Description! The root of evil! The material world is the source of evil and imperfection."

"And death? Only after death can the soul perfect itself, since in life it is tied to the material world?" I entered the discussion: "A floor above us, my ex-husband exists, even though he was murdered last night. Since he came to life immediately after his death, will he be a better man?"

"My dear lady, resurrection is neither permanent nor general. God does not change the laws of nature. In this light, every risen person must have once been dead."

"Not if he was Christ," I said.

"The lady herself uses the past tense… And your husband, if I may ask, in what sphere should he make improvements?"

"My husband was a lecher."

"In this matter, I would use the past tense very carefully. Further, a disease that can be cured by diet, should not be cured any other way." He looked at Averroes, who was now slumbering, and said: "Orange yourself and be ready to go. Ma'am, did you remember everything?"

I thought how terrible the change must have been for my interlocutor, leaving Córdoba, the collapse of his whole reality. And now, it did not carry the slightest importance for him. On the contrary, his exile allowed for his education, his creativity. In Córdoba, even though there are no more Jews, the residents will make a monument for him, and couples in love will sit at its base at nighttime. Their kisses will smell like red wine. In the narrow streets, their laughter will frighten the transparent geckos, chasing them from the dreams of the people asleep behind warm walls.

I would like, someday, to go to Córdoba with Narciso.

# BEING AFTER BETRAYAL 7.

||||||||||||||||||||||||||||||||||||||||||||||||||||||||||||||||||||||||||||||||||||||||||||||||||||||||||||||||||||||||||||||||||||||||||||||||||||||||||||||||||

I AWOKE NUMB, AS THOUGH THE BLOOD HAD RUN FROM MY ENTIRE body. I could not move my hands or legs. I could not find my voice in my throat. I had the impression that all these months I had dreamed had really passed. I was a bedridden old woman. I had not eaten anything. I was gaunt.

I looked at my toes and ordered them to move. I looked at my fingers and ordered them to move. I looked at my breasts and ordered myself to breathe. I had turned into an icicle…

This metaphor reminded me of Nora, and the memory awoke in me an anger and a fury, and pain, and jealousy, and hatred, and pity for myself, and a feeling of lost honour, and humiliation, and I screamed and tore myself from this powerlessness.

I raised my shirt and noticed that my body really had thinned that night. Long unseen muscles peered from under my skin. I looked like a young, athletic girl.

In the room upstairs, Narciso sat as I had left him. I said:

"Stay. We can try to start everything anew."

He was silent, crying.

"You do not need to leave. You were a good father to our children. They love you…"

Nothing, no response. Only the crackle of the fire beside him.

"Say something."

"I do not know what to say. Everything that comes to my head sounds unreal. I want to tell you that I know how I hurt you and it is too late to fix that. I want to tell you that I always loved you…"

"Shut up!!! How dare you say something like that?"

"See for yourself…"

"Say something that will change all this! Say something real!"

"See for yourself…"

He babbled something else in his voice like a beaten dog. I began to dance, stamping and shouting my farewell song to him:

"Betrayal, a splinter of glass / Crawled into my life, it lasts. / Your slut, she's cheap and fast / And because of her, my past / Reeks of shit. Is that it? / I'm no slut, not a bit, / And the acts that you commit / Have pained my heart, it splits / In half. We are finished. / All this you have diminished. / And I pray, may your shaft rot / For all the other women you have sought. / And all that you have given me / Is pain and hurt and frenzy / There is no love in thee / And not a drop of sensitivity. / You are dull, stupid, small / And I pray that you will bawl / Until you have repaid my tears / Through these many, many years. / The children will despise you. / You and I are through / Forever. So never, never more / Will you be my husband, you're / So cruel! You and your whore lover / You two can have each other. / You want our love and family, rather? / Those you will never recover."

He did not answer.

Down, down the stairs with a dying candle in my hands. I am going alone. Never again will I hear your tired steps on the stairs. Never again will I go with you. I am alone. Emptiness. The humpbacked shadow on the wall beside me. It's her. Her name is Solitude. She whispers in my ear, I am old, since he left.

He has left—since when?

Was he ever with me? He, Narciso, surrounded by mirrors, fixated on himself, mutilating and castrating himself in his autoeroticism. Closed and impenetrable. Withdrawn even from his own life.

Did he ever love?

Maybe once—his prematurely deceased sister. If he loved her and for his love he received death, could he love me without fear, fear that he would lose me too? In reality, when love dies, it leaves—a lack of love secures lasting. He did not love, so to protect? Why did he not protect me from himself? Was it my own fault? I—a moth, I—a bull seeing only the veil, not the sword. I—a mirror for Narciso and his reflection in it. Looking into me, he saw only himself. Listening to my words, he heard only himself. He touched me, but felt only himself under his own fingers. Loving his children, he loved only himself. All the tastes and smells were him. Narciso's world was himself, was Narciso.

A loneliness formed of himself. Beloved. Blindly reflected and blinded. Blind like love.

And I? I was your wife, Narciso.

Doomed to the impossibility of seducing him, reaching him with words other than his own. As a reflection, doomed to mirror him. I—mother of languages. Desperately and unsuccessfully calling the unity and the light before the creation of the world in Narciso's life. It was my voice and my words that declared:

"Fiat lux!"

And there was light.

Why did you not want to live in my world, Narciso?

Why did you not want us to be together?

You did not want to hear my voice, calling you there, where we could be together, where two become one. And even though we are only one, that one is everything.

It's all the same.

What do I have left after you, Narciso? Pain. Tubers on the shelf in the kitchen, onions like severed testicles. If I live until tomorrow, I will plant them in the garden, so that my husband will bloom every year. The pain will bloom in April as a punishment for the crime, and after that, some forgiveness? My husband, my flower with the bowed and embarrassed head. I will plant you by the pond, opposite your reflection. You will stare at yourself, without words, only silence. Only I will tell your story.

I am this story.

Narciso is me.

# DAYBREAK

## (ACT III)

# EXULTATION

*(In this scene, we flee Toledo in a flying machine,
which is steered by the thoughts of Narciso.)*

I THOUGHT OF THE UMBILICAL CORD.

I cut the last string holding me to the house. I cut it literally, not metaphorically. I watched as it fell onto the floorboards of my temple, my final hiding place on earth, with bloodstains on the stage. Genuine blood on a metaphorical stage.

I lifted very slowly, as in a dream, as a dandelion seed in the spring, above the walls, above the ceiling, above the roof. A light breeze pushed me past the edge of the roof, just above the warm shingles and onto the street, above the entrance to our house.

I heard a banging at the entrance gate. The pounding was coming from both sides. The sound came from within our house, it jumped up the stairs, to the top, to the top… and at the same time, a rumbling in the street, like a judgment.

I leaned down and understood that I must be delirious. I must be delirious, because what I saw could only be an illusion.

Before our gate the Inquisition's police force swirled, with a smartly-dressed gentleman in charge. When the doors opened, my wife, Esperanza Tomé, stood on the threshold in a blue dress, tight around her breasts, flattening her bust. I, Narciso Tomé, stood beside her.

I moved above the street, but below me I could clearly hear the gentleman speaking to my wife:

"Our guide! Lady, forgive me for disturbing you this calm evening, but I wanted to express my highest admiration and appreciation for your knowledge and your abilities of interpretation. The day, Ma'am, that you showed me El Greco's 'El caballero de la mano en el pecho' will always remain in my memory."

He bowed, sweeping his hat across the threshold, and then turned to me, standing four stories below the place from which I was observing the entire scene, and added:

"Sir, God must be gracious to have blessed you with such a wife."

Here, a series of bows, after which the gentleman continued:

"Are you, Sir, the only man in this house?"

I bowed there, on our doorstep, and spoke not in my own voice:

"Yes, but please come in and convince yourself…"

"This is not necessary." The gentleman held back his soldiers, which, already feeling welcome, had begun to surge forward like green algae in the sea.

"It will be enough, Sir, if you just show us your back."

"?"

"Sir, we are looking for someone who was injured this night, and we have reason to believe that his injury is on his back."

To my amazement, I, standing on the threshold, turned my back to the police forces and pulled up my coat and shirt. In this moment, the wind pushed me a bit further, beyond the edge of the roof on the opposite side of the street, and the entire scene vanished.

I knew what had happened.

On my back were written not only the meetings with Nora, her fingernails carving day after day, night after night, but also a tiny drop of blood, the payment her husband demanded for every second spent with his wife. The thrust of the sword.

They must have barged into our house, arrested us, driven us out where we stood, chased us through the city as it breathed a collective sigh of relief that it had been completed, that the slaughter of the innocent lovers would end just as abruptly as it had begun. I knew that they must have thrown us all into the dungeon, locked us up, condemned us, burned us to nothing, to dust, to ash that the wind would carry to Heaven.

It was I who had arranged this fate for them... I, who was moving further and further away from our home, our street, our city.

I did not understand anything, I did not want to understand, because in spite of the terrible fate that befell us all on the ground, I, the soaring nomad, was ascending into the sky, I was ascended!

My basket was small. It was large enough only to accommodate me, curled like a fetus, with two clay jars between my legs. The first jar, the larger one, was filled with water, in which the second jar stood, filled with embers. Just above my head hung a sail, bloated with hot air, like a soaring, magic mushroom, which carried me into the night, as far as possible from the past...

If the body submerged in water loses weight proportionate to the water it displaces, does the body raised in the air lose weight proportionate to the air trapped in the sail? But air weighs nothing, the heat carries it into the night, and catching the sail it pulls the basket, along with me and the jars filled with embers and so on and so forth, and higher and higher.

I was in Heaven.

Toledo t first into a web of bright streets, the veins on a leaf, torn at the edges by the walls of the city, washed by the Tagus. Beyond the river rose the gentle hills, from which El Greco once painted the city, where now the sheep grazed, and at night, the shepherds' bonfires suffered from insomnia. These hills, so similar to the mountain of San Martín in my home, Toro, reminded me of Esperanza. On those meadows, I swore her my love and faithfulness until the end of my days. I did not think that life's dullness would break my promise. That was the first and last time I was in love.

In love? How can I say something like that, after all this from which I am fleeing now? I say… Then I did not have to speak, then I felt, I knew that I loved, and my love was proof of that. She made everything possible and shared our happiness with those who found themselves close to us.

I remember your first touch, Esperanza, when you first took me by the hand. My heart stopped, my lungs filled with the sun, and my eyes, although they were filled with you, saw every detail as something extraordinary, to this point unseen, unique. Every leaf on the trees was pure beauty. And now I look at Toledo as an ashen leaf, a dying glow in the dust of the night.

Then I saw more of the same leaves, the whole tree of the earth, the tree of good and evil. And I understood that the earth is both Paradise and Hell and only we choose the place where we live. We are either Paradise or Hell.

I know, I must begin to speak about my feelings… Why did I do this… Alright, I will tell you.

It all started some ten years ago.

My father won or begged a commission for an altar and tomb for one of the Church's notable members in Toledo. Nobody in the family could go, so he sent me. I had a modest budget, enough to stay in Toledo for a few weeks, prepare a project for this tomb and convince the local investors that it was what they wanted. Everything was to be finished between Easter and midsummer.[26]

I stayed at an inn near the Jewish and Arab quarters. No, I honestly did not know anything about this inn. Its entrance was so near the

---

26 Narciso had probably finished his design before he left Toledo on the 6th of June, 1721, which would have been before he received a contract to complete the project. He returned to Toledo on the 27th of October, 1721, this time to work on the altar.

church that the beggars leaned their pans to both sides, towards the faithful and the transient. I did not forget what the pastor of our parish in Toro repeated, that demons always gather around holy sites, and this is why deals with the devil often happen in Rome.

Our investor, Cardinal Astorga, and his henchmen tried to suck the life from me. They sent a boy from the curia in the morning to ensure that already at matins I would be drawing at the table, and they let me leave only after the last Angelus prayer, during which I received my first meal. Besides this, I starved the whole day, drawing, measuring, correcting, sketching, writing letters to the cardinal and his secretary, correcting the secretary's letters before they reached the cardinal, changing reports, evaluations, checking local carvers, masons, builders, sculptors... Then discussing the final shape of the altar for hours with the clergy, the final shape that was never final but always changing, changing, changing...

Not surprisingly, the first few nights I slept like a stone. I rose in the morning and dragged myself to work. The first time I went to the tavern on the ground floor of the inn because the clergy gave me something for supper that I could not touch. It was clear that I was not getting treats from the cardinal's table.

I remember a surprise when I realized that everyone was eating in silence, emerged deep in their own thoughts. Even the innkeeper seemed to be listening to himself. I, too, began to listen...

The human mind, supposedly, has unlimited potential. Moses is an example of this. With the strength and will of his mind, Moses opened and dried the sea, squeezed the mountain and poured water from it, and smashed the walls of Jericho. Why don't we have the same potential? Apparently, we use the limitless possibilities of our minds to have meaningless debates with ourselves. Only those who do not argue with themselves internally—they can achieve something. I started listening to my thoughts.

When I first heard my own thoughts, I was upset by their banality. I discovered that I spent my time inventing conversations with the arrogant cardinal and his helpers. I pitied myself to myself, I convinced myself of my abilities and the injustice of my fate, which had sent me here, to Toledo. I realized also that my selfishness did not allow me to think of my family, and the sense of injustice whispered to me about the need to exact revenge on this life, that is, to put it bluntly—the need for entertainment. More precisely, I needed a woman.

I know what you want to say. If I equate entertainment with a woman, then maybe that is my problem, that I treat people as objects. Maybe. I suffered greatly, felt the pangs of my Christian conscience, sharing the tendencies of Onan. I was disgusted with myself.

Then I understood that the people in the tavern were not listening to their own thoughts at all, but to an especially quiet music, maybe a rhythm, something that was different from the beat of their own hearts. Mine too. The rhythm was quicker than any pulse, it was a pounding, a gallop.

The sound was coming from underground.

You know the kind of city Toledo is. Here, the gates of the abyss opened to swallow hundreds of people. Here, they sent the orders for arrests, sentences, thugs, public burnings, prosecutors, judges. Here, they perfected the auto-da-fé. Toledo is built on Hell.

The sound was coming straight from there.

So it seemed.

When I was returning from the cardinal's palace to the inn, the evil of the city never imposed on me. No stakes, thugs, death… On the contrary. The inn lay on the edge of the Jewish quarter, near the old Arab market where many religions and many ethnic groups sleep together peacefully.

Did I say "sleep together"?

It had just so happened that I had chosen to stay at an inn from which only alleys stretched, lit by red lanterns. Completely by accident. I did not know Toledo at all.

I decided I would get to know it. I began with the people in the inn's tavern. Each of them, and there were only men, after finishing their meals in focussed silence, paid, or did not, and disappeared somewhere in the back. I was sure that most of the clients came in through the entrance by the church and would go out on the other side of the building. After I finished my meals, I always returned to my room upstairs.

One day I gathered my courage and went into the back. The innkeeper stepped aside and extended his hand for a tip. When my tip exceeded the price of the meal, only then did his hand disappear behind his apron, and with his hand, the innkeeper disappeared as well. Before me, as you can probably guess, were a pair of doors.

Doors that opened onto another Toledo.

The entrance led to the basement, but at the other side of this basement was an exit to the street behind the tavern. Men came from the tavern to meet women from the nearby Jewish quarter, the Arabic Casbah and Chinatown. Pimps brought these women, who were kept in dark basements, consumptive and weak. All the pimps were the same, and all the women were different.

There were Turkish women with soft bodies doused in oil, belly-dancing and quivering. There were Hindu women from Khajuraho, with round breasts and hips, with bodies like rubber. There were red-headed Jewish women with strong legs and breathtaking necklines. There were black women with breasts so pointed they seemed to rip the air. There were black-haired Basque women, lush and restless, as well as fawning, lethargic Slovak women. There were small Asian women with children's feet and hairless abdomens. There were beautiful women from New Spain, tense, their eyes sharp and bright.

Some of the women were covered to their chins, and others were completely naked. Some of the women wore folk costumes, and others were dressed as elegant women of Madrid. Some of the women had elaborately braided hair, sometimes hidden under a scarf, a bonnet, or other form of decoration. Sometimes their hair was loose and reached their buttocks, or cut short, right to their scalp.

All the women danced, and they all danced differently, to a different melody. A melody that only they heard. There was, however, a small group of musicians, like black beetles sitting in a corner, but they always played the same rhythm. The dancers created their melodies in dance. Not only in the clink of their ornaments, but in the way that their dance changed the monotonous, rhythmic background of the music, turned it into a unique and diverse masterpiece, exploding like a firecracker above the city.

All varieties of the flamenco are the same for me, only the rhythm of the steps, claps, stamps, and cries individualizes them. Belly dancing is the ringing of metallic jewelry around rotating hips, but the individual bellies and hips of the dancers made each unique. African dance, as well as the dances from New Spain, had a rhythm beaten by the feet, strengthened by a guttural song. Japanese dance, full of laconic gestures and covered by a smiling mask, did not need any music.

Each woman was tethered. A rope, strap, or chain tied her to her partner, creating quite an impediment, especially in pirouettes. Although, I came to realize, only dances from certain parts of the world had pirouettes or twists. Other regions preferred a more static or stable form. I noticed, too, that in certain countries or regions, dancers rise in dancing, while in, for example, the dancing from New Spain, dancers slump in their dance, stamping heavily, accentuating the rhythm with a heavy step rather than a jump.

I also noticed that this two-levelled basement below the city was organized like the globe: the upper floor was reserved for the dances of the northern hemisphere, and the lower for the southern. Near the entrance, Andalusian, Basque and Catalonian women, and further women from Asia and from the New World, and at the very end, on the lower floor, danced women from the Antipodes, from Africa and Polynesia.

I was drawn to the women from the Antipodes. Exotic women from the bottom of the Amazon, from the depths of Africa... Especially one woman.

She was black, young and thin like a cat living on love and barley. Her hair was tied in a leather sash and stood upright. Her breasts were pointed and erect. The only ornaments she wore were metal hoops and bracelets—the hoops on her long neck and the bracelets on her ankles and arms. She was completely naked, if you did not count the thin leather bands on her hips, which rose in her dance, revealing a hairless abdomen.

She was the only one not dancing. It was difficult to call her performance a dance. She rose in the air.

She stood vertical, slender, her feet together, her arms extending along her body, her chin and breasts aiming somewhere before her. Absent. Afterwards, without any effort, she leaped from the floor and hovered above the earth. She fell, exposing the nakedness of her abdomen, knocking against the earth and again hovering in the air. Higher and higher. She was able to hang there for hours. At the end of her performance, the man holding her leather thong collected money from the spectators, threw on her something like a penitential sack, and they disappeared somewhere, together, into the black city. They never left through the tavern. Nobody ever left with them or followed them. The audience stood spellbound and then went looking for something less intense. A warmth, a softness, a smile.

I would return to my room upstairs, drink a glass of wine and sleep. One dream kept coming back: I dreamt of a dark woman, suspended above me, who would fall with open thighs on my manhood, bounce away and fall again… When my seed flowed from me, she became a dark night, and I would fall into a deep, restorative sleep.

I did not even know her name. Neither she nor her guardian spoke in any language known to me. I heard her name from an older man who often sat at the same table as I and watched her as I did. Maybe only with less desire.

And so it began.

Once, when we were alone at the table after the dancer's exit, I casually asked him:

"How does she do that?"

He tore a small scrap off his shirt and held it to the candle. The material caught fire, went out, and fluttered off away from the flame, from the table, farther and farther, where the black dancers from New Spain turned it into rhythm.

His name was Bartolomeu Lourenço de Gusmão, and he was a poor alcoholic who could tell extraordinary stories.[27]

I drank with him, made friends out of boredom. I did not believe a single word, but I liked his ability to bind together scraps of his reality. He was able to explain the mystery of flight with the example of Uhuru's breasts. Uhuru was the name of the dancer. He convinced me, even, that the flying machine of his design was here, in Toledo, and it served him to spy on the dancer in her bed. Of course, from

---

27  His story went like this. He was born in Brazil, where, at the age of fifteen, he was accepted as a novice with the Jesuits. Unfortunately, his hot blood allowed him to withstand the Jesuits only for eleven years. He fled to Portugal and although he studied philosophy and mathematics, he attained the title of Doctor of Canon Law. As a doctor, he gained the courage to write a petition to João V of Portugal, who was then king, asking him for an opportunity to present his airship, which he had been working on for many years.

The presentation was held at Casa da Índia. The small paper balloon rose from the earth and into the sky, carrying the world's first flying passenger, which was a small earthen jar filled with hot embers, sitting in the basket tied to the balloon. The king was sky-high happy!

Bartolomeu became a professor, and then one of the fifty members of the Academia Real de História. His earnings allowed him to build larger and larger flying apparatuses. One day, in a ship named "Passarola," Bartolomeu himself flew from the Igreja de São Roque in Lisbon to Terreiro do Paço, where he and his flying machine hurtled to the earth. With them, Bartolomeu's fame also plummeted, and envious professors wrote him onto the lists of the Inquisition.

He fled and hid beneath the wings of the Jesuits, promising he would stop his flying, if only they would save him from the stake, from which he would have risen, surely, to Heaven. The Jesuits sent him directly under the light, where it is the darkest, to Toledo. He flies no longer. He has no money for his machines. He drinks.

the moment I asked him my first question to the moment that we were walking together, holding each other up warmly, and staggering towards the Casbah, the Arab quarter, a lot of time had flown by, and wine too. Especially wine. Only, can you say in some language: "A lot of wine has flown." Flown from where?

Exactly.

We came across a small yard. To this day, I do not know how we got there. I know only that what happened next must have been orchestrated earlier by Bartolomeu.

In the Casbah, everything is shabby and second-hand. In contrast, the shed standing in the yard, and its padlock, were solid like nothing I'd seen. Bartolomeu had the key. We pulled from the shed something like a giant sack made of a thin, tanned skin almost transparent like parchment. A basket was tied to this sack. A basket— the kind that usually holds a jar to make wine. Bartolomeu pulled down a rope, which must have been attached to the roof, tied it to the sack, and pulled on it. Above the basket, in the air, something hung like drying laundry, something that had no shape, but that resembled some being or creature. A formlessness, an emptiness whose skin, once, had been filled. It reminded me of a monstrously large, empty scrotum, hanging upside down.

Bartolomeu pulled something else from the shed. A pitcher of embers. He lit them, carefully. Meanwhile, I inspected the surrounding houses. Nobody seemed to notice us. I could hear that someone lived in the houses surrounding the yard, but it was difficult to imagine who these people could be. A strong smell of spices, a guttural song, shadows on the ceilings seen from below. I tried to ask him about Uhuru, but he pointed only up, as though to the sky. I wanted to piss somewhere in a corner, but he forbade it, saying it would be useful later. I waited.

And an unexpected thing happened. Bartolomeu placed the jar with the embers in the basket, and the sack began to fill above him, it began to take shape, it swelled, and after some time it began to rise into the air along with the basket. The shape could not fly away, because Bartolomeu had tethered it to a stump, some tree that once grew in this yard. He persuaded me to get into the basket, which I shared with the burning jar, and then he loosened the tether.

I rose! Along with the basket, I slipped into the air very slowly, but noticeably. It took me probably half the night to the level of the windows above. Before I found myself there, by the shadows on the ceiling, I studied room after room. It was as if the shadows on the cave wall helped me to guess the essence of those who threw them or had long since abandoned them. When I rose to the second floor, I no longer had to look. My basket stood directly in front of Uhuru's window. I saw her, though I myself could not be seen. Behind the window, in the middle of the room, the hearth cast a strong, red light in which I could clearly see the pointed breasts and the leather tie on her head. She was naked, and her skin glistened from sweat or oil. In the light, she appeared as a figure poured in black glass. She knelt, she prayed.

For a moment I wondered, when she prays, does she imagine her God in her own image and likeness? thin, black, and standing above the earth. Or maybe she has other gods, hungry for blood, sacrifices, killing their children...

Before I understood that I was verging on blasphemy, I noticed that Uhuru was not praying, but that she was in a state of some ecstasy, as her naked body trembled uncontrollably. I thought this before my gaze reached above the edge of the windowsill. And then—oh, horror!—I saw that Uhuru was sitting astride not a horse, but a male individual belonging to her race. Not only that. She was having sex with this individual!

I should not have been shocked by what Uhuru was doing. After all, I came here to spy on her. What had shocked me was the manner in which she was doing this.

In my mind, sex did not always have to be initiated by the man, but it did always place him in a privileged position. The man was on top, he straddled, covered, possessed. The woman, to some extent, was always subordinate, giving herself, receiving the man. The roles were divided and the boundaries between them ran along the axis above / below. Even when a man mounted his better half from behind in order to feel her breasts or to desecrate the holy sacrament of marriage by practicing sodomy, this hierarchy was maintained through the structure of the position of intercourse.

The people from which Uhuru came must be so different!

The man lay on his back unmoving, and he writhed in pain or pleasure from time to time. The woman knelt above him, sat, straddling him and his hands, taut along his body. The man was imprisoned, incapacitated, controlled. She seemed to be static. Her legs held her partner's body, her bosom was taut, her arms raised above her head like a dancer teetering on a ball, and only her hips, bum, and waist vibrated at the rate of a heart after a long run. This part of her body, linked with the man, swirled like the wings of the hummingbirds of New Spain.

The miracle of floating in the air was nothing compared to these new and wonderful forms of sexuality. I was struck not only with the idea that each of their group, strain, or family might have a different culture of copulation, but by the fact that the way in which Uhuru was dominating her partner was so incredibly similar to my dream!

And so, slowly gliding upwards and passing the floor that housed their den, a certain thought occurred to me. If, in other cultures, women dominate men, and in my dream I am dominated by her, then maybe I, too, am "different." Maybe I too need a different sexual culture, which is, after all, only a different culture...

Unfortunately, the word culture no longer applied to the scene that I was spying on.

The man beneath the raging Uhuru was probably unable to control himself any longer, because she—suddenly and without warning—began to slap him, beat his face with flourish, pummel him briskly, beating, clapping some rhythm belonging to the desert or the wilderness rather than the Casbah in Toledo. She must have, in this way, kept him on the brink, because she stopped beating him, and—with her arms raised above her head—vibrated while letting out a squeal or prolonged whistle, so high that it was almost inaudible, like the song of an exotic bird.

Suddenly everything froze. Uhuru dropped her arms and stopped vibrating. Then, slowly, as though tired, she pulled herself from his member and dragged herself along his body, leaving on his black skin a white trail of thick milk. The man shook with disgust, but he was her submissive. He might have been crying. Because when she knelt above his face and poured the rest of the milk straight on his closed eyes, he trembled, as if shaken by sobs.

The scene startled me to the point that I remembered that I was hanging in space. Just as Uhuru hung above her lover, I sensed that my flight was coming to an end. The climax came in the form of Bartolomeu howling below me in the yard. He could hold my vehicle no longer, and he demanded that I quench the fire immediately and return to the ground.

Quench it—with what?

"Urine!" Bartolomeu shouted.

Unfortunately, I was so excited by my voyeurism, and maybe also by what I had seen, that my cock stuck out of my pants, and was unable to fulfill this wish.

I tried to get him to obey. It was useless.

Below me, Bartolomeu was crying that he could not hold the rope any longer, that I would fly away, that this was the end.

Oh, if only it could have been! I would not be where I am now, and this whole story would not exist. Why did I not fly away then with the vision of Uhuru under my eyelids, with the hunch that I knew nothing about the lives of these wild creatures, or not wild creatures, people, that I knew nothing about the coexistence of humans?

Then there, in the air, hanging above the earth, as though in meta-physical ecstasy, I understood that I wanted to return. I wanted to go back to earth, to normality, because living in it I knew that maybe something would happen, something I felt already. Maybe my sexual otherness would collide with another sexual otherness...

I listened to Bartolomeu, I tore the shirt from my back and, shielding my hands, gripped the jar of embers and tossed it into the void below me. It exploded in sparks and the howls of my partner. My vehicle lurched, jerked upwards, and then slowly—although much faster than it had previously climbed to the height of Uhuru's window—began falling directly into the burning embers.

When I landed, the vehicle caught fire and burned in the blink of an eye. I fled.

What happened later is boring and I will spare you of it. It was Hell. Bartolomeu wanted to kill me for destroying his flying machine and demanded that I pay for it. I, without a cent to my name, begged the cardinal for a bit of money, because the design of the altar was already finished. Unfortunately, the cardinal's people found my drawings unacceptable. According to them, I had no idea about architecture— I would not get any money for my work, because they had already hired a new architect, which had increased their expenses, for which they would sue me. For days Bartolomeu harassed me, demanding that I pay for the reconstruction of his burned vehicle. Without any money, I promised to pay and finance the entire project if Bartolomeu got me into bed with Uhuru. Why did I demand Uhuru from Bartolomeu? I guess only because it seemed to me to be quite impossible for him to achieve.

If the cardinal had taken a different architect then maybe in Toledo there would stand a different altar, and I would be somewhere far away... If Bartolomeu had not been an alcoholic, believing in my words... If I had not made the silly joke of demanding Uhuru's body from him... Everything might be different.

Finally, after receiving an advance from the cardinal for the construction of the altar, I gave almost all of it to Bartolomeu. I had to remain in the city for a few more weeks to settle matters related to the construction of the altar, and then the message came that Bartolomeu had bought Uhuru, who as a slave had changed her name to Ahara. They had pierced her nose with a hoop like a bull's, as a sign of servitude, and she was waiting for me in his shed.

When I came—Bartolomeu was dead. Uhuru was gone. Next to Bartolomeu's body I found a new flying machine. I did not try to guess what had happened. My imagination in those days was filled with images of humans mating—I imagined the old Bartolomeu, dying from the exertion of attempting to rape his slave, or having a stroke from the excitement, and so she fled. She fled, because who would believe a slave, a black one at that, that it was not her who killed her owner, but his lust?

Maybe I wasn't so rotten after all, sitting with the inventor's corpse in his shed, because I also thought maybe his heart had simply broken at the thought of what he had committed just to build another machine. Maybe it was not him, but I who was guilty of everything?

Guilty.

I hated that term from the language of ethical bookkeeping. Guilty—it solved the need for grief, compassion and redress for those harmed, bah, even the need for guilt or consciousness of causing harm. Guilty—so absolve me, Father, and in a moment the balance will once more sway to me.

That night I took the body of Bartolomeu to the Jesuits. I knew they would bury him. I wrapped his flying machine in felt and buried it, covered it in dirt in a hole on some construction site, some house that was under renovation, where they were repairing the foundations. I could not see anybody, and it seemed as though the renovation had finished, and the trenches had already been partially buried. I threw it in and covered it up.

Could I have imagined that my wife would convince me to purchase this very house, that she would lead yet another renovation, she would dig up the basement, she would find the doors (which I did not know existed), that the decayed felt would let loose the machine's springs, which would invade our basement, our reality, charge between the legs of my wife?

You think that there is only one answer. There is one and it is: no. Nobody would have been able to foresee all these coincidences. It's impossible. Too improbable, too complicated.

You're mistaken.

Somebody is watching all this from above, somebody who invents our stories, writes them into our lives. Somebody. Some Supreme Author sees everything before it happens. This Supreme Author can be either a man or a woman, because after all, every male story has its counterpart in a female story, and vice versa. Each Odyssey is also a Helleniad, even if nobody has written this second story, or has not found it yet. Someone has already invented all of this, and so it is possible. We only reaffirm, with our lives, that everything that can happen—will happen.

Right, isn't this a comforting theory? My wife would say that once again I am washing my hands, that I do not want to take responsibility for my actions, that I am being cheap.

Not really.

There, above the filled-in excavation, I did not yet know what I was thinking about. Only ten years later, in our basement, when I tried to piece together this machine, carried it to the attic, hid it, and then lied to my wife about it—then I understood what I had been thinking about above that excavation.

If in every crime there is a moment before we commit it, if this is a moment in which we make a decision, we agree to commit this crime, we acquiesce, we allow it to happen, and so there—above the symbolic grave of the flying machine—I understood that even if I had buried, burned, destroyed, forgotten about the flying machine—something had already happened, and I had allowed it to happen. It had all started with my loneliness in Toledo, my exhaustion, my conviction that I deserved more, and finally—my descent into the basement with the dancers, my desire. This flying sack was a sign that something had torn me from reality and carried me into the unknown, that I was no longer in control of myself.

Out of control, I had the affair, which is difficult to even call a love affair. And the fact that I had it with Nora means nothing in particular, because anybody else could have been in her place. I was ready, internally, I invited the possibility into myself. The flying machine is not only a sign, but a metaphor for my thoughts. I believed that it was possible to have a second life, hidden from others, right before their eyes, a second life floating a few feet away from the earth. This moment, when the corpse of the machine awoke and crawled into the basement, this moment should have awoken me. Unfortunately, I was already speeding downhill, too weak to stop myself. I hid the machine, which now carried me from the city of my madness.

Is this real?

But I had seen myself standing on the doorstep and the captain of the guard with his henchmen. But they had already discovered the wound on my back and dragged or beaten me, Esperanza, the children, the maid, and the dog... Anyway, what might death mean to me? After all, he, her husband, had already pierced me through, killed me.

Where am I and what am I doing here?

I imagined that this flying sack was a space from which we do not see reality, only our projections. In that yard, where I had spied on Uhuru, I might not have been there—it might have been only my fantasy, my imagination feeding me images. Just how, a moment ago, hanging above our street I saw something that I could not have seen, because at that precise moment I was somewhere else.

Where?

Somewhere outside of time and space, my flying sack had disembodied me. Non-corporeality. How can an object fly, an object that is much heavier than that in which it flies? The sack must be either an optical instrument, giving the illusion of movement (and, at the same time, life), or an otherworldly vehicle that carries us to the afterlife (which would mean that I am a corpse, from which all blood has flown).

Immateriality.

I tore off my clothes and pulled off my shoes. I threw it all in the flames. I tore off my bandages, which Esperanza had treated me with, dipped them in the hot water and washed myself carefully. And then, naked, I lay in the bottom of the basket. I told my soul:

"Shhh…"

I told myself to wait without hope, because there was no hope for me. And I told myself to wait without love, because there was no love for me. And although faith remained, it was just faith, I had stupidly left hope and love behind me. What do you think about, when you are on the way to a place where you are no longer, as you are no longer in the place from where you set out?

I could only wait.

I waited.

At the bottom of the basket I lay like a fetus. I felt very lonely and I missed the smell of my children. I wanted Esperanza's touch. I felt a terrible pain in my stomach, an emptiness, which nothing could fill.

With my body, I held the jar of hot water, which held the jar of embers, the way I had once held Esperanza's body when we fell asleep. I felt that this memory would never again become flesh. I spoke her name aloud and I felt that this name would never again become flesh for me. I spoke my own name and I slid into darkness.

In the darkness I heard the flutter of owls' wings, because what else flies at night? Another bird joined the first one, and together they circled my basket. And then they sat on its edge, and I was convinced that this was a demon in the form of a griffin, and an angel disguised as a flying lobster. They both dug their talons and pincers into my body, searching for my heart and soul. But my soul was quiet and difficult to find, and my heart was no longer a heart... [28]

---

28  (Yes, this is already the end of my confessions...

Too few dramatic details?

Am I speaking too generally or too metaphorically about my fall? You cannot respect the fact that there is no more, and there will not be any more, because I—Narciso, who is telling this story—I am probably dead, silent, cooled off, the end. You demand more? You do not want to let the narrative end in the place that it, itself, has chosen.

You see, to your question "Why?" I can answer only with what I felt before I arrived at my affair. I felt enormous disappointment with my own life, maybe self-pity, an ocean of frustration, in which there were hidden dead waves of hope for the future, icebergs of cold, a Mariana's Trench of hurt feelings. Maybe I did not know how my life was supposed to be, and this is the reason I did not want it to be as it was.

When frustration rolls in, only memory can speak of what it was like before the wave. And when it disappears, there remains debris, fragments, warped algae. Then one believes, as the thunder rumbles and the lightning strikes separately, that you can balance this matrix of frustration, desperation, and loneliness. Yes, loneliness, because even when someone beside you dies and dries up alone, you feel only your own pain.

A lack of sympathy? Loneliness is a state in which sympathy for others rarely appears. Maybe only sometimes when another welcomes you into his or her own solitude.

I wanted to die with the narrative, in part because I have nothing to say, but also because I refuse to share myself with anybody. No, it is not emotional stinginess that is stopping me. Why do you need to know all this? Is it so you can submerge yourself in someone else's swamp, submerge yourself in the fall, enjoy the view of another's pain, or demand repentance, regret? But this does not explain the "why?"

Why?

I do not know. Before it happened, I remember only the feeling of regret, pain, frustration, that life was passing, I am dying and I have no winnings, no compensation for my efforts. Yes, I wanted a prize for living. Paradise—now. Instant gratification.

*

The basket crashed into the ground, and I lost any remaining traces of consciousness. I might have been in New Spain, or in Africa, or somewhere near Toledo. I knew that I had crashed in a place where there were slaves. Above me leaned a figure with a hoop in her nose. Maybe it was Uhuru...

---

Instead I brought Hell. I know, I hurt people without knowing it, without even thinking about it. Maybe selfishness, in order to get its fill, has to take satisfaction from others. In order to have luck—do you have to deprive others of theirs?

Did I not know that I was lying to myself? No. Maybe I was not even lying to myself. Then, when I was betraying my wife I was almost sure of the existence of separate worlds, in which my actions might have a limited range, might not interfere with the other worlds. Isolated worlds. In one I am a good father and husband, and in the other, a stud, a bull, a ram, mounting and straddling anybody before me.

Anybody could have been my lover?

What a horrible word...

Words, the language of ethical bookkeeping, moral accounting that reprimands with words. Lover, romance, extramarital affairs, adultery, a jump to the side, on the side, a lack of emotional connection...)

# HIDING

*(Scene in which doña Esperanza Tomé becomes Narciso Tomé.)*

⁣|||||||||||||||||||||||||||||||||||||||||||||||||||||||||||||||||||||||||||||||||||||||||||||||||||||||||||||||||||||||||||||||||||||||||||||||||

BEFORE THE POUNDING ON THE DOORS, I, DOÑA ESPERANZA TOMÉ, who is telling this story, buried my face in my husband's discarded shirt. With closed eyes, I traced the journey from his mornings, foamed scented soap and tart aftershave, through his workday and the full sweat of the quarries, to the stale odour of Narciso's lust. I crept step by step with his dreams, the sweat from his nightmares, I felt the smell of the liquor that washes his shirt and the smell of the south wind that blows through it as it dries on the string, and which imbues Narciso's shirt with the smell of dinners cooked, fried, baked, braised in kitchens and restaurants throughout the city. It seemed that I could even smell the aroma of blooming apple trees and dandelions beneath them, on fresh-cut grass, saliva leaking from the open mouths of sheep bending down in silent contemplation of their digestive systems. I was thinking of the sheep woven into Narciso's underwear and felt the black pearls left behind, the remainders of sheepish meditation. I inhaled the sour smells of sheds and barns, where old straw and chaff is kept and where the chaff mixes with old dung. Sniffing his under-wear, I recognized the smell of urine and something else, a smell that I remembered well from my dreams. I found his pendant, from which he never parted. A small silver medallion cut in the shape of a Cross of Jerusalem.

And I cried.

I dressed myself in Narciso's smell and descended to the kitchen, to Petra's room, to the servant's room.

The servant's room was small. There was enough space for a bed and a wardrobe. On the bed, Petra dreamt her final happy dream. I called through the open door:

"Petra, wake up…"

"Oh, Ma'am, you're here? Please, please come in…" She slid over to the wall, pulled back the blanket and invited me in, half-asleep.

I took a step toward her, bringing a candle into the room. Petra paled and cried:

"Oh, it's you, Sir?!" She quickly pulled the blanket to her chin. A blush of shame crawled into her cheeks, horror at the fact that Narciso was visiting her and that perhaps he had realized what she, Petra, felt for her employer, for me.

"Petra, it's me. Don't be afraid. Put on your blue dress. You will be my wife."

She stared at me like I was mad. She was afraid.

"Petra, today I am Narciso, and you are doña Esperanza Tomé. If you betray me—I will kill you."

"Ma'am, you know that I would never…"

I knew that tonight I would wait until the rooster crowed three times.

Years of practice in theatre school helped us to exchange faces. When the pounding on the doors came, we were ready.

I opened the doors and saw, with fear, that on the threshold stood the older gentleman, whom I had led, with Nora, through the sacristy. Before I could gather my thoughts, he addressed Petra in a thunderous voice:

"Our guide! Lady, forgive me for disturbing you this calm evening, but I wanted to express my highest admiration and appreciation for your knowledge and your abilities of interpretation. The day, Ma'am, that you showed me El Greco's 'El caballero de la mano en el pecho will always remain in my memory."

He bowed, sweeping his hat across the threshold, and then turned to me, standing a step away from Petra:

"Sir, God must be gracious to have blessed you with such a wife."

Here, a series of bows, after which the gentleman continued:

"Are you, Sir, the only man in this house?"

I bowed as best I could and spoke not in my own voice:

"Yes, but you may come into our house and become convinced of this yourself..."

"This is not necessary." He held back his soldiers, who, already feeling welcome, had begun to move forward, ready to convince themselves of my truthfulness. "It will be enough, Sir, if you just show us your back. We are looking for someone who was injured this night, and we have reason to believe that his injury is on his back."

I turned and wanted to run. My back? I would have had to take off my dress, petticoat, corset, underwear, but, being Narciso I lifted my coat and shirt, and bent forward, so that I could watch the scene behind me through my legs set wide apart. Being a man has its advantages.

The gentleman looked disapprovingly at my shoulders and muttered:

"What a strange family. The wife is gifted with the mind of a man, and the man has a woman's back... I wish you a good night, master Narciso."

They left, and I could not straighten up. I heard a pounding on the doors of Westefania and the cries of the gentleman. I looked at the sky and saw above the canopy in front of our home an amazing array of stars. I saw Cassiopeia and Orion, and above them, somewhere far away, I saw an angel. It might have been, of course, a fallen angel. Perhaps it was the devil. Its figure had remained in the sky throughout almost our entire conversation. I had tried not to look at it. Then, when I stuck my back out towards the gentlemen and his guard, the devil was gone. Before he vanished, his great wings glowed with some interior light, as though he were filled with embers. I did not see his legs, they had been curled, but there, where his penis should have been, the devil had a face, amazingly similar to another face well known to me. I was almost certain that the devil had the face of my husband, Narciso.

*

We went back to the kitchen, where I finished the wine. Petra fell asleep with her head in my lap.

There are these moments of complete security, when something terrible has passed, and something worse has yet to come. Moments without concern. The evil beyond the door had not yet vanished, but it also had not yet crept in, come knocking. The thought amused me. I realized that I only had to wear Narciso's clothes to begin to think like him. I only had to dress up to get a taste of the risks.

I, doña Esperanza Tomé, who is telling this story, I always recognized the principle that responsibility for our choices and for our guilt should be consistently adhered to in our lives. Narciso loved to gamble. He risked everything and he lost everything. Even himself…

Dressed as him, would I act like he did? If I allowed myself this tragi-farce of a disguise one time, must I be faithful to this choice?

*

I spent the rest of the night listening to the darkness fade outside the windows, waiting for the roosters to crow.

*

At dawn I was on the construction site.

I am sure that Tomé Sr. recognized me disguised as Narciso, but he told everybody:

"From today, Narciso alone will direct the project. Listen to him. I…I must rest."

Nobody said a word. I gathered everybody and we went to the altar. It was nearing completion, although it was difficult to say to what degree it was finished. The upper part was shrouded in darkness, and although the sun fell on the interior of the cathedral, it lit only the base of the altar. I thought, what a waste of years of my husband's work, and his father's, and the rest of the family's. In these last years, they produced piles of rubble, scrap metal and stucco. Why is all this human energy going to waste? I breathed the stale air of the cathedral, hoping that Narciso knew what he was doing. I was almost ready to admire my husband, who had hurt me so…

I do not know the world in which You live, but I am sure that our worlds are as far apart as Spain and New Spain. Mine was divided into small kingdoms, principalities, provinces, countries. Each part had to be different, or wanted to be different, differing in language, culture, social customs, or history (because this was the easiest craft). The differences divided us, causing wars, attempts to equate differences. For nothing.

Despite these wars, my divided, proportioned world was governed by an otherworldly power, a global institution not only standing above all these divisions but drawing benefit from them. This institution was the Church—in their words, structured in a way unparalleled, to the degree that it existed without an army, military police, security forces. Well, maybe with the exception of the Inquisition… How could a utopia like this be possible in my times? I do not know. The only explanation might be psychological slavery, the necessity or the need to belong, an unquestioned acceptance of being controlled by something that did not necessarily promise a better tomorrow, but a better oblivion, Heaven.

Were there no free thinkers in my times? Some were burned, exiled, imprisoned, were ordered to denounce their ideas, or to sit quietly. Free thinkers were free to think in silence. The same as all the others. There came a great separation, an opposition between kind exteriors and the truth hidden in darkness. Narciso was the same. He hid his affairs and his work, which I watched with growing anger. I needed revenge. I already knew how to destroy his memory and his altar in one fell swoop.

A moment later I was begging the archbishop for an audience, for which I had to wait half the day.

"I'm sick of your damned family, master Narciso. If you came for money, that's too bad, because I will not give you a penny more. From this day, I will penalize you for violating your contract. And what! Your family has been sucking me dry for years, demanding money, money, money. What do I have to show for it? Shit! A mountain of debris and decoration, which nobody sees anyways because its alleged beauty is shrouded in darkness. I am like your nanny, always birthing, helping, doing for you what is yours to do. Have you ever noticed that everything that you make is unfinished and defective? Everybody requires that I have money ready, materials ready, people ready… When will this all end?! I demand that the project is finished by next Sunday. Not a day longer!!!"

Did I agree with him? I stood silent. I did not know that this was what conversations between men looked like. He went on:

"Anyways, the public prosecutor came to see me… Some two days ago. Today we pray for his health. He barely breathes. He had no evidence, but, after all, his word would be enough… Apparently it was reported to him that your father, Narciso, is a Freemason.[29] If this is true, which I refuse to believe, you would be standing today before him with your entire family. My memorial would have to be razed. All

---

29   It's difficult to say what the cardinal is talking about here, because records of Freemasonry appear only in the year 1717.

this work. All of my work! Out, out! Get out of this city and let your story die. Cursed family! Out! What are you waiting for?"

Silence.

"Your Eminence. I came to beg for forgiveness for the fact that your memorial is not yet finished and that it is shrouded in gloom. I came to beg for Your Eminence to allow us to cut a window, which would crown Your Eminence's work and reveal the beauty of the altar. Thanks to the genius of Your Eminence and the blessings of the Most High, we have been able to build a unique altar. I want to bring it into the light of day... It is not right to hide the light. Not for us, Lord, not for us, but for the glory of Your..."

The cold of marble and thick walls. Here, all the materials were expensive and genuine. He had not been so generous with the materials for the altar.

"To His glory, Narciso. His, not mine."

Even in modesty, vanity remains vanity.

I left in silence. Apparently, it was his bidding.

*

A week later, the cardinal's men forcibly removed me from the site. This time, I did not need to wait for an audience:

"You must immediately cease and finish! Today everything was supposed to be finished! Who gave you permission to destroy my cathedral, Narciso? It was reported to me that you have covered the entire ambulatory with scaffolding and that you plan to break through the walls. If you touch the dome, the entire cathedral will collapse. The entire cathedral, not just the ambulatory. The choir behind the main altar is like a keystone, a key in a vault. Remove it or destroy it and the rest will collapse. At least, this is what they told me... I can only add: The end! Today it has to be cleaned up, finished, handed over to the curia. And you, out of here! I do not want to see you, I do not want to hear about you, I do not want to have anything to do with you. Leave Toledo as fast as you can and go as far away as possible!"

He was right. I had learned as much during the renovation of our house. Domes, the structure of ceilings and their supports, although they carry the most themselves, they are very delicate. It is enough to puncture them in the proper place, as a vein, and the building dies, becomes ruins, collapses into rubble.

In this city, they tell the legend of the wise wife of the builder of el Puente de San Martín. The builder made a mistake in his calculations, and it was only during construction that he understood the bridge would collapse as soon as the scaffolding was removed. His wife, wanting to save him, burned the scaffolding, the bridge fell, and he built it anew, setting a sculpture of his wife into the bridge's central arch. I sometimes wished to find myself beneath a collapsing building. The pain pushed me to this, the pain of a broken heart—yes, Narciso, you broke my heart! The shame of being betrayed and my lost dignity pushed me to thoughts of suicide.

I pitied the children, but anger blinded me. I ordered them to hammer in the most sensitive spot. I wanted to destroy, to smash the cathedral. I stood below, waiting for it to collapse on my head and bury me with my anger, my lack of honour, and my unbearable pain.

Unfortunately, Andres's workers had placed the scaffolding so that the dome rested on the wooden structure. It hung above my head and did not want to fall. Not only that. It became even worse.

When the first stone was removed, I was blinded by anger—blind. Instead of stones on my head, a beam of light fell from the black above me, hit me right between the eyes and forced me to turn. And behind me, in the bright sunlight, stood Narciso's altar.

Stood?

If stone can seethe, then Narciso's altar was boiling. Like lava in the crater of Vesuvius, it bubbled with sculptures, gleamed and steamed with polished stones and metal plates, exploded with gestures, figures in the clothes of cardinals, bishops, and citizens climbed higher and higher, and processions of naked bodies, unclothed.

Light.

An otherworldly light fell into the stuffy cathedral, and instead of crushing it, it held it from falling. Moment after moment, the light washed, lifted, animated Narciso's altar. Like a child with building blocks, the light built a brightness, materialized in immaterial memories.

Oh! There we are, at the top, some ten years ago, sitting at supper like the apostles in the cenacle, and Tomé Sr. predicts our trip to Toledo. Oh! And there on the four corners of the altar, the men of the Tomé family stand like archangels. First Andres with his shield, then Narciso with a lily, and the fragrant Diego. There is Tomé Sr. ... Everybody is there, everybody, only I am missing...

I began to scream with all my might, to stop seeing, to return to the darkness before the breaking apart of the stone above the apse.

I screamed until the entire family gathered, the clergy, the church servants, the stonemasons, the woodcutters, the plasterers, the students and apprentices, the most miserable helpers and the unwanted beggars, cripples, the sick, the grandfathers and church hags. Some knelt with devotion or stood as though petrified, their mouths open, hands folded, spellbound by the light, this moment, and Narciso.

They probably thought that I was struck by the beauty of "my" altar or delighted with the idea of disemboweling the cathedral. Maybe they thought nothing. What was happening before our eyes was theatre. My cries roused the crowd, which also erupted with pleasure when the light animated some new element, some undiscovered figure, a dark detail.

In the end, I lost my voice.

Someone took me by the shoulders, pulled me from the church and threw me into a carriage, which took me to the cardinal. And he, once more, told me to leave the city with my family, looked me in the eyes and said:

"You have changed so much, Narciso…"

I could not utter a word with my torn throat. With a hand I gestured in the direction of the cathedral and invited him to go with me to see the altar. I do not know how, but I was able to convince him wordlessly to come with me. He gathered his retinue and went.

They filled the entire apse, head to head, deathly silent, especially when the cardinal knelt and spread his hands as though he were having a vision. Maybe he really was having a vision. A soundless vision, disrupted only by my wheezing.

I could not cope with the massive delight, I could not stand the pain, bear the awareness that I was alive. I could not. I ripped a long pole from the scaffolding and swung it into the stucco and kitsch. Nobody flinched, nobody stopped me, forbade me. They all looked at me approvingly, as though I was Moses parting the sea, or a rock in the desert from which the water of life would spring.

The light fell precisely on the central section of the altar. Through the deepest darkness, it cut through the ambulatory to the centre of the altar where something small hung, like a heart, a dove, a cloud, and from it metal rays spread outwards, piercing the mass of angels and plaster figures. I hit it with all my might…

There was the sound of a gong, as though something was about to begin. They all looked at me. Blood and fury flooded my eyes, and the crowd awaited the spectacle.

I fled, I ran out with the stick in my hands. If they wanted a spectacle, they were going to have it. Behind the wall, at the back of Narciso's altar, stood a medieval altar, which housed the monstrance. If I cannot die by the cold stone—I will die in the flames at the stake for my sacrilege. I ran to the main altar, and they behind me, panting with impatience. Maybe it was because they were crowding me, but when I swung the stick to smash the tabernacle and the Most Holy Sacrament, my cloak became tangled. I stumbled and had to prop myself up on the stick so as not to fall. Instead of smashing the tabernacle, I stood the stick beside it.

Crushed, beaten, I glanced at the cardinal. He was delighted:

"Genius! Narciso, you are a genius… Of course, I already knew that it must be so. At the same height…"

As I was tangled, so was he, only in his lies. His roar filled the entire cathedral:

"Cuuuuuuuuuuuut!!!"

Some of the clergy were already placing the ladder. They lit incense, rung the bells. The monstrance was removed and given to the cardinal. Tomé Sr. handed Andres the tools, Andres helped Diego climb onto the ladder, church boys in white coats spread white cloths on the altar in a rhythm commanded by the cardinal, who leaned from behind the monstrance. Behind him, the mob, thickening with each moment, filled the cathedral. The beggars, the cripples, the poor, the unemployed and those who had abandoned their work, lured by others in anticipation of the extraordinary.

Diego commanded the chisel efficiently. After a few strokes, as if fate were knocking on the door, we heard something fall on the other side, on the side of Narciso's altar. Diego stepped back and revealed the hole that he had broken in the wall behind the tabernacle.

And then, a "miracle" happened.

Through the hole in the dome of the apse, through the ambulatory and Narciso's altar, through the hole cut in the tabernacle, one of the last rays of the day fell on the face of the local cripple, a church grandfather propped up on crutches. He lifted his hands to his eyes, and—inevitably—the crutches fell to the floor. To many, it must have seemed as though he had thrown them away. The blind cripple, not knowing what to do, took a few steps forward…

Those who stood nearest rushed to his spot, so that the light would fall on them too, so that they too would be healed. Soon, on the church floor, lay a twitching mountain of maimed bodies, lame beggars and amputees. Around them sprawled a field of walking sticks, dentures, beggars' hats and mugs.

The cardinal ordered it all removed, closed the cathedral and knelt on the spot where the last ray of light had fallen. Nobody remembered that I had wanted to commit sacrilege. We received the money for the completion of the project and there was no talk of leaving the city. It seemed that life was back to normal.

At least, it appeared that way. But breaking through the wall behind the main altar of the cathedral transformed the city.

# FALL

*(Narciso meets a series of unfortunate events after
landing in a strange and unknown place.)*

|||||||||||||||||||||||||||||||||||||||||||||||||||||||||||||||||||||||||||||||||||||||||||||||||||||||||||||||||||||||||||||||||||||||||||||||||||||||||||||||||||||||||||||||||||||||||||||||||||||||||||

FOR A MOMENT I BELIEVED THAT UHURU LEANED ABOVE ME. AT THE same time, I understood that I had arrived in a country of slaves. Being in a country of slaves, I myself became a slave. And then I stopped believing. The figure with the ring in its nose was horned like the devil. I was in Hell. I felt terror, and beside the first horned figure a second and third appeared... They surrounded me and began to hold court.

None of them opened their mouths, and yet I heard them clearly:

"Is he dead?"

"Does he know where he is?"

"We must tell him..."

"First, make him speak!"

"Speak!"

"I am... I was Narciso Tomé. I was an architect, husband, father, writer, teacher, traveller... I had started many things at once, but I never finished any. I always wanted to start something new, be somewhere else, be someone else. Reaching for the place where I was not, this drove me, it was the engine of my transformation and the source of constant frustration. I lusted, unable to reach, attain, unable to stay in one place, unable to stay myself…"

Here one of the mouths murmured:

"Unethical… But what is ethics and what is ethos?"

"It depends on how it is written. If with epsilon, it is habit, custom, or attachment to something. If with eta, it is a place of dwelling."

Another mouth spoke up, and then another. I was silent.

"Ergo, since he was neither attached, nor dwelled there, he is not ethical…"

"Why are you so concerned with the meanings of words? Let's ask him about the existence of ethics. Into what ethics was this man born?"

I felt obliged to speak:

"A Catholic ethics. I was born into a Catholic ethics, more precisely, a Catholic ethics of a small town named Toro, which lies in the province of Zamora."

"Oh, that's a very good ethics for you! It gives you the goal of the supernatural, to which you should strive even after death. And just in case, it also gives you an innate target, which you seek before you die. You are always on the road, so neither here nor there. If you deserve the sanctifying grace, you will achieve the first target. But to reach it, you must realize this second target, a satisfaction of material and spiritual needs, in accordance with the moral order established by God."

"This ethics should instill a sense and a love of good in you, mold you in a moral beauty, and show you the way to realize it, give you zeal to do what is good—and a disgust for evil."

They talked so much that I had to stop and interrupt them:

"I think I mistook that innate target with intimate, and so I became an onanist before I became an atheist."

"Eeee… but you're not an atheist. You've read about God, after all."

"Is that not the whole point of fiction, that you read about something that does not exist in your tangible reality? If it doesn't exist, can you only believe in it?"

"You believe in your reason, Narciso, right? What have you read?"

"A brief treatise on God, man and his happiness, and then also 'Ethica, ordine geometrico demonstrata.'"

"Baruch…"

"I think it's Benedict Spinoza."

"That Jew?"

"Jewish or not, his method seduced me, the *more geometrico*, like Euclidean geometry, in which only a few true propositions create a whole, expanded study. Spinoza formulated assumptions like mathematical propositions, then built on their claims, proving them mathematically and verifying them by confronting the facts."

"Do you think you exist? Because it does not look like you think. See how your ethical relativism has led you to the conclusion that knowledge of the harmonious unity of the self with all of Nature, if accepted, grants the only possible happiness."

"To accept something, you first must know it."

"And God? The unknowable can only be accepted on faith."

"I believe! I believe, like an Egyptian slave building the pyramids. No! Not like an Egyptian; I am a slave from Toledo. My altar reigned over me and controlled me for years. The work was more important than I— it was not at all creative, but the method dominated me. I stopped being human, became a tool, an object and, for the cardinal, a value in and of myself."

"You alienated yourself…"

"Yes, I alienated myself to save myself! Save myself from reification—items, agreements between people. The house was not a place to live, but something that I had to have. Marriage was not an extension of love, but a social contract. Even values began to rule us, control us. This was supposed to be life? This was supposed to be freedom?"

"In your case, Narciso, alienation consisted in the fact that you lost your human characteristics by drowning in yourself."

"You gave up on the possibility of changing the world, Narciso. Your alienation became a commodity fetishism. Your altar could have been beautiful because of your work, or not beautiful, as a product, commodity, a thing in and of itself. You treated humans like clients, too, or like commodities, objectified, deprived of specifics."

"Fetishist!"

"Pervert!"

"I don't understand…" I spoke truthfully, because the discussion had gone above my head: "I, a fetishist? What is that?"

"A fetish is detached from its actual object. You desire characteristics, not the object or the person who has them."

"You, Narciso, have an entire collection of fetishes. One of them is agalmatophilia, because monuments and statues excite you. And then agoraphilia, your fetish for public spaces. Acrophilia, erections at great heights, huh? Acrotomophilia, you get excited by the mutilated body of your partner. Acousticophilia, sing, and you get hard. Ablutophilia, you wash yourself and the water excites you. Anasteemaphilia, did you even know that you prefer shorter partners? And then autophilia and autofetishism, your own body makes you spasm, even as you hurt yourself. Dendrophilia, you become stiff from the touch of wood and trees. Doraphilia, you get stiff while petting fur. Teratophilia—you love the hunchbacked, the lame, the deformed. Just look at your altar. Gerontophilia, you love old women, you pervert! Heterochromophilia, skin colours bring you to orgasm. Hygrophilia, you lick the wax out of ears, sip jizz? Candaulism, because bragging about your woman in front of other men makes you hard. Xenophilia, you love fucking women without knowing who they are. Mammaphilia, you weren't sated in childhood so still you need to suck nipples? Both? Three?! Ozolagnia, from a single smell, you stand, hard as Hell. Speaking of standing—podophilia, you pleasure yourself with feet. And that's not all—urophilia, although it's difficult to piss with an erection…"

"At least I don't suffer from coprophagia and necrophilia…"

Nobody listened to him. All the beasts turned their heads towards the herd of calves running on the horizon. The court had ended, and the beasts raced away. In their trot, they resembled bulls.

It became quiet. With my ear to the ground I listened, as somewhere in the depths of the earth, a heart beat. Maybe it was my heart, beating after death. Then, quietly, as though on tiptoes, there came footsteps. I looked at the horizon, where I saw a group of angels slowly approaching me. As they approached, their wings transformed into rakes, tridents for dung, flails, and clubs. They circled me and began their judgment:

"Is he breathing?"

"Ehhh, he's probably dead."

"Shhh, he stares, so he lives."

"Does he know where he is?"

"We should tell him."

"Bludgeon his carcass. Since he fell from the sky, he's a fallen angel, so a devil."

"How can he be a devil if Hell has not swallowed him?"

"If he's neither an angel nor a devil, then he's a human. Bludgeon him!"

Before the first strike fell, I cried:

"¡Hola! I am not a carcass, a devil, or an angel. Especially not an angel."

They stopped for a moment, but began anew:

"He speaks with Castile and León accents. He's foreign. Bludgeon him."

"Who are you?"

"I am…I was…" I felt as though I had something to say, but they did not listen, only whispered amongst themselves and then spoke their judgment:

"Since the bulls did not kill you, we will also leave you in peace. You can live in this pasture and you will clean it, but you will never leave the valley, and you are not allowed to wear clothes."

Then I realized that I was naked, and I was ashamed.

Then began days of humility and madness. Entire days I tended the pasture, collecting the bull and cow dung with a primitive wheelbarrow and carrying it to the edge of the valley. When it dried, I returned it to the shepherds as fuel. In exchange, once a day I was given a bowl of soup, after which I was often ill. Through these first days, the vomit and diarrhea almost killed me. Luckily, a small stream ran through the valley. It flowed from the enclosures of the shepherds and fell into a chasm. Not only did I drink from this stream, but I washed myself in it, and the herbs I found along its bank allowed me to regulate my digestion. I had no idea what these herbs were, but chewing them brought me relief, filled my stomach, killed my pain.

I spent the entire day in the pastures, and at night I found myself a relatively comfortable place in the branches of one of the few trees. The first morning, after a night spent in the tree, I noticed tracks, by which I understand that my flying machine had crashed on the edge of the chasm and then fallen into it. When the shepherds found me, there was already no trace of it. The chasm was at the south edge of the valley... And so I must have been flying south.

The valley was surrounded by tall and steep mountains, like a ring. There was no beginning or end. Each point at which the steep rocks began was also the point at which they ended. There was no escape from the valley, except for a tunnel that the stream pierced through the mountains, covered by a wooden building where the shepherds lived and from where they brought out their bulls. The only way out of the valley was not a way out for me.

Why was I studying the valley? Of course I dreamed of escaping it. The walls of rock around me, my bare feet, and my lack of knowledge when it comes to climbing quickly ended my dreams of crossing the mountains. The chasm in which my vehicle rested was not very big, but deep and steep like the walls around the valley. Sometimes I lay at its edge, studying the fall of my flying machine, its insignificance. I had no chance to save and repair the vehicle, to fill it with embers. How similar I was to it. Fallen, broken, without life, without fire.

Maybe that's why I preferred to sit in the tree. The bulls did not threaten me, I could see farther. It also hurt more. Slowly, oh, so very slowly, I began to understand what it was that I had done.

Sitting among the branches did not offer me an opportunity for survival. I had to come down, work in the pastures with my wheelbarrows, and then beg for a bowl of shit from the shepherds. Collecting the dung always brought the risk of coming into contact with the horns or the hooves of the bulls. Through the first few days of my gathering I was roughed up, but alive. Several times, a bull knocked me over, and I was trampled once. It hurt, and so in my first brushes with the bulls I tried to bounce myself off their speeding bodies before teaching myself how to dodge them. After some time, even without using my hands, I was able to jump far enough out of the bull's path that I would be safe. When my wounds on my back and chest healed, I rubbed myself in their dung, but the smell did not scare away the bulls, which reacted to movement and threw themselves blindly into attack.

One such attack occurred when I was stretching, standing on some rock, next to my loaded wheelbarrows. I turned and realized a bull was charging right at me. I had no time to dodge, so I jumped straight up and straightened my arms before me to protect myself. I knew that in a moment the horn would rip me in half.

And then something extraordinary happened. My straightened arms landed above the bull's horns, on his back, and threw me into the air. I flipped through the air above the galloping bull and landed in a wheelbarrow. My day's work was for naught, and I had to gather all the spilled dung once more, but I was happy.

From the times of my architectural studies I remembered the story of Leon Battista Alberti, an architect working for that exceptional bloodsucker, Sigismondo Malatesta. I could not remember his architectural achievements, but even so, the piece of information that made the greatest impression on me was that Leon could jump from a standstill to the height of a grown man's head. I do not know if I became a better architect by leaping that bull, but I was impressed with myself for this feat. From that day on, every morning and every evening I tried to jump into the tree, I jumped instead of walking, I circled the valley hopping like a frog, or I lay on my back and tossed stones into the air above me with my legs. I chewed more and more of the herbs by the stream, I ate almost all the leaves on the trees. The work in the fresh air, the water and the herbs strengthened my body. The constant exercise improved my muscles. The first weeks in the valley thinned me immensely, I was much lighter. I was becoming a different person. Different physically.

My previous escapes from the bulls, the jumps and dodges, were replaced by leaps over their backs. I was often bruised, all my muscles ached because I often tumbled to the ground, slamming my elbows, knees, and head. After weeks of work on my balance, I taught myself to fall onto all fours, and then to land on my two feet.

The shepherds began to feed me better, and even gave me an old shirt and a pair of stinking pants. One day, a group of dignified-looking gentlemen came to the valley. I was given some rags, placed into an enclosure with an especially powerful bull, and I heard:

"Corrida!"

Only a simpleton would make such a joke. Bullfighting, for every Spaniard, is a holy symbiosis between human and beast. In the history of bullfighting, each side has met with death. Most often, it is the bull that is killed. It is then quartered, sold, eaten. The bull does not have much of a chance against the whole group, who works together in order to tire it, make it lower its head, reveal its weakest point, the shortest path to its heart. Break it. And when it is no longer a beast, there is nothing left to do but kill it. Not just in any old way, but in such a way as to demonstrate the mastery (faena) of the bullfighter (torero).

The shepherds did not expect the bull to die, because I could not kill it with my bare hands. Everybody waited for my slow death.

Each corrida begins with a parade (paseíllo)—the bull chased me around the pen. Then, heralds (alguacilillos) ask for the keys to the gates, through which the bulls enter (puerta de los toriles)—I cried for them to let me out. This aroused only general merriment and the amusement of the audience, which began to place bets. I wonder if anybody bet on me?

After the formal section, we come to the three parts of the corrida (tercios), the three sections. In the first, the matadors use a wide cape (capote) to fool the bull. I did not have a cape. So, I removed my shirt and tried to tire the bull with it. It was torn into shreds on the bull's first charge.

In this section, the picadors (picadores), on horseback, stab the bull with long lances. I had neither horse nor lance, I had only my ability to dodge. When the bull attacked, I jumped up, jumped over, and somersaulted above him.

"Bravo!" the observers roared, safely hidden behind the high fence. I tried to tear a splinter from the fence to have something to plunge into the beast's back.

The fence would not give. I did not succeed as a picador. I managed to break off two small pieces, with which I moved into the second section. In this section (la suerte de banderillas), flagmen (banderilleros) stick small blades with coloured flags attached to their shafts into the back of the bull.

Jumping over the bull, I managed to plunge my two splinters into him, but they, protruding from his back, became obstacles for me as I jumped above him.

I do not know how the bull felt, but I was staggering from exhaustion, entering the third part of the corrida, the "suerte suprema." As a toreador, I should have unfurled my muleta and brought a sword. I did not have either of these things. Instead of a muleta, I used my pants. As for the sword… No, I will not compare my manhood to the sword. Naked and hanging, it became the object of jokes and whistles. I had to use my intelligence.

Twice I was able to direct the bull towards the gates of the enclosure. The gates trembled in their foundations, but they did not give way. The third time, my jump was unsuccessful. I flew above his horns, and then his hooves caught me and slammed me into the ground. As for him, he fell into the gates with all his might and demolished them.

I lay on the sand in the improvised arena, listening as the shepherds tried to catch the bull, as they killed it, as they argued with the gentlemen about their money, which they had won with their bets on my life, and as they angrily parted company. They left.

Death had spared me. Once again. Why?

This last fall, the cold of the horns, the rough hair, and the circles under my skin. The toss, which had sent me far into the centre of the enclosure, only this finally awakened me. Until now it was as though I had been dreaming, a dream that, like a thread, had woven itself into my existence, my half-life. What had this time been, from that moment when the sword pierced my back, slid above my diaphragm, not catching my lungs, my heart, my aorta, and exited through my breast. I had lived, even though I did not believe it. My escape from my city in my machine, the flight above the mountains, here, to the bulls, my meeting and living with them, day after day, until this most recent fall. My body was telling me that this is life, because I hurt, I am hungry, I shit, I pant. My head was telling me that this could not be true, because nobody has survived a sword plunging into their back.

I awoke to life. Suddenly I wanted to speak, but I had nobody to speak to.

The shepherds changed their attitude towards me. Perhaps the money they had won muffled the smell of dung surrounding me. It was not an illusion that after the corrida they had gained a respect for me. Further, they allowed me to sit near their fire in the evening, listening to their nonsense. They did not chase me as before, throwing stones. I received a new shirt and pants.

During these evenings, when their stories were drowned by the pain and rumble of my stomach, I learned, to my surprise, that some Narciso Tomé continued to live in faraway Toledo (how far could Toledo be from the valley?), that his altar spread a heavenly light and healed the masses that visit the city. Nobody paid attention to my cries (how crazy I must have been then!), that I was that architect who built that wonderful altar. If they had diagnosed me then with madness, I could have ended up like my flying machine. I inferred from their conversations (although maybe it was just my imagination), that the architect (me), after building the altar, was rebuilding the cathedral.

The thought that somebody was pretending to be me was a hundred times more painful than all the wounds I had received since the beginning of my stay in the valley. I was not frightened for my pride and ego, but about the fate of my family. While I had been gathering bull shit, somebody else had been living in my place, somebody else had been living my life…

A great sadness came over me. Did I have a right to call Esperanza's side "my place"? Not only had I rejected it, betraying my wife, I had even fled, renounced it, I had not faced the executioners of the Inquisition, had not defended my family… I was not sure if I even knew what had actually happened. Impossible explanations for what I had heard from the shepherds floated through my head. I imagined that the Inquisition had stationed somebody in my position, maybe my whole family had been replaced. I did not want to think about what had happened to my real family.

Every time I thought "my family, my children, my wife," I was seized by a boundless grief. The impression that I had no right to those words, that I would never again be able to use them, that I did not know their meaning.

Still, from the moment I had heard the rumours about myself, the fear for those closest to me and the belated longing and regret for what I had lost and abandoned did not leave me. I did not have a hope of escape, not a hope of contacting anybody beyond this valley. And then fate gave me an opportunity.

One day, the dignified-looking gentlemen returned to the valley with some even more dignified and stately looking gentlemen. Without hesitation, the shepherds threw me into the pen with an even more intimidating bull and shouted the same command as before:

"Corrida!"

Once again, I was fighting for my life, and the more dignified and stately looking gentlemen were betting with those less dignified, who probably wanted to win back some of the money they had lost the last time. The shepherds were responsible only for organizing the fight between the bull and myself but were probably also counting on some winnings.

I was not about to pretend to fight with the bull. I had no reason to tire him or force him to lower his head. I had no sword. I could delude myself that one of the gentlemen would throw me his sword at the last moment, but I could not count on any help. This time, the bull was larger and more powerful than before. Jumping over him demanded greater strength and was much riskier than in the battle with the first bull. We stood before each other. Him with his massive head lowered so his wide horns were at the height of my chest, and I again with my shirt in my hands instead of my cape and muleta.

The physical superiority of the bull saved me. The first time he lowered his head to hit me, his horns almost touched the ground. I had to survive only until the bull tired itself out. I crouched, I fell to the ground, I dragged my shirt through the dirt, trying to make the bull's horn catch on the arena. A few times he threw me, his horns landing on my back when my dodge was a bit too late, but finally, with his full force his horns plunged into the earth. He stumbled, but the mass of his body could not stop itself, and he flew into the air, breaking his neck. He collapsed, fear in his eyes, and he trembled with terrible convulsions, once, twice. He died.

I had killed a bull. I had never done it before. I did not take his life. I killed him in order to save myself. I or him, I told myself. He would have been killed anyways. He would have had a moment of glory in Madrid, and then he would have been eaten by those same people who would have cheered him that very day.

The more stately looking gentlemen paid the price of the bull to the screaming shepherds, paid the less-dignified gentlemen their winnings, and then turned to me, asking me for my name. Without thinking, I said:

"Cinarso Meto." Nothing better occurred to me than to rearrange my name.

They asked me, also, if I would like them to do anything for me. I wanted to write a letter. They gave me paper, and I wrote:

*My Dear,*

*Can I address You in this way, after what I did? I know, I do not have that right, because I lost it abandoning You, abandoning our life. I know that I hurt You, that I broke Your heart. I broke my vow of fidelity. I did this and I cannot hide it, erase it, or cover it up.*

*And even though I know that it sounds absurd, I feel that it has always, always only been You that I have loved, even when I was with that other woman.*

*I know that this does not fit in Your imagination, in the boundaries of Your ethics. But I lived beyond those boundaries, lived in my divided reality, where in one world I was a husband and father, in a second an architect, in a third somebody else, in a fourth… And so on, and so on.*

*Why did I do this?*

*Selfishness, I was lost in my selfishness. I regretted my wasted life, which had settled on a sandbank, I regretted my wasted art, which already was not a craft, just ordinary prostitution, I regretted my wasted marriage, in which we appeared to each other as strangers. You with Your self-pity, broken by the pain of reality, and I with my self-pity, torn by ambitions, frustrations, appetites.*

*Selfishness is not self-love, because if I had loved myself, I would have loved my life, I would have lived my life and felt good in it—I would not have sought a different life, satisfaction in my lack of fulfillment, regret for myself, regret that the world did not recognize me.*

*Why did I become the lover of another woman? Was it only because I could? Or was it from powerlessness?*

No, I do not want to say that I succumbed, that I was seduced, that this all happened against my will, against my consent, somehow beyond me. I experienced powerlessness as a lack of authority, the inability to enforce my will, being a subject, subordinate, forced into something that was not my own choice.

For all this, I could take "revenge," dominating, subordinating another person to myself, denying their humanity, making them my subject, subject to my will. I stopped being powerless, I had authority and I could even see myself as the most wonderful lover—and who was I?

After all, I was not even her lover! This woman—who does not even have a name—was an object to me. She was ruined and probably ruining me to the same degree. She was a pretext for me to realize my sexual fantasies. And all this in secret from You, the children, friends, the family, bah—especially from my employer, the cardinal. Necessary lies, half-truths, understatements and concealments—I created an entire false reality, which I manipulated so that nobody could have guessed where I was and what I was doing. It seemed to me that I was beyond time, beyond bourgeois morality, beyond the social order.

At the same time, on a daily basis, I was subordinate to so many dictates, standards, controlled by so many people, and I felt that this was a secret hidden before everybody, something of my own, something private, which could not be taken from me because it is hidden.

My conscience? Do I have a right to speak of my own pain after the pain that I have caused You? When I was returning to our house, first I looked in through the window. I saw You inside, You, the children, Your mother, our dog... And I looked at all this like a ghost, like somebody who had died in this life, who had committed ethical suicide, departed to the afterlife. I lived with You, waiting for that moment when I would become invisible to You, like a ghost, catching on Your sleeves and hands. I waited for this moment when I would hear: "Something haunts..."

*I was so dead inside that I was unable to find any tenderness towards You, any love. I was unable to find my feelings, and even if I had found them, I would have been afraid to speak of them. I was unable to speak of them. I had been so eloquent, translating my altar in the cathedral, but I was unable to utter a word to You.*

*Do these words not reveal how much I did not live in my own life, how I was not fit for it, or it for me? I lived a stranger's life, I was living a stranger's life, not living.*

*Can I understand, now, what I have done?*

*I am somewhere else and I am someone else. Someone who understands Your hurt and Your pain. If there is no longer a return to You, please accept only that Your love, before I trampled it, has given my existence meaning and purpose. The children, which You bore, have brought me incomparable happiness and are the greatest gift, a reason to live. The nights with You, full of love, will be what I take with me when I leave this world—the memory of tenderness and joy, when we opened ourselves to each other, full of light and happiness.*

*Here where I am, the ground is dry and thirsty for blood. And although this is probably the most prestigious breeding ground of bulls in the Sierra Nevada, the services that I impart to them represent the depth of my fall and teach me humility, from the depths of which I want to thank You for Your love.*

*Humbly—*
*Cinarso Meto*

They promised to deliver it to the address I indicated in Toledo. They left. The shepherds denied me food. The first night after I had sent my letter, when I brought the dried dung to the edge of the valley, they chased me away. I went to sleep hungry and anxious about my letter. For the next two weeks I begged and negotiated until my situation changed radically.

As evening approached, a group of riders tore into the valley. I was lying down to sleep under my tree, and I did not see everything. At first, I thought I would have to fight another bull. The visitors murdered the shepherds, slitting their throats and desecrating their bodies. They burned the wooden structure at the entrance to the tunnel, which connected the valley to the rest of the world. They opened the enclosures and drove the bulls into the chasm.

In the arena, a bull dies quietly and with dignity. Thrown into the chasm, it roars and moans in agony of its broken horns and bones.

The killing of the bulls scared me more than the deaths of the shepherds. I buried myself in a small hole at the foot of the tree, knowing that death awaited me too, and the lament of the dying animals had made clear to me that the cruelty of the visitors could reach farther than their blade.

When everything became quiet and the visitors were burning the wood from the dismantled enclosures and preparing for sleep, somebody found me hidden at the foot of the tree.

They dragged me to the fire by my hair, shouting and cursing horribly in some unknown dialect until their leader came out of one of the tents they had put up after the massacre of the bulls and shepherds. Most of their clothes were tattered, shabby, or hanging. They were tanned, but not dark-skinned. Their leader, however, was slim and black like the night. He wore horse-riding boots, fine trousers, and a solid coat. Tucked behind his belt he had three pistols. Although it was night, in the light of the fire I recognized the face. Not knowing if what I saw was the truth, or if my fear had robbed me of my reason, I fell on the ground and said:

"Uhuru!"

And to this she, because it was her without a doubt, although she was dressed as a man, answered in a deep voice:

"My name is Ernani."[30]

She took a torch from the flame and held me by the hair, staring long into my face. She stared so long that I felt exhausted.

I was still kneeling before her when she put her hands in the pockets of her pantaloons and clearly got an erection. The front of her pants puffed up considerably, and from the flaring hole, something emerged that was shaped like a mace or a short club. Then Uhuru, who covered this object with the tails of her coat, shoved it into my mouth. Before this object passed through my lips and began to penetrate me, I saw that its tip was a clenched fist with a pointed index finger that had, in part, broken off. Instead of a penis, Uhuru had made a prosthesis from the Jewish pointer for reading the Torah.

I preferred not to think about how many times this object had violently deflowered a virgin or sodomized an ambushed gentleman. The object read me from within, page after page, shallower, deeper, shallower, deeper. And in my head, only some thoughtless pain prevailed. I could think of nothing, I felt nothing, maybe only this headache.

---

30  Of course, Narciso is too frightened to think straight at this moment. You, however, Dear Reader, should know that this is an allusion to the story of Don Juan. This story tells of the great love between Elvira and Prince Don Juan of Aragon, who hides as the bandit Ernani, and is the disinherited son of King Philip I, who is also the father of Don Carlos. Elvira lusts after her uncle and guardian, the old Gomez de Silva. Elvira also desires Don Carlos, who has arrived at de Silva's castle, tracking Ernani, who is disguised as a pilgrim. Hospitality prohibits de Silva from seeing Ernani. In vengeance, Don Carlos kidnaps Elvira and takes her to Aachen, promising her freedom in exchange for the bandit. Ernani, knowing the intentions of the son of the monarch, explains to de Silva the king's plot. They swear an alliance and decide to pursue Don Carlos in order to take Elvira away from him. Ernani, as a sign of honesty, gives a horn to de Silva—if he hears its call, he will get out of the old man's way. Their alliance is discovered, and Ernani and de Silva are sentenced to death. Elvira saves their lives by begging for the grace of Carlos, who has just become the King of Spain. When Elvira and Don Juan are married in Saragossa, the horn sounds. Ernani, fulfilling the oath he has given to de Silva, kills himself with a dagger.

Even the roars of joy behind my back grew quiet and slid away into some deaf emptiness. Everything ceased to concern me. I was even unable to feel shame.

Finally, my humiliation was over. The object was taken from my mouth, and I was kicked from behind and marched off to her tent.

We sat across from each other. With my tongue I checked if I had lost any teeth. I felt a metallic taste in my mouth. I had found myself beside a woman who, years ago, I had coveted and paid money to spy on, and who now decided my life. I was? I thought? I waited, rather. He who waits expects the unimaginable, that being will begin again. No thought suggested that I was alive. Only the breath flowing into me and leaving through my nose, only the air testified to my life.

"Bartolomeu, the other one, we watched you dance together…did he buy you? Auuu!—" Slashed across the face by her whip, I fell silent.

"Shut up, the way you shut up then. You paid to see me naked, so that my body was naked before you. You did not want to know who I was. I was an object for you. An object of your desire. Do you still want me? Here is your chance… Pour out your seed. Here and now, before me, or… we'll cut off your balls and shove them down your throat."

Uhuru spoke fluent Castilian. With her whip she poked my crotch and beat me on the head, urging me to take my limp member into my hand and start masturbating. I thought about her body, but the fear of castration could not awaken my organs to something that once came with ease. Now I was shut in her tent, one on one with the object of my desires. But between that desire and this moment stretched an ocean of time, stretched a journey—hers and mine—to a point in which, for my former infatuation in her vulnerability, I had to pay. Beaten and helpless, I lay in the dust of her tent and wept.

My sobs drowned in her quiet voice:

"Between one and the other, between a man and a woman, there is no clearing, no passage. If there were, it would be an expectation of the openness of something that has already been closed in a circle, in a vacuum. Returning a stranger's gaze, you recognize his impenetrability. There is no hope for a bridge built over a precipice or suspended in nothingness. A bridge built in the expectation—but in a vacuum—of the passage towards something."

"The mind can stop here and wait. Because waiting anticipates the unimaginable return of (to) the beginning."

"However… The modest back-and-forth movement within the woman constitutes the almost unfounded base of the relationship, where everything can take place without the fall into the abyss. This movement takes place before all phenomena and designation. When a woman touches herself intimately, or when women touch themselves intimately without the need to traverse boundaries, this state is the base upon which the phenomenon of distance opens a clearing for the thinker, becomes understandable. The interior relationship."

"Delight, which takes place within her, her delight, her own delight, which he will never be able to assimilate and will only be able to take part in with her—this is the pain that the thinker cannot bear. Unless… offering or offering up himself, as a being, in which she can discover a space to develop what she must say."

"What must she say herself…"

"Life, or rather being in our time raises questions about the sexual destiny of every being: does ecstasy begin with erection or with ejaculation? Is the goal of the erection that man always preserves a distance in relation to each other and to the whole, or, rather, is its purpose the production-emitting of seed to the outside, so that it can be thrown out or projected? Can both these situations come into play? How are they linked? By the tension between them?"

"Put simply, does a conscious being "here-and-now" bring both erection and ejaculation into the present, through its residence in language? In what way does erection and ejaculation determine time and space depending on language, how it reveals and develops."

"Language, precisely, would be technology—architechnology, architectonics—for men to shape their lives in the design of their sexuality."

"And love?"

"Turning to the other—looking reveals differences and penetrates them, becomes a ground to discover what is common. Loving thought must always anticipate concern, which remains in the boundaries of being, which has been entrusted to oneself. The ecstasy of the lovers is the space of the return of these tropes in the direction of the common."

"Language does not express the essential. It reveals itself as an excess of what makes a man a man. What is said, exchanged, presented or represented will never be anything more than excess, which is needed for the necessary conditions of life. Man never spoke out of necessity. Maybe in the distant past. Forgotten. The path on which the past was lost. The abyss, opening. The discovery of the origin of man as something unnecessary. An animal generating a mutuality between earth and sky. Occupied with death, not life. Uprooted from birth, from development—in a world of projections, in a world of dreams."[31]

I did not understand a single word of what she said. I so tired that I fell asleep during her speech. The next day, Uhuru strapped me to her saddle and we rode out of the valley, in which there were no more bulls. Only clouds of black crows vanished into the chasm at the edge of the pasture.

Beyond the tunnel, a different world began.

---

31  Clearly, Uhuru has had the opportunity to read, absorb, and manipulate the contents of other peoples' brains and books. The above passage indicates that one of the texts that Uhuru has assimilated is *L'oubli de l'air chez Martin Heidegger* (1983) by the philosopher Luce Irigaray.

# ENTRAPMENT

*(Doña Esperanza Tomé, disguised as Narciso Tomé, uses Maja, the
former shop assistant, to deceive doña Nora del Pulpo, whose body,
not too long ago, doña Esperanza used to betray herself with her own
husband, who she now pretends to be.
The sentence above reflects the complexity of the reality of
Toledo after the events described two chapters previous.)*

IIIIIIIIIIIIIIIIIIIIIIIIIIIIIIIIIIIIIIIIIIIIIIIIIIIIIIIIIIIIIIIIIIIIIIIIIIIIIIIIIIIIIIIIIIIIIIIIIIIIIIIIIIIIIIIIIIIIIIIIIIIIIIIIIIIIIIIIIIIIIIIIIIIIIIIIIIIII

AS I SAID, THE PIERCING OF THE WALL BEHIND THE MAIN ALTAR IN
the cathedral violated the order of the city. First, the routine of daily
life was shattered by the uninterrupted flow of masses of cripples, sick,
and pilgrims lured by the rumours about the miraculous light shining
from the tabernacle in the cathedral. These people did not just occupy
themselves with the cathedral, but they polluted the neighbouring
streets and alleys. Because they needed something to eat and somewhere to sleep, hostels, inns, and taverns multiplied faster than rabbits.
In addition, everything immediately grew more expensive in the city.
The wealthy pilgrims had to pay, and the poor begged for a piece of
bread or a bowl of soup. The poor slept on the street, which not only
paralyzed the city, but also caused an influx of thieves who robbed
the poor and the rich to the same extent. Gangs of thieves fought for
control of individual streets, murdering without mercy. People were

afraid to go out at night, and in the meantime the curia, which was making the most money, ordered work on the altar only in those times when the sun did not fall through the dome. Apparently, the workers would often block the hole and stem the flow of light. And the flow of light through the tabernacle meant a flow of money into the coffers of the church.

First, the curia eliminated free entrance to the cathedral, forcing even the church beggars to pay tribute before they could return to their places in the church. Then they closed all the gates, allowing only those who could afford to buy entrance to the cathedral. Finally, the place where the light falls in the chancel was fenced off, and entrance to the lit space was preceded not only with the purchase of yet another ticket, but also rigorous questioning as to the reasons for wanting to be exposed to this wonderful light. This was explained as a necessary check for decency, as it turned out that many of the people who could pay for all three stages of the pilgrimage to the light wanted to expose, before the Blessed Sacrament, parts of their bodies that had been affected by impotence, venereal disease, or underdevelopment.

The fact that the wonderful light was only available to those who could pay for it meant that pilgrims were often placed in a position where they needed to acquire money in a very short time. Usury, prostitution, theft, and gambling covered the city like a thick skin of filth. In addition to these, the most sophisticated forms of extorting money fulfilled the city's new image of corruption and stupidity. Shops that sold devotional items began to carry objects associated with the wonderful light almost exclusively: bottles that had capped the light within them, medallions on which the light had fallen, shadows traced on pieces of paper... The demoralization touched everybody. Even the apprentices and assistants to the builders began to sell their passes to the construction site to those who could afford them.

Then came a letter from Madrid or Rome and everything ended. The dome was covered, and entrance to the cathedral was free again. Many people in the city lost their sources of livelihood, many could not come to terms with this; the hole in the wall had changed too much about their lives... As for us, we worked without pause. First, we enlarged the hole in the roof of the cathedral and secured the structure against collapse. The new window appeared as a means to spy on God from beneath the rough waves of the apse. The periscope was decorated with frescoes (from the fingers of Andres) and sculptures that were once rejected as unfit for the altar, and that had been stored in the shed on site.

Once and then—it seems that it was the same time, and yet, how different they feel. Once I felt that I loved and that I was loved. Then I lost everything. Once it seemed to me that I was united with Narciso in a feeling that had no equal in the world. Once I understood he would not return, then the cracks began to spread through my reality.

One day, while working on the window in the apse, I saw a woman. Maybe her look drew my attention. When I looked at her, she was already walking towards the sacristy. I saw only her profile. She was beautiful and young. She had a small head with smooth combed hair tied on top in a heavy knot. A long neck gently sloping to her shoulders. Her corseted breasts were firm and her belly and waist fell flat to the folds of her dress.

I came down from the scaffolding and went into the sacristy. I had not looked in here since my time leading groups through the cathedral, those groups where I had met Nora. The sacristy in Toledo was always more of a museum than a church facility. Along with my favourite El Greco, "El caballero de la mano en el pecho" there was also "El Expolio." The hand on the heart of Christ being torn from his bloody clothes corresponds with the same gesture on the breast of the gentlemen, turning this significant gesture into a painterly mannerism.

She sat in the far corner by a primitive easel. It is difficult to say what feelings I had towards her. She was only a servant of that hated woman through which Narciso ruined my and our life. On the other hand, it was her who, betraying her mistress, ended a sequence of betrayals...

"Maja?"

She turned and looked at me curiously.

"Do you recognize me, Maja?"

"Everyone in this city knows you, Sir."

"And you?"

"I…I know, Sir, who you are, but I am not happy to know you."

"Once we saw each other often, Maja."

She rubbed her forehead in confusion. She tried to concentrate or gather her thoughts, and then:

"I do not remember, Sir. The priests told me that I lost my memory…"

"The priests?"

"Yes, the priests took me in. I work for them now. I copy the paintings for devout parishioners."

"And what's your name?"

"Like you said, Sir, Maja."

"How do you know, if you lost your memory?"

"The priests told me…"

"Did they also tell you that you have a great talent?"

She did not speak, only looked side to side, as though fighting her thoughts, desperate and sad. On the verge of collapse, looking me in the eyes, she whispered:

"Help me, Sir…" Slowly, she raised her skirts. Before I could react angrily, I was shaken with indignation. Maja's abdomen was locked in a wrought-iron chastity belt, metal panties with terrifying teeth and spikes enclosing her anus and crotch.

"How can you clean yourself in something like this, child? Did the priests do this also?"

"No, apparently I was given it by the same person who took my memory… Quick, Sir, you must flee!"

A preacher entered the sacristy. He did not even try to hide the fact that he had been listening to us. Maja bolted, but I stayed and faced him. He was the same man who slapped Narciso on the back in my first dream. Feigning surprise, he said:

"Master?! What are you seeking here?"

I do not know how often the "master" blushed, but I was red as a beet:

"I am always seeking talent that wields the chisel or brush. This one is very talented… How did she arrive at the rectory?"

"We are keeping it from her, but to you, master, I will tell the secret…"

I leaned closer to him and then…the scaffolding fell around the altar. If I had not gone after Maja, I would probably be lying like my workers under the beams of the scaffolds. Dead. Once I sought death, once I wanted the cathedral to collapse. Now, the ceiling had already been secured, and it hung above the altar without the scaffolding.

I learned that it had not fallen on its own, that somebody had sawed it down, somebody who had wanted to delay our work. Not even for a moment did I suspect that somebody wanted me dead…

Still, the chastity belt that Maja wore hovered in my mind. During my years of searching for the hole for the key with which I came to Toledo, I had so much practice that now, I believe I can see locks inside-out, I see the combinations of latches, the shape of the key, and I can even tell you where in Toledo you can find such a lock. Now, I was certain that I saw before me the key that could open Maja's belt.

I should have thought about my safety immediately after Narciso's disappearance. Men died almost every night, near the cathedral, on our street, or behind our house. All of them were Narciso's age, similar in stature, usually dressed like me. They always died of one thrust of a sharp blade planted in their back.

I tried to return home with someone from the site, I closed my doors, checked to make sure everything was locked. Several times I felt as though someone was watching me, standing beneath our window in the night, crawling by the doors. Sometimes it seemed to me that someone was spying on me at the church. And then finally, it happened…

"Narciso, it's me…"

Before me stood a woman with a small head, her combed hair tied on top in a knot, with a comb in the shape of a fan stuck in it. A dark veil flowed from under her hair, covering her neck, shoulders, and breasts. I saw her face, a dark Arabian face or the face of a Jewish woman from the south. She might have been sick. She panted, breathed quickly, and her breasts—completely different than those I remembered—squeezed by her soft corset, heaved to the rhythm of her breath, as if they were losing air.

Many times I had looked at her through her eyes, I had seen her in the mirror, somehow differently.

"Who are you?"

"Narciso! Come back to me! I can take care of you… We were good together, right? Just once, just one more time… One, single time. I need you…"

I was outraged, I could not speak, but I felt that I could kill her with my bare hands. The woman standing before me did not remind me of the Nora from my dreams, did not remind me of the Nora who visited me in the sacristy. Whoever she was—she was growing old before my eyes, graying, wrinkling, hunching, falling apart, like somebody, somebody who had risen from the grave… She looked at me like a blind man. Maybe she was blind? Indeed, as somebody who was—to Hell with her!—so close to my husband, how could she not see that this was not Narciso, but I! I, doña Esperanza Tomé, disguised as my husband.

For a moment I believed Nora was blind. Quickly, however, I remembered that I had looked with her eyes, I had looked at him, after all. Had I ever looked into his eyes through her eyes?

The blood surged in me, and because I was unable to speak like a man in front of women, or just generally, like a man, I simply paraphrased the cardinal:

"I am sick of your damned desires, Nora. If you came to give me money, then go ahead. To this day I have not received a cent for the project I did for you! You sucked me and my family dry, you damned us all to Hell. And what do I have in return? Shit! A hole in my back and a hole in my breast. You used me like a bung, like a churn to make butter. You calmed yourself with me. Yes, you used me and hurt me. Look how many people have died because of you, how many you hurt beyond their mortal wounds... Get out of here, you bitch!"

"But you loved me..."

"Never...!"

"Prove it!"

"Come back tomorrow..."

I fled. I fled from the city, as far away as possible from that stuffy cathedral, the emptiness, the cold and the dark of the aisles, the apse, the chapels, I fled beyond the city walls, into space, through la Puerta de Bisagra. Leaving the city, I reversed history and abandoned reality, fleeing into legend. Cid, taking Toledo from the Moors, rode through these gates once after seven years of siege.[32]

I walked along the walls in the direction of la Ermita Basilica del Cristo de la Vega, where Christ hangs crucified with one arm lowered from the cross.[33] And further, to the Tagus, to Baño de la Cava, where the last king of Toledo, Don Rodrigo, instead of occupying himself with ruling, spied on Florinda, the daughter of Count Julián, in the

---

32 Alfonso VI and Cid Campeador conquered Toledo in the year 1085, destroying the old gate built by the Moors.

33 Legend says that under this cross, Inés de Vargas and Diego Martínez made their vow of fidelity before Diego left for war. When he returned in glory, he did not care for the faithful Inés. Inés asked for help from the ecclesiastical court. The judge demanded the testimony of the sworn witnesses of their vows, and then Inés called Christ as her witness. Christ lowered his arm from the cross and said: "I swear it."

Diego married Inés, and to commemorate this marriage in Toledo, after the Easter holidays there is a festival of love, and renewals of marriage vows.

baths, and then slandered her. Demanding vengeance, Julián brought the Moors to the city, which they captured and ruled for three hundred years,[34] until the time when Cid ... And so on, and so on.

And so I came to el Puente de San Martín, on which the image of the builder's wife reminded me how much Toledan wives have done for their husbands, especially when they have needed to be saved from trouble.

My indignation passed. The walk made me realize that my anger, even if it is real, does not make sense in this magical reality. I returned to the city and went to the market. Once, I came here every day. Usually I would come home with full bags, having spent most of my time in the section of the market where they sold cheap, second-hand junk. At those stands I would buy clothes and rework them for myself, for the children, for him. There, among the stands, there was a shop that sold metal rings, bars, padlocks, old locks—scrap collected from the ruins of the city and the surrounding area. Among the scrap lay bunches of keys. I began to choose one, two, three, like a spell that would open Maja's steel panties.

The dealer watched me, first indifferently, then attempting to conceal his interest, and lastly with open curiosity, until finally he spoke:

"Ma'am, the key that you seek is not in my possession...but go, Ma'am, to the Jewish quarter. Right behind Cuesta del Cambrón you will find Noah's shop with the stuffed animals... Ask there."

I had been here once. In a dream, in Nora's skin. Now, I was in Narciso's skin. I was here as somebody else, so I had never been here before, although here I was.

An inflated fugu fish hung above the entrance. Behind the creaking doors, rows of animals stood, hung, or rested on shelves, reminding me of Noah's ark, if it had not landed on Ararat. Hidden behind his

---

34   The Moors appeared in Spain in the year 711.

stuffed animals, the owner himself appeared stuffed. He stared and stared, until he said:

"Master Narciso, it is an honour for me."

"How do you know my name?"

"Everybody knows you, ever since you spilled the 'light of Narciso' all over us, the sick and the crippled."

"How absurd! It is a regular light, and it was not even I who ordered the hole cut…"

"The hole in the church—this by itself is unusual! It might just be light, and it might be regular, but because of it I have lost my impotent clients, the cold and tepid, infertile, those seeking love… in a word, everybody, with the exception of amateur taxidermists… But you, Sir, look like somebody who wants to stuff something himself…"

"I am looking for a key for… a certain piece of clothing."

"How valuable this clothing must be if it is held under lock."

"It is the clothed that is valuable. She is in the garment, which is locked by key."

"Master Narciso! I thought that with your pick you could open any lock, even one that is made of ice."

"The thing is, Noah, I do not have a pick."

"And your fame? Any bank could break it for you."

"Fame does not matter when you need to unlock a chastity belt."

"But Master! You should not remove a chastity belt. If it guards, or if it imposes, without it there is only licentiousness. A man and woman can have a lot of fun, orally. Conversations, for example."

"I think that ours has reached its climax. Can you help me?"

He opened a wardrobe, which contained a collection of chastity belts, shackles, and prostheses. There were small devices, like metal sanitary pads, and large ones like armour for the abdomen. Belt-traps with hidden teeth, spikes, and blades in alluring shiny openings. Belts for women and belts for men. All closed, sometimes with elaborate locks or padlocks, and none with a key in the lock. I wondered if within each keyhole there also lurked lock-pick spikes, teeth, or blades…

From his collection, I pointed to the lock that appeared to me to be the nearest to the one on Maja's chastity belt.

"Master, do not ask me for the key, because if it is for this belt that you seek a key, I have already received payment, and how could I receive a second for the pick to its lock."

Oh, how I was stupid! How could I have expected that I would convince him to issue me a key, if there even existed a spare? I looked into his eyes, remembering everything I knew about Maja and her mistress. I thought long (my thoughts must have been painted on my face), until I arrived at "*Majaaa!!! I curse you! To the end of the world you will be young, you will want and you will be wanted, but you will never know fulfillment, you will want it forever as I want it in this moment!!!*"— and I said:

"This woman has been cursed with something more terrible than a chastity belt…"

Noah shuddered, and the astonishment on his face turned into a spasm of terror. He gathered himself and after some thought, with an uneasy smile, he whispered:

"Sir, look at the lock, see the crank and the gears in the hole. I am sure that you have seen something very similar to this mechanism?"

"Hmm… Maybe you are right. The belt I have seen has a padlock more delicate, maybe not even a padlock, but a brooch, something circular, a small head… Yes, a head with an eyelet… Like the head of a fan!"

As I ran out, Noah bowed, and then closed his shop forever.

*

"Maja?"

"I do not know you, Ma'am."

I was dressed in my old blue skirt, which I had given to Petra long ago.

"I came to help you… I will help you take off…your underwear, if you do something for me."

She nodded, and I continued:

"Do you see this medallion on 'El caballero de la mano en el pecho'? Paint my portrait on it."

"El Greco's painting?! I will not touch it!"

"How do you know that it is El Greco's? If you do not want to touch it, then wait for somebody to touch you before you rot to death in your metal panties."

She was silent. She looked at me:

"Ma'am…stand here…" Maja whispered, and then wordlessly painted my portrait on the medallion. My lost face, written on El Greco's forgotten painting. It was lifelike. Identical.

Had I forgotten that I was a woman? The time since Narciso's disappearance had taken its toll. I bent down to Maja's knees and lifted her skirt. The breeze blew the smell of her dirty groin, unwashed vagina, unwiped anus. I spread her legs and brought my face close to her crotch. Feces, urine, sweat. And into this smell, I hissed with disgust, fury, envy, hatred, pain, anger, pain, disgust, pain, pain, pain, as though I was beckoning someone, cursing someone, calling someone from beyond this world:

"Nar-Ci-Soooo…"

The belt opened like a fan and fell from Maja's crotch to the stone floor with a thud.

I wrapped it in a scarf and left without a word. Maja fled through the other doors, also without a word.

What happened to me, I will tell in a moment. What happened to Maja, she can tell by herself.[35]

---

35 The day that doña Esperanza Tomé (known then as Narciso Tomé) has described happened in the year 1732. I was sixteen years old, then. I remained in the sacristy until the year 1799. If you can count, then you know that I spent sixty-seven years there. The day I left the sacristy, I was eighty-three years old, and still I could not die.

I stopped counting years and I stopped wanting to die. Before that day came, I had suffered more than words can express. For many, my pain was no pain. It was a simple desire, lust, need, insatiability. During the days I copied paintings in the sacristy, and during the nights I bought lovers. I gave my body to young boys in the hopes that one of them might satisfy me, I sold my body to rich men, the lazy and lecherous, in order to pay for brutes, who I ordered to possess me until I felt bliss. Nobody satisfied me. Wanting and being unsatisfied, I slept with probably all the boys and men in the city and its surroundings. Finally, I started to poison myself with herbs that were supposed to soothe my senses. I stopped seeking fulfillment. I agreed to be insatiable.

I also understood that in addition to the curse of insatiability, I had received the curse of endless youth. After days filled with work and sleepless nights drowned in wine, sweat, and sex, I returned to the sacristy without a trace of my life of revelry. I continued to look young and naïve, as though I was sixteen years old. When I had my fortieth birthday, I began to colour my hair grey and paint wrinkles on my face. I was afraid that they would burn me at the stake if I did not age. From the fiftieth year of my life I began to wear a veil during the day, and to walk with a cane. The priests were not interested in my age. I made them money with my forged paintings, I guided visitors through the cathedral and sacristy, sometimes I cooked for them or allowed them to violate me from behind, hidden in the recesses of the rectory. None of them looked at my face, maybe they did not even see that I had one. I too thought that I had lost my face, painting doña Esperanza Tomé's on that portrait of El Greco.

I regained my face when Francisco José de Goya y Lucientes came to the sacristy. He painted St. George and Christ. He stared at my paintings, and one day he lifted my veil. He was deaf and did not ask anything. He was not interested in my age, and he did not inquire if loving him gave me pleasure. He was a lover full of passion, and he knew the art of love like nobody else in the city. I went with him to Madrid. I was his model. In truth, nobody knew that I painted for him, paintings on which he signed his name.

I am particularly proud of two. They were large canvasses, on which I painted life-size portraits of myself. Two self-portraits in the same, reclining pose. In one I was nude, in the other, clothed. These paintings restored my life. I began to age. In Francisco's workshop I met the Spanish prime minister, the Duke of Alcúdia, Manuel Godoy. He bought my two paintings and my body. Of course, I did not tell him that I was as old as his grandmother (Manuel was born in the year 1767). Before I met him, he had served as a bodyguard for Charles IV, before becoming the darling and then the lover of the queen. In the year 1792 he became the prime minister and was referred to by his people as "The Prince of Peace."

When he was with me he was passionate, mainly because he thought I was sixteen years old, and I satisfied his failed marriage. His wife was a cousin of Charles III, the Duchess of Chinchón, Maria Teresa de Borbón y Vallabriga, the daughter of Infanta Luisa de Borbón. She was a perpetually depressed woman who liked dogs and horseback riding, and was humiliated by her husband at every turn. Can I say anything to defend Manuel? Only that his marriage had been arranged by the Queen Maria Luisa, for the purely selfish reasons of controlling her lover. When it became known that I was sleeping with Manuel, somebody tried to kill me, but after that first failed attempt I was left alone. I was forced only to leave Madrid.

Amazingly, all this time, Goya was able to remain friends with Maria Teresa. He often painted her, her family, her uncles.

When I disappeared from Madrid, my paintings disappeared from Manuel's collection. He was thrown into prison in the year 1808. After his release, Napoleon's plots forced him to flee Spain. First he went to Paris (where I helped him to forget about prison), and then to Rome (where I was by his side when he died in the year 1851). I was 134 years old then, although I looked like a sixty-year old woman.

And Goya?

Because of my paintings, Francisco was arrested by the Inquisition in the year 1815. The prosecutors wanted to know who had requested my naked image. Francisco said nothing (how was he supposed to admit that the majority of his paintings after the year 1799 were done by me?), lost his position as court painter, and went insane. Before he died in 1828, he wrote to me that the person who posed for his "La Maja Desnuda" was María del Pilar Teresa Cayetana de Silva-Álvarez de Toledo, the Duchess of Alba. The jealous fool.

Today my self-portrait hangs in the Royal Palace, the Prado, in Madrid. Only, the Palace has been turned into a museum.

\*

I was waiting for her, disguised again as Narciso. I knew that she stood behind me.

"Do you want to know if I loved you? Go to the sacristy. You remember how you told my wife that 'El caballero de la mano en el pecho' looks like me? It's my portrait. The woman I love has been painted on his medallion…"

To this day, I do not know if I really heard her light steps in the direction of the sacristy, if there really came a cry of fury, if I really heard a scuffle and a smack like a slapping. I do not know if somebody ran out from the sacristy and towards the offices of the Inquisition. I know only that I was suddenly seized with terror, that my life was ending, that the ex-mistress of my ex-husband was about to report me and completely destroy my family.

Instead of racing away, packing what I could, taking the children and fleeing, I went to the sacristy. Maja stood beside the easel. One hand smoothed her skirt, and the other held her red cheek:

"Look, Sir, what that hag did…"

Under El Greco's painting lay Maja's brush. My portrait had disappeared under the gentleman's coat. Almost entirely painted over…

I ran home.

Petra was agitated. Apparently, the prosecutor's wife—Nora—had come banging on the doors. Petra had not let her in. Nora had taken away all the letters that had come for us that day and run towards the market.

There are these moments in life in which, not knowing what do to, we commit the greatest mistake:

"Petra, this woman will destroy us all! Oh, if I could I would kill her!"

"I will kill her for you, Ma'am."

I knew that Petra was willing to do this. I held her, or maybe I held myself against her, seeking a moment of calm, serenity, suddenly terrified of the possibility. Terrified by what might happen to Petra. Torn by pain, gratitude, and hatred, I pulled the chastity belt from my scarf.

"Ma'am! Why? I will never betray you. Never! With no man or… anybody else. You know that."

"This is not for you, but her. So that she cannot seduce anybody else! May her snake thighs ensnare no longer! So that until the end of her life, she will never again have what she has taken from others."

No sooner had she gone that I began to regret it. Instead of packing and fleeing, I sat stunned. I was afraid that I had sent her to her death.

Meanwhile, Petra followed the trail of our abandoned letters, scolding letters from the bank, loan offers, the useless pamphlets we threw away each day, which now Nora threw away behind her. She ran through several streets, and on the Calle del Ángel she saw that a house in the Jewish Quarter was in flames. As she pushed through the crowd of onlookers and those who were trying to quench the blaze, a puffy and stuffed fish exploded out of the heat and flames. Apparently, the owner had burned inside.

Nora was in the crowd. She lost consciousness on her way home. Somebody had hit her in the back of the head. When she regained consciousness, she realized that her abdomen was shackled with the same chastity belt that she had given Maja, only the lock had been destroyed. The letter she had stolen from Narciso Tomé's home was still hidden in her bra.

# ENCHANTMENT

*(In which we travel with Narciso, not knowing where, or why.
Once again, we avoid still more deathly dangers, until finally...)*

||||||||||||||||||||||||||||||||||||||||||||||||||||||||||||||||||||||||||||||||||||||||||||||||||||||||||||||||||||||||||||||||||||||||||||||||||||||

WE WERE RIDING NORTH. FIRST BY A THIN PATH CUT THROUGH BY
deep ravines, then by a sandy scree, until we arrived at milder, almost
shady slopes. All the rivers, and there were not many, flowed south. I
realized that we were in the Sierra Madre, on land that had been abandoned by everybody except the most fearless robbers. It was foolish
to venture into these parts, and few dared to. Only in exceptional cir-
cumstances did travellers risk crossing these mountains. So on what
did these legendary robbers live?

Strapped like a bag to Uhuru's saddle, I hung from both sides of
her horse, lying on my stomach with my hands tied behind my back.
I had no idea why she took me with her. She could have killed me like
the rest of the shepherds. Was it the fact that I was not one of them
that saved me? And if that had saved me, then for what?

Whenever we stopped she threw me to the ground and surveyed
my naked body. She looked at me, but not the way I once looked at
her. She looked with contempt. She was returning my gaze. When
I tried to look into her eyes, she would always whip me in the face.
Humbly, I averted my eyes and stared into the ground. I think I was

sick, because every time she stared at me my head began to hurt, I felt weak, I fell asleep. I preferred to look at the ground.

I looked at the ground from the horse as well, while we rode. The ground in the Sierra Madre was different than anywhere else. Its surface seemed to be preparing itself for the future, as if sensing that it would be the scene of bloody battles for many years after our passing through. Porous as leather, it sucked down everything on it. When I lay on the ground during stops and rests, it seemed to me that my body was also being sucked into the depths, piece by piece. When my ear pressed to the earth, I heard the soft hiss of air coming from somewhere deep below. What was under the surface, I did not know. I did not care.

From the position of one being viewed, I began to learn about the group, bandit by bandit, their tendencies and their hierarchy. I had no idea how they could accept Uhuru disguised as a man, and why they did not question her position. I did not understand how this entire group could be obedient to one woman. Not only obedient, but committed, efficiently performing every command. Bah, sometimes it seemed that Uhuru did not even need to issue orders. The bandits understood her intentions. As though they were being directed by her thoughts. It was difficult for me to understand how this was possible.

Often we would be riding in single-file, when suddenly, without warning, Uhuru would tie my legs, cut me loose from her saddle, and throw me to the ground, and usually at the same time from behind the mountains, or behind a turn in the road, or through an opening in the rocks, a coach or carriage would appear, or a wagon, or a group of riders. Before I sank to the ground, the bandits, spread out along both sides of the path, would throw themselves on the passersby and kill them or throw them at Uhuru's feet. She would stare at them until (and usually they did not last long) each of them slumped on the ground, or she would rape them with the same instrument that she had once shoved into my mouth. Then the bodies would be buried, we would eat the travellers' food and drink their wine, share the spoils, and I would have to, once again, climb onto Uhuru's horse and we would ride on. At night, I would pitch the tent for her. I usually slept outside, a rope tied around my feet.

One day, I noticed on one of the bandits an earring that resembled a pendant I had seen on the breast of one of the men to whom I had given my letter to Esperanza, long ago, in the valley of the bulls. I felt uneasy. If Uhuru controlled the Sierra Madre, she might have killed the stately looking gentlemen whom I had entertained with my bull-fighting. I wanted to ask Uhuru about the fate of these gentlemen, but anytime I tried to speak I was hit in the face before I could finish my question. It was only when I stopped trying, when I was exhausted and weeping, lamenting my soul and myself, that she told me:

"One of them made it to Toledo."

How did she know what I wanted to ask her about?

Apart from Uhuru, nobody from the group approached me. Sometimes only the cook, who, with great skill, prepared the animals they killed, portioned them, fried them or cured them and fed the entire group. Only he would give me something to eat, and -only when Uhuru was not looking at me. The cook was silent and always absent-minded. He would usually throw me some scraps, which I would have to eat off the ground. It was he who taught me not to piss or shit where I lay. At first he would throw the food onto my excrement and wait until the hunger overcame my own disgust. When I learned not to wait for food in dirty, sandy, overgrown or infested places, then he started to feed me himself, letting me eat from his hand. My arms were tied behind my back.

The cook carried the mark of death. I do not know what it was, but in his movements, his face, in the way he worked with his hands, there was something cold, a cadaverous cold. Can evil be a part of a man? And if so, how can evil be measured? I had seen, after all, how these bandits slit throats efficiently, crushed their opponents' skulls, how they shortened the suffering of those broken. I never felt the evil in them that carried on the cook. Maybe it was because the bandits did their work skillfully, with no emotion. The cook prepared the animals with a strange delight. Soon I would realize why this person made me afraid and anxious.

The route of the group's march was a typical nomadic trail. It was not ordered, it seemed littered with obstacles for no apparent reason, fickle, arranged only around the direction that Uhuru sought. The rest followed her, tied by invisible bonds as strong as mine. Sometimes we cut across trails, paths, rivers and streams, sometimes we moved along them, breaking off suddenly sideways without any sense or logic. After some time, I began to understand the sense in this erratic movement, because often other wanderers, travellers, and their groups would fall across our path, and everything would begin anew, starting with Uhuru throwing me from the horse. Plunder, murder, burial, the erasure of our tracks, feast and drunkenness, and then back on the road. Once or twice among the travellers there were women. Nobody raped them or slit their throats. They were sent back from where they came. The only person who had the privilege of "raping" the captives was Uhuru, but she did not murder anyone, did not spill any blood. Until that night came that brought with it a series of unexplainable events.

It was raining. In the Sierra Madre, it rains very rarely. But when it rains, it seems that the entire water supply of the sky must be poured onto the earth as quickly as possible. The water was falling unevenly, like walls, whipping the ground, which after the first few moments was sated and could not continue to absorb the rain into itself. Rushing streams formed on the surface and ran in unpredictable directions, like steel snakes, winding together and apart. Somewhere below our hiding place under a hanging rock the water thundered, water that a moment earlier had not been there. Beside our mountain flowed dried bushes, rocks, until finally a waterfall sealed our hiding spot. Time stopped. The steady hum lulled everybody to sleep, including the horses.

Shhhhh…

I awoke and before I could even understand what was happening, I felt terror and fear. Something had happened, something terrible and irreversible. Catastrophe.

Before I could open my eyes and see anything, I became aware that the rain had turned into a gallop. The rain had stopped, and in its place was the pounding of nearing hooves. At the same time, in my sleepy field of vision, through the smell of the rain and the dark of the night, in a single flash of lightning I saw the body of Uhuru, tense as a spear, flying towards the first galloping horse. The bolt lit the blade in her hand, which slid under the left shoulder of the horse galloping a step away from me. Uhuru fell under the hooves of the horse running just behind this first one, rolled through the forest of horse hocks, hooves, and horseshoes, and fell flattened and motionless on the other side of their path.

The first horse, as if unaware it was dead, kept running for a few strides, and then lost feeling in its front legs, and as if the ground beneath him had collapsed, he fell to the earth, slamming his straightened neck and breaking his back. The rider flew from the saddle and fell like a stone some yards away.

With the fall of the first rider, Uhuru rose from the earth. Slowly she pulled herself to the rider, covered him with her body, and slumped still. Meanwhile, the cavalcade behind the first horses tried to slow or stop themselves, assuming that some wild animal had thrown itself on their leader. Horses at the forefront of the group tripped on the body of the first, and the others reared, bumping into each other in the dark. Neighing and tumult.

I do not know if I awoke at the same time as the rest of the bandits, but after the first lightning bolt, another flashed and thundered. This time, it was a salvo from the bandits' side.

Cries of pain and shouted orders were added to the neighing and tumult.

With the third bolt of lightning, I saw that half of the horses and their riders were writhing on the ground in convulsions, and the other half was firing in our direction. How could they have missed me? I do not know. Above the lament of the horses and the dying, a fierce roar of hatred and fury rang out, after which I heard the surviving bandits clash with the surviving horsemen.

Flash after flash of lightning revealed men locked in mortal struggle, as Laocoön. The flashes made clear that the horsemen were better armed, and also that they were perversely cruel in their murders by dark. I heard one of them running in my direction. When another bolt of lightning flashed, I saw the approaching rider lunging at me with a rapier.

Darkness!

My breath stopped, and my heart beat too quickly, bursting my chest. I knew that the rapier would rip the air from my lungs as it tore me apart. When another bolt flashed, my potential murderer was dead. He lay beneath the smiling cook, who had plunged a kitchen knife into his eye. I fainted.

When I regained consciousness, Uhuru was sitting on a makeshift chair, her head bandaged and her arm in a sling. The remnants of the group were burying the corpses of the riders and bandits. The one remaining rider was the one Uhuru had thrown from his saddle, killing his horse. The man was richly dressed, and it took me a long time before I saw him as the innkeeper, the owner of the tavern in which Uhuru had danced many years ago in Toledo.

After burying the dead, Uhuru ordered the cook and I to tend to the survivor. We tore his clothes from him, all of which the cook took. We washed him in the dying stream, shaved all his hair and, naked, tied him by his hands to a cord, which we hung from the rock overhang. The cord was long enough that he could reach the ground if he stood on his toes. We tied two boulders to his ankles, which stretched the innkeeper like a string. The entire time, he did not defend himself, he did not try to fight with us, he gave himself up to his fate. With contempt, he looked at the faces of the survivors, who Uhuru had ordered to sit in a circle around him. I sat with them, trying not to stare at his impressive genitalia, which looked monstrous after the shave.

The hanging innkeeper whispered prayers while the cook sharpened his knife. When he was finished, he brought a canteen filled with some concoction he forced the innkeeper to drink. Uhuru said to the prisoner:

"You forced us to sell our bodies, to expose them to everybody, although they never saw deeper than our skin. What is it about skin that you never had enough of it?! You won't speak? You'll be able to stare at your own skin all you want! We will give it to you as a gift…"

Without a word, the cook cut him from his Adam's apple to his penis. The innkeeper screamed terribly, but he did not lose consciousness. Slowly and precisely, the cook skinned the man's chest, separating the thin sheet of the epidermis from his muscles. From under the white skin, dotted with age-spots, bloody muscle fibres emerged, blue and red veins, white sinews, yellow deposits of fatty tissue. The blood flowed in narrow rivulets down his legs and soaked into the earth, mixing with his excrement, which he could not stop. The concoction he had drunk must have blocked some of his suffering, because although he screamed in pain, and his face remained frozen in an expression of supreme astonishment, he retained his consciousness. He began to lose it only when his entire front, like a coat, hung from both sides of his body, and the cook began to remove patches from his arms. Each time the innkeeper's head fell forward the cook would pause his work and revive the flayed man. He brought everybody's attention to the precision with which he had been able to keep the nipples intact so that they remained, undamaged, on the removed skin. When a mountain of skin hung from the innkeeper's hips like a shirt, the cook poured the remainder of the concoction down the man's throat and hastened the skinning. The cries of the innkeeper became inhuman gibberish and wheezing.

Nobody was allowed to leave, and a few of the less resistant robbers began to vomit. The sun was high in the sky, and the stench grew unbearable. Only the cook was unaffected, and continued to skin as if in a trance, pour water, revive the man and tear away his skin.

The innkeeper's final agony began when the cook showed him the skin he had removed from his torso, shoulders, and arms. The innkeeper noted the skin with his eyes and hung, without feeling. Above his head, tied by the cord, his white hands, still covered with skin like gloves, raised themselves to the sky in a gesture begging for the mercy of death. When he returned to life, his hoarse cry forced a few of the bandits to plug their ears. Uhuru, from her seat, whipped those who turned away from the spectacle or plugged their ears, until the innkeeper became silent, which was when the cook castrated him and gagged him with his removed scrotum. The blood that flowed from his crotch ended his life. He hung in silence for the last time, and only the slick sounds of the skinning knife mixed with the buzz of the flies drawn to the dead.

I had never seen a human body beneath the skin. Apparently, when the Lord created the angels, they did not have skin or genitals. Maybe they looked like the innkeeper. His face, however, his skinless face, frozen in a grimace of ecstasy and disbelief, looked nothing like what we call an angel's face. Isn't it the angel Gabriel who tells the Blessed Virgin, "Do not be afraid"? You could die from fear looking at such a body, let alone such a face.

The cook showed everybody that the skin he had torn from the innkeeper remained in one piece. The continuous fold of material from the ankles to the crown of the head did not resemble anything like what it was this morning. In the morning, as it covered his bloody and knotted body, it had given him expression, protection, a way to touch the world, which it protected him from. Now it hung from the hands of the cook like Michelangelo's self-portrait in the Sistine Chapel.

"You are free," Uhuru told the bandits: "My destiny is fulfilled. I will return to Toledo. You may go where you please. Each of you will receive your share. You"—here she turned to the cook and pointed to me: "You can take him for yourself. He's yours."

The cook was a strong man. He was panting still, after his most recent murder, when he tied my hands and dragged me to a pool that remained from last night's storm. He threw me into the water, which had a salty taste. He washed me thoroughly, scrubbing my feet and hands with soapstone, which also had a salty taste. He ripped the dirt of many weeks from me, the smell of bull dung, the dust of the roads of the Sierra Madre. I did not defend myself. It gave me pleasure.

"Why are you doing this, my good man?" I asked him, touched by his concern for me.

"What do you mean, why? I want you to be clean."

"Clean, for what?"

"I like clean skin."

"Wait, wait. What do you have in mind? What do you plan to do to me?!"

"Skin you. The same as the other one."

"What?!" I tore myself from his hands and ran downhill, but he caught me, knocked me down and overpowered me. He tied my hands and feet behind my back with the same rope and carried me back to the water. He pulled a razor from his sack and began to shave me.

I shouted, I cried, I argued, and I begged:

"But you cannot skin me! It's murder!"

"Murder? Now it is murder, but before you looked at his body and you did not stop me? You helped me tie him, wash him. You participated in that murder, right? In your case, this will not be any murder, just…a skinning." He laughed deeply, excited for this impending pleasure.

"Why me?!"

"I received you as property, right? I could use you as a servant, but I do not need a servant. I want your skin more than you. I will take only the skin, I will leave the rest to you."

"You cannot kill me! I…I have a family and kids."

"You're lying. You were shit, a piece of garbage. You were lucky that we did not kill you immediately, like the rest of the shepherds. Except they were normal people. You were already a piece of scum."

"No, that's not true! You do not know anything about me!"

"Shut your mouth, because I want to shave you, and I do not like cuts on the skin. Shut up, I say!"

I thought of dozens of impossible escape plans to get free from the grasp of the worst of the bandits, who had decided to shave me before he would skin me. After weeks in the valley with the bulls, my hair had grown long and covered my face. As the cook slowly shaved my face, a look of disbelief grew on his. As he was trimming my beard and moustache, he stopped. He was sitting astride me, and he turned my face first to the right, then to the left:

"Unbelievable," he muttered, and returned to work.

Suddenly he paused and said:

"You look just like master Narciso."

"I am master Narciso."

"You are master of shit. He was my last client in Toledo." I understood that he, too, had met somebody who had disguised himself as me in Toledo, and who was building my altar, as the shepherds had said.

"Ask me anything you want, and I will prove to you that I am Narciso Tomé."

"Yeah? Tell me, what did you come to purchase at my shop?"

It was over. I felt his knife on my skin even now, as he shaved my moustache and beard...

"Listen, everybody in Toledo knows you and everybody comes for the same thing. Ask me about myself, about me, about my altar..." I bluffed, but I saw that he was considering it.

"Why am I doing this, "master"? Can you describe "your" altar, you shithead? Do you remember the two bronze plates? What is on them?"

"On the left, a priest gives David his sword, and on the right Abigail gives tribute to David."

"A fluke. You went on a pilgrimage to Toledo… as you can see, the light did not help you. Since you want so badly to get out of your skin, I'll skin you."

"What else is there to tell you?!" I began to scream: "You are blinded by your need to murder, your need to spill blood and you will not even consider the thought that you are going to slaughter Narciso, in front of whom, not that long ago, you bent to the floor in your shop, you merchant! It was enough to smell human blood and already you cannot see with your own eyes? Come to your senses! Help me get out of here, and you will not regret it!" I was lying, of course I was lying that I could pay him for the favour, but I wanted to live. I escaped the sword of Miguel, the knife of the Inquisition, the horns of the bulls and the flails of the shepherds, I avoided the knives of the bandits and the rapiers of the riders just last night, and now I was supposed to die skinned by this madman?

"Anyway, if you cannot recognize me, you fool, at least sharpen your knife well." I had given up, I had lost my strength, when I understood that, in reality, I had not avoided anything, that something had watched over me. I myself had done nothing…

He sat and sharpened his knife. He picked at his fingernails and continued to sharpen. Nothing was happening. The group did not pay us any attention. Uhuru as well.

"If you do not believe me, ask her."

"That day, when you came to my shop… When I left Toledo, I fled… I fled by the Sierra to Andalusia. Nobody caught me or passed me. I joined this group, and a day later we found you. Even if you had left Toledo with me, you could not have passed me, become a shit-shoveler… The road takes time."

"Unless you fly. I flew in a machine built by Bartolomeu Lourenço de Gusmão."

His face changed.

"But he has been dead for ten years."

"Eight. He died in 1724."

"How did you have his machine?"

"I kept it."

"Where is it now?"

"Broken, in the same chasm as the bulls."

"Bartolomeu... He could talk all day about flying machines, about his flights. He explained the mechanism, he left drawings. He always needed money. He never had any. He tried to persuade me too, to finance his machines. I remember, just before his death, he received a sum and ordered an immense amount of skins from me... No, not human. I did not believe that something heavier than air could fly... But I built this machine for him... He never paid me for it. And you flew, in my machine, all the way here? Well, brother, you're lucky..."

Then he looked me in the eyes and said:

"Master Narciso, I am sorry for my eagerness to skin you. Nobody knows what hides inside a man. Sometimes, this something comes to the surface in a haze, without will, without morality, when the possibility of uncontrolled use emerges. I had skinned thousands of animals, birds, and reptiles, but man—that was the first time. You are right, I killed him. Not anybody else, just me. It is not right, I know. I have no right to kill, not even a crook, and not you. I return you your freedom, Sir. I never had a right to control it. I lost myself. I was afraid of that woman... No, not this one here, but that one in Toledo. The prosecutor's wife. I was afraid of this one too. Tell me, were you able, at least, to open the chastity belt?"

The person disguised as me in Toledo now also tries to open chastity belts. As a precaution, I said:

"Oh, yes, Sir. Thanks to your help, of course."

"And what am I supposed to do now? I cannot return to Toledo, you neither. We are both fleeing from the same woman."

"Go to France. The French are more open towards innovation and...they do not have the Inquisition. Build another machine like the one you built for Bartolomeu."

"Sir, my grandparents were named Goldberg. They had to change their names to Monteoro. I am Noah Monteoro. But this cannot be my name in France."

"Change it again. Change it to Mont-gold. Montgolfier sounds even more French! Start a family, maybe your wife will give birth to a few sons. Name them Joseph and Jack and let them fly along with you."[36]

---

36 Noah Goldberg, known in Toledo under the name Noah Monteoro, after the events transcribed above, did, in fact, settle in France, in a small town named Annonay, south of Lyon. He never returned to the profession of skinning animals. He opened a small paper mill, married, and his wife bore him two sons, who, as Narciso suggested, he named Joseph-Michel (1740-1810) and Jacques-Étienne (1745-1799). History, and especially French history, attributes them the idea of filling a balloon with hot air in order to overcome gravity. But that's not all! This same history says that the two brothers were the first people who succeeded in overcoming gravity. But You, Dear Reader, and I know, that it went differently.

On May 5, in the year 1783, the citizens of the city of Annonay were able to admire the "first" balloon flight by both brothers. A balloon with a diameter of eleven metres made from paper, silk, and taffeta, filled with the hot smoke of burning straw and wool.

On September 19 of that same year, in the presence of the King Louis XVI and his court, the two brothers released their balloon in Versailles. This time, in the balloon's basket, there was a duck, a sheep, and a rooster. The balloon rose to almost 480 metres before it fell into the forest at Vaucresson, some 1700 metres from where it had started. The only fatality of this flight was the rooster. The sheep and duck survived until dinner.

On August 26 in the year 1785, another of the Montgolfier brothers' balloons was ready for flight. This balloon had a diameter of sixteen metres and was twenty-five metres tall. In the basket stood Jean-François Pilâtre de Rozier, a professor of physics and chemistry at Reims, as well as François Laurent, the Marquis d'Arlandes (1742-1809). The balloon rose from the gardens of the Château de la Muette in Bois de Boulogne. The flight to a height of 960 metres

"And you, Sir?"

"I do not know yet. All my life I have fled, I have disguised myself as somebody else, I wanted everything that I did not have. I lived strangers' lives... Out of fear of my own. One day, I have to come face to face with my own life."

\*

The Sierra Madre had ended long ago. We were moving in the direction of Toledo, mostly by night and by empty trails. Our horses had their hooves wrapped in rags and bags over their snouts to muffle their neighs. By day, we hid in forests, caves, and pits. We stole food from the rare villages and taverns. The bandits, although they had regained their freedom, preferred to follow Uhuru. She did not care whether she rode by herself or with others. She suffered. Her arms, legs, and head were wrapped with bandages, sashes and slings covered her body, which nodded in the saddle at the front of the cavalcade. Cavalcade? We were only a few survivors in rags. We were like a pilgrimage of the sick, crippled, tattered.

It was dawn when we arrived at the Sulphurous Swamp by the old crossing of the Tagus. The crossing was gone. Nobody carries travellers across this river anymore, because nobody ventures out in this direction. Many years ago, when the swamp was adjacent to a clear, fast-flowing, and wide river, it became active. The sulphurous gasses began to poison the forests on this side of the Tagus and transformed the region into a nightmarish setting. A forest of stumps, black trunks and boughs stood ankle-deep in the blood-red gore. During the day, gasses animated the surface, so that it appeared like boiling blood,

---

lasted approximately twenty-five minutes and ended safely in Butte-aux-Cailles, about eight and a half kilometres away.

Soon, on September 26, 1785, Jean-Pierre Blanchard crossed above the English Channel, from Dover to Calais. From this time, balloons filled with hot air have been called "Montgolfier."

or a sheepskin hidden beneath a crimson mist. By night, here and there fires lit up, and flames flew through the empty and dead forest, hissing, gurgling, howling. Still, a road wound this way, an old forgotten trail along the Tagus, which had been closed because of fear and superstition.

We were riding along a sandy gully between the water and the marsh, and we were about to turn onto the trail when before us, a carriage approached. A black car, black horses, and black wagon. They would not have noticed us, were it not for the bandits' instincts, which moved them to attack and kill whatever came along. Somebody spurred their horse, somebody jumped on the driver's seat and stopped the carriage. Already the driver was falling with his throat slit, already the coachman was bleeding into the sand, the horses cut from the wagon, the trunks broken open, and the passenger pulled from the carriage and thrown to the ground.

The passenger was a woman in a blue dress and black veil, from under which shone a bright neckline. Before Uhuru could yell "Stop," two bandits tore her dress over her head, and through her starched petticoats they plunged their hungry desire into the passenger's abdomen, one from the front, the second from behind.

Never before, while travelling through the Sierra Madre, had I seen a bandit commit a single rape. The only person who "raped" was Uhuru. Nobody else. Now, when the group was no longer a group, just a collection of independent robbers, nobody respected Uhuru's orders. Before the rape began, already another was lowering his pants as though waiting his turn, or abandoning the coachman to reach for his fly, or forgetting about the horses, the trunk, the carriage. A rape is not a trophy, and before it began, it shook me in a way I had not expected. I cried "No!" and I was ready to stand against the bandits, against inevitable death, standing in the way of their desires, standing to defend this unknown woman.

Was I really standing to defend her?

My conscience, which I do not remember from my times in Toledo, objected to this act. I could not stand any more violence, the domination of one person over another—I could not.

I spurred my horse and threw myself towards them, when a cry, a terrible cry of pain and suffering caused my horse to rear and throw me to the ground. The cry was coming simultaneously from the throats of both bandit rapists and flew around us as quickly as the blood from beneath the petticoats of the victim, until it suddenly turned into hiccups, which threw both bandits into fatal convulsions, spasms, and finally hysterical howls. They were gone before they came.

A pool of blood, in which three bodies lay, marked the centre of the group. Nobody moved. The hands that had lowered pants and opened flies froze. It was deathly silent. Only the gurgling of the sulphur, only the wheezing terror in the horses' nostrils, and then a fearful flamenco's rhythm tapped out by the fleeing hooves. In the silence that followed, from within the dress thrown over her head, a hand reached out; a hand gripping a copper fan. The fan opened fully and sliced the quivering bodies of the two bandits. It cut off the penises, which had been plunged into the victim. The front and the back. And then the women lifted herself from the sand and blood, brushed off her dress and stumbled toward the swamp. We stood as though paralyzed, staring at the two mutilated bodies lying in the blood, like parentheses, from which all meaning slipped away. Only Uhuru had not lost her cool. With an outstretched hand, she raised her pistol, hesitated a moment, trying to overcome her weakness, and then came the shot.

Maybe it was her wounds, exhaustion, or whatever else, but Uhuru missed. Only the marsh behind the back of the traveller exploded in blisters of fog. Uhuru lowered the pistol to her belt and pulled out a second. The woman began to run further into the marsh, fleeing from the coming bullet.

The next shot ripped a red wound into the tree right beside the woman's veil, and the second smoking pistol fell to the earth. Uhuru pulled her third, her last, and without aiming, fired. The traveller was already on the edge of the water and tearing through the thick, black, and dried bushes. There was the sound of a bell, like a strike on metal, and then the splash of a body falling into the water.

I realized that this was not a woman, but one of those mechanical figures, machines that moved like humans, made entirely of metal. Everything was made from metal. Even the fan. The two bandits must have plunged into the gears…

I was shocked. I lay stunned, as though I was a pillar of salt, as though I had stared at the thing forbidden, at some old memory, which had returned me to events I had never admitted, and I realized that this could not be a machine, but a person. I knew the woman from the carriage. I knew those movements, that dress, that person, but I could not remember from where. I reached farther and farther into my memories and there was nothing there. As though I had no memory, or I had lost it after the woman had been shot. Or it was different still, as though the memory of the valley and the bulls, the journey to this place, had taken the place of a different memory from a different life. I understood that if I did not accept both my memories, I would cease to be. Or I would be partial, remember selectively. I remember, therefore I am?

And then I realized that I was alone. I rose from the earth in a bloody mist. My head rang after my fall. The smell of blood and fog mixed in my nostrils. On the trail there lay four bodies, the trunk and the carriage, but there was no sign of the horses, which had fled after the first cry. There was no sign, either, of the bandits, if you do not count the marks on the sand. Uhuru had vanished.

Now I tore through the dried bushes, the blackened rushes, and the dead sedge where I had seen her last. I tried to remember everything, recall everything. And then the memory of the journey in the carriage "returned" to me, the carriage we had ambushed. Was it I inside it? Was I with the woman who had been shot by the other woman who was disguised as a man?

When I reached the edge of the dead but bubbling water, I almost thought I had been the woman in the carriage. So, am I a woman?

My head hurt, but it seemed to me that my thinking was logical and I did not feel confused by the fog, which thickened around me. Beneath it, beneath the fog, the dark water covered the marsh. I did not see anybody, did not hear anybody. Only the steady splash of the water on the shore, below the place where I stood, only the irregular sound of bubbling. Like a whisper, a call, a summoning to the centre of the marsh. There, below, some shape came to life, moved in the surge of water. Tatters, inanimate matter, not belonging to nature. Or to a completely poisoned nature. I knelt down and reached. I pulled from the water something like a blue sack, out of which fell a copper pot, grinning at me with sharp teeth on its front and back. I dropped the sack in the water and it stuck in the mud. The pot looked like metal panties, with holes for the legs and torso. Predatory panties, with hungry, toothed openings underneath. The front had a small lock, made from the same metal, as elaborate as the head of the fan. From this opening, a black leech crawled then fled, writhing, into the dark depths. From there, from the depths (if a marsh has depths), something floated to the surface like a giant lizard, or maybe it was only the deep that opened her eyes and called me more clearly than before. She called me by my name.

I heard her splash:

"Nar-ci-so… nhaaa… ciii… sss…"

*

I do not know what happened. I felt free. I put the wet dress over my weeks-long nakedness, looked at myself in the pond and saw an old woman's face, which someone had shaved for me. I did not want to give myself to the whispering darkness, did not look in its direction, did not wonder whether I was in the pool, whether I was a woman.

A letter was tucked into the folds of the wet dress. I opened it and saw before my eyes a blue map painted of spilled ink. Seas and lakes flooded singular white islands with words, which had lost their meaning in the sick water of the marsh. I read the beginning:

> ...
>
> ...*address You in this way? I know, I...have that right, because... life...I cannot...hide it, erase it, or cover it up.*
>
> *And...I know...always, always...I have loved, even when I was...*
>
> *I know that...I lived beyond...boundaries, lived in...reality, where...I was...And so on, and so on.*

And then there were only spots, muddled sentences, diluted words, a blurred meaning until the end, where the last few lines survived the flood:

> *I lived...life, I was living...life, not living.*
>
> *I am somewhere else and I am someone else...If there is no longer a return...Your love...give...my existence meaning and purpose...The nights with You, full of love...leave this world...the memory of tenderness and joy...light and happiness.*
>
> *...the ground is dry and thirsty for blood. And although this is...the Sierra Nevada...I impart...my fall and...humility, from the depths of which I want...Your love.*
>
> *Humbly—*
>
> ...

All this surviving gibberish was written in my hand. Uncertainty returned again. Was it I, disguised as a woman, who was carrying this letter to myself? And now I stood above the marsh. The marsh—and its nature—reduced the mechanical toy to its mechanical abdomen, which stuck in the mud and—if I am not mistaken—lies there to this day.

The dress, blue as the sky through the cracks of the red mist above, dried on me, and drying, fit tightly, as though it had been tailored for me, holding me, possessing me, constricting me, taking away my will like a straitjacket for a madman, like soft shackles, like a wedding dress, demanding from me the word "Yes."

Crying "No," I ran through the wicker brush on the banks:

"I am not what is human in you, what has survived your fading in the swamp. The machine and the lizard. No, no, I am not a lizard. I am myself. I am myself. I am myself."

A fear gripped me, a fear whose great eyes would not close to the branches beating my face. I fled from the fear that the humanity of the figure and the machine hidden in the swamp fled with me, like a dybbuk, a ghost, a demon, a leech, a tick that had already crawled under my skin and was writhing, crawling to my skull, to devour my brain. Before it reached my head, I ripped it from my body and crushed it with my bare heel.

Whatever had been human, had been reptilian or machine, remained behind me, it was only the memory of it that I could not refuse.

I returned to the trail and without searching for any traces of the robbery, I went north, in the direction of Toledo. Did I go to recover myself? Rather, to recover something in myself. When I met the first pilgrims hurrying to the city for mass, when they greeted me, and I returned their greeting to them, I felt that I was alive. This was my life. I went with them.

# DEATH

*(Tomé Sr. explains the plot and, for the last time, attempts
to claim authorship over the entire story.)*

||||||||||||||||||||||||||||||||||||||||||||||||||||||||||||||||||||||||||||||||||||||||||||||||||||||||||||||||||||||||||||||||||||||||||

"GET OUT, ALL OF YOU GET OUT AND LEAVE US ALONE. LEAVE THE
window open. This noise does not bother me. On the contrary, I like
to imagine how it is made. I was listening to the tools and imagining
the whittling of jar after jar, like spools of the holy book—because
wisdom will remain, golden curls—because our children and grandchildren will also remain, angelic feathers… But what am I talking
about! No, that is not what I wanted… How does it look?"

"Almost finished…"

"What do you mean finished, what is finished?"

"The altar, Antonio."

"I am not asking about the altar—how does it look?"

"The coffin? Beautiful, modest and bright, well-built, strong. It
basks in the sun, so that its warmth…"

"It basks? Ha, ha, ha! You, too, speak funny. Let's drink some wine,
shall we? Nothing can hurt me anymore, right, Narciso?"

Without a word, the person named Narciso slowly filled two cups.
He gave one to Tomé Sr. and sat with the other at the head of the table.
They drank in small sips, holding the wine in their mouths instead

of words. They did not have to hurry— at least one of them had all of eternity before them. From the yard came the sound of hammers pounding the casket. Clouds of poplar fluff, like condensed heat or barely discernible angels, floated on the air, warmed by the coming of spring.

"I wanted to apologize. It was I who prepared this fate for you. Everything is my fault."

"Now? Give it a rest..."

"No, no! I really need to tell you something. I do not intend to pound my chest or say goodbye to you in some special way, since I have already said goodbye to everyone. I want to tell you why I destroyed your life..."

"You, Antonio?"

"Listen, this was very long ago... Some two hundred years. May, in the year 1484. One of our ancestors was neither an architect, like you, nor a sculptor, like me, nor a stonemason, like my father, nor... He was a ferryman on the Tagus. He had a barge in a place that was called the Forgotten Ford. Maybe once it was a ford, but in his times the Tagus was too deep, and to cross it you needed a barge. Now this place is called the Sulphurous Swamp. It took only one night for the river to become a swamp, and it happened precisely in May of that year...

"Those were probably the darkest years for Spain. King Ferdinand, hungry for money and land, and his dog Torquemada, murdered and confiscated the property of the murdered. Most of the robbed had allegedly converted, had been baptized, and did not admit to their old faith, or only admitted to it under the influence of torture. The machinations of the Inquisition were so disgusting and so efficient that Pope Sixtus IV issued a bull, wanting to prevent a massacre. Ferdinand wrote a letter to the pope, accusing him of protecting the Jews, and the pope withdrew. He hung the bull. This allowed Ferdinand to appoint Torquemada to the position of General Inquisitor of Aragon, Valencia, and Catalonia, all simultaneously, uniting the Spanish Inquisition under the rule of one man. In addition, Aragon combined with Castile through the union of their rulers, and so the Inquisition there also fell under the control of the general. Torquemada… He will always be remembered as a bloodthirsty executioner and a monster. And yet, he did not kill that many people with his own hands. The General Inquisitor created figureheads in each region of Spain. The machine, oiled by blood, worked more efficiently, because each small Torquemada wanted to be a greater Torquemada than the original. From Córdoba to Barcelona, the Inquisition's 'Philosopher's Stone,' which was of course a tombstone, turned the bodies on the stakes into gold in the royal coffers.

"Did everybody drop their hands and passively watch the destruction of their neighbours? You see, now our family is very neutral, uninvolved, meek and quiet. Once, it was not like this. This ancestor had passion in his blood and he suffered from a sense of justice.

"And so he joined a secret group conspiring against the Inquisition, which amounted to automatic excommunication. Because it seemed to them that they were fighting with the devil's machine, they began to dabble in magic. Maybe it was 'white,' not black magic, but I do not think they understood what they had unleashed. Alas, just as violence begets violence, madness only incites madness."

Tomé Sr. began coughing and covered his lips with a handkerchief, on which red spots, like wine, appeared. When he came to himself, he added:

"We are doomed. We, the whole family. As long as we do not wash the disgrace from our name… Perhaps, we have already rehabilitated ourselves."

He was lying on the pillows, parchment, transparent. He looked out the window and closed the sky under his eyelids. And then again he opened his eyes wide, trying to convince himself that he was alive and that he saw before him the image from beneath his lids. He was lying and listening, as if the rhythm of the hammers and the planers guaranteed the beating of his heart. He took the warm air in through his nose, carefully, not too deep, so as not to undermine anything in his disintegrating body. His big hands, which once shaped boulders, now sought rest on the bed sheet that covered his body.

"...he called his assistants. The first two he sent to Aragon. One was named Pedro Arbués de Épila, and the second—allegedly Gaspar Juglar. This second stood in the way of our ancestor, who was to remove him. Drown him, when he crossed the Tagus.

"Nobody knows what happened. Our ancestor spoke some angelic spell and with a heavy heart began to drown the Inquisitor. With a heavy heart, because as a ferryman he was meant to protect people from the water rather than drown them. Before Juglar drowned, a storm broke. It was as though something else had joined the fight for the body of the Inquisitor, as though the angelic powers were not sufficient to end the impending career of the Inquisitor, a career that would blossom soon. At some point, above the struggle appeared a cloud in the shape of an immense buttocks, and with one fart it transformed the entire region into a dead swamp with infernal vents. Speechless, our ancestor released the man from his hands.

"The half-drowned Inquisitor was saved by the witch that lived by the Forgotten Ford on the Tagus. A few days later, after regaining his strength, he rewrote and trimmed the auto-da-fé...

"On this day, our ancestor and his entire family were cursed. Men died too early, the children were born weak and sickly. The women were lonely. For generations we have lived in poverty, despair, and desperation... And it will be like this until we manage to escape from the tasks imposed on our family two hundred and fifty years ago..."

Outside the window the noise ceased, and silence gripped the room. Tomé Sr. listened. Voices in the yard. The man who had been building the casket had paused his work. And then he had begun to joke with someone else who had brought him water:

"...apparently, in the Jewish Quarter, there lives a black herbalist who can cure all sorts of ailments. Ahara, or something like that. She heals without herbs, actually. She listens, looks, touches...and that's it. It's gone. But she hides, because now anybody can be accused of witchcraft. I've also conjured up a nice box, huh? Ha, ha, ha! Oh, if the rich would hire the poor to die for them, then the poor could live in prosperity…"

When the hammer started again, Tomé Sr. continued:

"I found a descendant of that Inquisitor. They have grown thick with fat, which was melted from the Jews, and now they are named de Juaclac. The last of them is Miguel de Juaclac. I came here for him. Yes, I was looking for work and stumbled upon him, as a representative of the cathedral's community. The altar was only a pretext to find him and… Well, yes, I wanted to kill him. Only, it turned out to be very difficult. With God as my witness, I tried many ways. Until I finally went to his wife's shop… I pretended that I wanted to buy a fan, that Narciso was my old friend, that I must return to Madrid, and I gave her a note for Narciso Tomé… No, I did not know that it would lead to an affair… I knew that Miguel was so jealous that he would pull his sword and demand a duel… This was the only hope."

The person named Narciso had been sitting on the edge of their chair for a long time, and now they rose suddenly, knocking over the chair and throwing their cup to the floor. The glass shattered into many small pieces, bloodying the tile with unfinished wine.

"What?! You risked the life of your son, his entire family, maybe even our entire family, in the name of some bullshit curse? You would be happy, fool, if we had all died because of your revenge, and you would believe that we would suffer no more?! No one would be poor, unhappy, desperate, in pain, because nobody would exist! No more children would be born weak and sick, because there would be no more children! You madman, I should smother you with this pillow so that you might get to your coffin quicker. I spit on you and you disgust me. You disgust me twofold, because not only did you want all of us murdered at the hands of a stranger, but this entire time you have not cared where your son is, this son who allegedly removed the curse from your family by getting himself stabbed! Because from the very beginning you have known who I am!"

"Where is Narciso?"

"I do not know! He dissolved into the air like poplar fluff, he fled, straight to Heaven."

"He will return... return... turn..."

"How dare you, Antonio, how could you?"

"And you, why are you not seeking him? You cannot forgive him?"

"This is not about forgiveness, it is about a broken heart. How long does it take to mend a broken heart?"

"He will return, return, because he loves you, as no one has loved..."

"Then why did he betray me?"

"...loved, only you did not want to see it.È

Now they both wept. Tomé Sr. pleaded quietly:

"Forgive me. Forgive me, forgive. I know it is all my fault... I have brought everything on you. I am at fault for what Narciso did..."

"Oh no, Antonio. You are simply trying to explain your stupid vendetta. You are not to blame for anything. That woman seduced Narciso. You had nothing to do with it. You had her meet him? So what. You see yourself... I forgive you. You did not break my heart or ruin my life, somebody else has done that, and I allowed him to. I forgive you. You may die peacefully."

In this moment, from the yard came a cry:

"I am finished, Antonio! My work is done. Goodbye!"

Tomé Sr. looked at Esperanza and asked:

"Give me a hug at the end..."

"Are you afraid, Antonio?"

"It's not that I'm afraid of death, but that I would like to be there when it happens."

And when he was lying like a child in Esperanza's arms, with a fading voice he said:

"Persevere... and do not be afraid. You are the hope of the family. Without you... What can I tell Him?"

"Tell who?"

"Well, God. I think I will see Him today..."

"After what you have told me here today, I would not be so sure...
Tell Him, whomever He is, to shave that beard and stop being our
Father. Ask Him to finally be a Mother to us..."

Tomé Sr. probably did not hear these last words. A streak of light
fell through the open window, bright, warm, almost material. Over
that streak, like a bridge over the abyss, climbed the last breath of
Antonio Tomé, and from behind the closed doors, quiet sobs rose to
bid farewell.

Esperanza went to the window. Over the sloping roofs of Toledo,
the sound of the cathedral bells carried. Far beyond the city, beyond
the Tagus and the suburbs on the other side of the river, the hills
rose gently, the sheep on them like white drops of milk, from which
someone will make cheese, like they have done in the years before,
like they have done in the past, like they have done always.

Only Tomé Sr. will no longer be there. His world will go with
him, and from his window, the roofs will no longer drop to the river,
beyond which there will no longer be hamlets and hills, and on them
nobody will let the sheep graze, nobody will milk them, nobody will
make cheese. In his world, even I will not be there, standing in the
window, like my husband, wondering— in whose world do the sheep
graze on that side of the Tagus? In mine—doña Esperanza Tomé's, or
in his—Narciso Tomé's?

On the other side of the Tagus, the hills resembled the landscape
of Toro, the hometown of Tomé Sr., they resembled the hills on which
I first kissed Narciso, and I understood that I loved him.

I opened the door to let the weeping family enter. The thought
struck me that the two worlds—mine and Narciso's—do not exist,
that we had always been together. Even when we were apart, his reality
tore into my dreams, his escape ended with what I am: at once both
him and myself. This unity with him, which I always dreamed of, has
been a part of me since the day he left. I know that he is near. He will
return, to complete himself, because we have always been one.

# IMMOBILIZATION

*(A chapter that appears in this place only for historical credibility
and can be skipped by those for whom the story we are telling
is more important than chronological accuracy.)*[37]

||||||||||||||||||||||||||||||||||||||||||||||||||||||||||||||||||||||||||||||||||||||||||||||||||||||||||||||||||||||||||||||||||||||||||

THE PILGRIMS WITH WHOM I WALKED HAD LONG SINCE LEFT ME
behind. My feet, calves, thighs seemed to wade through a mass of
memories, fears, uncertainties. The past caught my knees and took
away my breath.

I was returning without knowing to what.

When I saw Toledo, I had only enough strength to fall to my knees.

Kneeling, I felt, was a gesture that meant two things. On the one
hand, like a pilgrim, I was ready to kiss the ground, which I took as my
own, and on the other hand—I felt that on my knees, I would not go
forward, I could not, I did not want to. Joy and bitterness. Bitter joy. I

---

37  The death of Tomé Sr., which happened in the previous chapter, has its place
in history in the year 1730, so two years before the completion of the altar in
the cathedral in Toledo. The following chapter, "Completion," occurs on the day
of the consecration of that altar, so June 9, 1732. To somehow deal with this
passage of time, we have introduced an additional chapter, "Immobilization,"
which links these two events.

was filled with a desire to meet Esperanza, to meet my wife, but I also knew, I felt that I was not ready for this meeting. I was not myself.

I crawled from the road to a slope and hid behind a boulder where I was face to face with Toledo. So close and yet so far. Beyond the pastures, sharply falling to the river, beyond the river, the city climbed sharply to the sky. When you look at it, first you always see Alcázar, the castle where people were burned at the stake and fought with the bulls, and then the cathedral, the synagogue, the monasteries by the walls. But a city is not only its largest buildings, but its houses, small blocks covered with small roofs… At least, that is how they looked from this distance.

I wondered how something so small could have lasted me for so many years. And at the same time, this pile of rubble swam towards me like the Promised Land. The Tagus was bleached and gilded with milk and honey. Clouds of poplar fluff flew through the city like a host of angels, flying towards these hills and away, as though this was not a city, but unreality.

Maybe, indeed, this city was not real, maybe it was only a vision of my soul, a mirage, Fata Morgana, because I saw it too clearly for my eyes. After years of work on drawings, often by lamps, after dark, until late, my eyes had weakened, lost their strength, lost the ability to see things farther away than the tip of my nose. But now I could see clearly. House by house, farther and farther. Rows of buildings lining streets, detectable only by the gaps between their roofs. Bricks, stones, tiles, pigeons, and cats on roofs.

Windows like ants, tiles like grains of flour.

I recognized houses. Ours—abandoned, without a trace of life and the house of my father. When the cathedral bells rang, somebody stood in the window of his bedroom.

How did I know that somebody stood there?

In the black hole of the open window somebody appeared in a dark coat with dark hair, but a bright face. This person held his hand on his breast, a familiar gesture.

Yes, it was me.

I, Narciso Tomé, who is telling this story, stood in the window of the house of my father. And I, Narciso, this same Narciso, lay on a slope opposite the city staring at myself. So, it is true that I still live and I am rebuilding the cathedral, or else somebody is impersonating me, has entered into my skin. Why?

The meadows below me rolled down towards the river and smelled like the meadows of my youth on which Esperanza and I loved each other. How did I know that it was love? After all, I chased others, I was infatuated with other girls. Why her? We were not two halves of an apple, nor did I believe in God's plan. We were more like two suns, which found each other in the cold cosmos and joined so that the light would always now accompany us.

There—I, the one she sustained. Here—the one, who should not exist.

*

I lost track of time. Evening came, and night. Huddled beneath a boulder, I saw shooting stars, and then dawn broke and the dew fell on me. Around noon I had to cover my face, I could not look any longer. In the night it became cold and I think the rain fell. In the morning I was awakened by the sound of bells on sheep that grazed nearby. The shepherd stared at me for a moment, then walked away with his sheep. I did not feel hunger. I felt nothing.

The next day, the shepherd sat with me and opened his bundle. From it he removed a piece of cheese and a handful of olives.

The olives were fat and juicy, the cheese salty and delicate, a sheep cheese. It seemed a bit dry, but its taste opened like a flower in the mouth. A true manchego. I had never eaten one better.

The shepherd said:

"How come Moses never entered the Promised Land? After all, he could part the seas, squeeze water from a rock, but when he arrived at his destination, he had to die. He wandered with the Jews through Sinai for forty years, until a new generation of pilgrims was born, until his people were born again. For Moses, that was his life, he lived in it, he completed it, for the rest of them—no. When life hangs on you like loose clothing, or squeezes you like a bad shoe, then it is difficult to live. Maybe your time has not come yet. This might not even be your Promised Land. Maybe this is Jericho… Before these walls fall for you, you may tend the sheep with me."

Then, like a good shepherd, he threw a lamb across his shoulders and walked ahead.

I, unlike him, was not a good shepherd. My sheep went missing, they ran not knowing where, because there was nowhere to go. Sometimes I went missing, staring at the city and forgetting about the sheep. Nothing was happening. The sheep always returned to the pens themselves, required milking. My shepherd, whose name I do not know to this day, did not call me by any name, as though we were not people, but nameless ghosts. Wanting to help me and save me from chasing the sheep across rocks, he suggested that I take up cheese preparation. And this is how I became a cheesemaker. You will probably think that this is a completely silly resolution for my return pilgrimage to Toledo. Maybe You're right.

In the production of cheese, time passes slowly, and the body does not tire. One has a lot of time to think. No, do not worry, I will not bore You with the thoughts that passed through my head in those times. I only want to share a few reflections with You.

First of all, I realized that manchego cheese is only prepared with milk from Manchega sheep, typical of this area. The milk must be fatty, and then it ferments in the heat, a heat lower than body temperature. If you add the yeast of a different sour milk, it can go bad in the duration of a single mass (and time on the hills is measured by the bells of the cathedral, the same as in the city).

Is this not a description of my fall, the souring of my soul?

And then then you have to cut the loose cheese into pieces as thick as your thumb. I felt the cold steel of Miguel, who wanted to cut me down. The cold of the steel became a fever. The cheese should be warmed, as though it has a fever. Let the whey drain from it, as the blood drained from me in the flying machine. What remains must be kneaded, choked, kept under pressure, the way I was in the valley with the bulls.

And once it has formed, then the manchego cheese is rubbed in salt, or dipped in salt water. The way I was dipped by Noah in the salt pool, rubbed with the salty soapstone... How much salt remained in me after those baths, I do not know. In a manchego, the salt should not exceed one-tenth of a quarter of the weight of the cheese. And then the cheese is left to mature.

And here comes the worst part: how could I enter Toledo without "maturing," since manchego must mature for at least two months?

Often, the cheese is aged for longer, a year, two. It must sit in a well-ventilated and humid place. All cheeses are similar because they are squeezed from the same mold. The sides of the cheese have the same design as my skin—I pressed a thickly knotted felt (esparto) onto them, which I received from the shepherd to cover my body, which had burned bronze, like the skin of the cheese. On the top and bottom of each wheel of cheese, a flower was stamped.

During cheesemaking, there is time for more than thought. I studied Toledo.

First of all, our house was not abandoned. I saw us eating breakfast on the terrace on the roof. I saw Esperanza, the children, myself, just as I had been in the window of my father's bedroom. I longed for them, I pitied myself for being here, not there. I longed for Esperanza, for the children. I thought that this, what I was now involved with, I had initiated with my affair. Meeting with Nora outside of time and outside of the knowledge of other people, living in pockets of time, directed me to this forked road, where I was both here and there. There I am a good father to the family, and here—a derelict who does not have the courage to humble himself, to apologize and return to his place. As who? As reformed scum? And then what will happen to that other one, the good and the respected one?

And what will happen to me when that other one discovers my existence?

In moments like this, I focussed on my work in earnest. It helped me not to think. Some three months after meeting the shepherd, my first cheese was ready. The shepherd examined it thoroughly, tapped it and smelled it, and then cut a triangular piece from the top to the bottom. A wedge with the edge of the wheel as its base. He turned it on its side and cut off its skin, which was the best part of the cheese, cut off the top, which had the same shape as the base. He looked, smelled, squeezed it between his fingertips, until finally he put it into his mouth. He chewed with his eyes closed.

When he had finished, before he had even opened his eyes, he said:

"If you have somebody in the city, you should give your cheese as a gift."

Roughly every two weeks, a trader who bought our cheeses came from town. I could have sent it through him, but I did not. Before it came to this, I had a lot more to understand. Wanting to control the taste of the cheese, I decided to separate the sheep (and therefore their milk) by the pastures in which they grazed. We had the milk of sheep that grazed on the steep, northern slopes, where the grass was sharp and mingled with dry herbs, and the milk of sheep that grazed on the southern, sunny slopes. There was a herd that grazed low, near the Tagus, and a group from the summit, directly opposite Toledo. The cheeses made from each type of milk matured for two months before we could give our verdict on which was best. For the shepherd, the pastures were unimportant. The art was in the mixing of milk and the modification of the final product's taste with the help of the salt rub. After a few months, he acceded to my innovation. The cheeses with the lowland milk were the best for pasteurization. The milk from the northern slopes was best suited for lengthy maturation. Those from the slopes opposite Toledo were ready in two months without pasteurization. These slopes were also my favourite.

Once, already after sunset, at the time when the entire city falls on its knees before open windows in order to speak their evening prayers, it seemed that I could hear the clatter of knees, the creak of the floorboards, the whispers of prayers. It seemed as though the prayers did not flutter off to Heaven at all, to the feet of the throne of the Most High, but that they flew here, to the meadow, drowning in the grasses that, tomorrow, the sheep would nibble. I understood why some sheep, while grazing, would raise their heads and bleat plaintively:

"Beeeeeeeeeeh…"

I imagined that they had landed on some forgotten, painful prayer.

And then a revelation came to me. I understood what I was doing there, and what I should do now. My slope across from Toledo did not only accept prayers, but the souls of the dead. Like the morning dew, they clutched the blades of grass, were lost in the throats of sheep, and processed into milk, into cheese. Into my cheeses, which, returning to the city, secretly smuggle souls, which then enter the bodies of those who will, one day, return them to the slope, where the shepherd and his sheep will again take care of them.

I saw myself as a craftsman of metempsychosis, one who allows souls to return to the city and to remain with their loved ones. The cheeses I worked on suddenly grew into secret vehicles for the soul. I understood that I myself, my being, my soul, must restore myself to my body in Toledo, so that I could complete my return. I knew that my cheese needed to be sent to Narciso Tomé. I also knew that month after month I would send pieces of my soul, drowned in the cheese, until my whole body would return there to Toledo. Our design would be a different symbol, which I would print on my cheeses. If he is me, then on his neck hangs my old medallion, with which I have never parted. A small, silver medallion, cut in the shape of a Cross of Jerusalem.

The shepherd allowed me to print this symbol on the cheeses made from the slope lying opposite from Toledo. I spent an entire Sunday molding a new lid and bottom for my cheese.

Then I began to work on my cheese.

After two months, when my cheese was ready, I met a messenger who I could trust. It went like this.

The moon that night was full and bright. Sitting in the grass on the slopes and holding my cheese to the moon, I stared at the fading town and did not notice when night came and when I fell asleep.

A grey-eyed boy woke me:

"You're reeling, man, like a drunkard. How did you get here?"

Behind him, a ray of dawn chequered the eastern clouds.

"I erred from the path, and because I am not Titan, I had to rest. And what are you doing here so early?"

"Before the sun's burning eye drinks the dew and dries the day, I must fill up this basket with herbs, herbs that can return health or take it away. After all, the earth is not only a grave, but a womb from which we have all come, all of us suckling different virtues. Thus, it is such a miracle, the grace that hides in herbs, plants, and stones. The cheapest of them can sometimes help, just as the best can harm in excess. Good lives through evil, when we have too much, and evil sometimes reveals itself through good. Inside the innocent flower, the remedy that heals sits right next to the poison that buries. The smell revives you or soothes your senses, and the taste kills, leaves you without will. Similarly, in the soul, evil and good go together, and when the worse dominates, soon the rest of the man spoils, dies."[38] And then he looked at me and said: "It's a family thing. We have a tendency to dramatize."

He sat beside me and from beneath his hood, his red hair spilled. I asked him:

"Why are you not working at the forge, blacksmith?"

---

38  This is a paraphrase of Friar Laurence's monologue from Shakespeare's Romeo and Juliet, Act II, Scene III.

"Then, I forged excess for men, and now I am able to give them what they lack."

"Love?"

"Health. With my wife, I treat the sick, but she must hide herself, so I gather the herbs that her patients need. I come here every full moon. Do you also need something?"

"Yes. I would like you to take this cheese into the city for me. I would like you to give it to Narciso Tomé."

I do not know if I dreamed this. Throughout the entire month I wondered what this meeting could have meant, and if Italo took my cheese, or if some animal ate it during my sleep. At the next full moon, however, I waited for him and gave him one with the Cross of Jerusalem for Narciso, and a second, a regular one with a flower for him and his wife. In this manner, I gave Narciso twelve cheeses. After twelve, I bid goodbye to my shepherd and went into the city.

It was Sunday, the 9th of June, in the year 1732.

# COMPLETION

*(In which the altar in the cathedral in Toledo is finished, and doña Esperanza receives the honour attributed to her husband.)*

||||||||||||||||||||||||||||||||||||||||||||||||||||||||||||||||||||||||||||||||||||||||||||||||||||||||||||||||||||||||||||||||||||||||||||||||||||||||||

BLACK MARBLE ON THE FLOOR, A BLACK BED BEHIND BLACK CUR-tains, black silk instead of linen, black satin instead of drapes. Somewhere in all this black the white Madonna hangs, with the same complexion as the dying man.

So this is what the cardinal's bedroom looks like.

"I am trying to enjoy myself until the end. I still want to catch that witch. Bring in the boy!"

Somebody besides us is in the bedroom. The doors pour a wave of light into the chamber. A small and thin boy steps uncertainly across the threshold and drowns in the darkness.

"What is your name?"

"Giacomo Girolamo Casanova, Your Eminence."[39]

"And when were you born?"

"On the second of April in the year 1725. In Venice, Your Eminence."

"You do not need to only call me 'Eminence,' boy. We have so many beautiful words. You may call me 'Your Exaltedness,' or 'Your Worthiness,' boy."

"Yes, Your Worthiness, Your Eminence."

"Why have you come to our city?"

"…"

"Do not be shy! Anyways, we both know why."

"In that case, Your Worthiness, I came to admire the altar of Your Eminence, Your Exaltedness. But…I saw that everything that is famous and beautiful in the world loses something if we trust the descriptions and illustrations of writers and artists, and we must go to see and admire it for ourselves."[40]

"Shut up, boy, if I have not asked you. And then, then where did you go? Where did you go after you visited the cathedral!?"

"I went with my family to, His Sublimity, the witch."

"For what?"

---

39   Giacomo Girolamo Casanova (born in Venice on April 2, 1725, died on June 4, 1798, in Dux, Bohemia, now Duchcov, Czech Republic).

His father, Gaetano Casanova was an actor and director. He married Giovanna Maria (Zanetta) Farussi in 1724, an actress of extraordinary beauty. In his childhood, Casanova suffered from nosebleeds, and nobody predicted a long life for him. His life was dominated by strong women, such as his mother and the witch (who healed him of his nosebleeds). The parents of Casanova left him under the care of his grandmother and left for London. Zanetta and Gaetano returned to Venice in the year 1728. Casanova's father died in 1732, and Zanetta refused to give her hand to any and all suitors and decided to raise her children alone. Soon, however, she left Venice and settled in Dresden, where she became a member of the Comici Italiani.

40   A quote from "Histoire de ma vie," G. G. Casanova.

"Since my childhood, I have been haunted by, Eminence, nose-bleeds, and my father thinks that I will die prematurely. But she healed my nose. It does not, Your Worthiness, bleed."

"How did she heal you?"

"…"

"HOW!?"

"She put, Your Worthiness, into my nose, and then she pulled it, Your Sublimity, out and…and then she attached, Your Exaltedness, to…she attached, Your Eminence, to my weenie…"

"Did she say something while she was doing this, boy?"

"She said that true love is love that sometimes arises after sensual pleasures, and if it happens like this, it is most often an immortal love. All other types of love become routines after some time, or are pure fantasy…"

"…Your Worthiness."

"Pure Your Worthiness fantasy, Your Eminence," Giacomo repeated.

"Can you find her again?" The Cardinal asked.

"But I am healthy already…"

"Well then, go to Hell! Take him away."

"Cardinal," I spoke in the darkness, once Giacomo had left: "This woman who is called the witch has not hurt anyone. She has clients because she hides herself, but if you allow her to operate out in the open, nobody will be interested in her." And, changing my tone, I reminded him: "You wanted to see me, Sir."

"Is it finished…my work…?"

"If you are asking about the altar, then yes. Sir, I beg you, order the curia to pay for our work before your time runs out…So that you may live as long as possible."

"Money, money, money! Narciso, I want to give you something more valuable. I am giving you immortality."

"Sir, our benefactor, I do not need immortality. I have children who need something to eat, something to wear."

"Narciso, you will be famous! People will write books about you. Do not reject my gift. It may be my last."

"Sir, you know that I gave you all of my talent. Not only I, but my entire family toiled for you. Since our father died two years ago, we can barely cope. Give us just half of what the curia owes us. Just a quarter."

"Do not argue with the dying! I am finished! This is my will. You must sign the altar before it has been blessed. Bless the altar on the first Sunday after my death. My body will rest beneath the altar after its consecration. On the first Monday after my funeral, you will be officially appointed to the position of Maestro of the Cathedral in Toledo. For your lifetime. Do not think this altar is anything important. Anybody can whip something up along the lines of the Churrigueresque. I will tell you something else. At the end of my life, I have learned another lesson. The synod sent me to Córdoba. Brrr, a terrible city. It is as though the Moors left it only yesterday. The houses are all the same, the university, the people. Once, there were some Jewish and Arabic scholars there. Marmalades and Avocadoes..."

"Maimonides and Averroes."

"Whatever. What made the biggest impression on me was the mosque. A city of arcades. A forest of columns with a roof on stone horseshoes and a cathedral built bisecting this forest. A barbaric place, which could never be turned into a church. Why did they send me there? They wanted me to see the monument to Cardinal Pedro de Salazar. One small figure, life-size, sure, but only one. And look at my altar! Hundreds of people, angels, saints. Everybody, everybody, except for me! You think I have not noticed that you have put your whole family into it. Your daddy, your brothers, even your servants. And in the centre, who? The Blessed Virgin, with the face of your wife..."

"Oh, no!" I protested, but he would not allow the interruption.

"And the Baby Christ with your daughter's features!!! Yes, yes, yes! You will burn in Hell for this vanity. And only my protection will spare you from the fire beyond this life... The one thing that is good, and that we have created together, is the skylight through which my soul will fly into the vastness. I want my altar to be called 'Astrolabium,' after my name... Go now, Narciso. Well, go now, go..."

"I am not Narciso."

Silence, and then a cry:

"Everybody out! I said get out! Nobody! Don't you dare eavesdrop..."

In the darkness, the doors allowed shadows to pass before being extinguished. He was panting, as though he were about to die:

"Do you really think that we are all idiots?! Do you want to ruin everything?"

"I only want to say that I am Esperanza Tomé, who pierced your musty cathedral with the light that I brought to your monument. My name should appear on your monument."

Snarling, he prayed. From the mutterings, words leered:

"...Thy will be done... Get my confessor and go, finally... Esperanza Tomé."

*

The mass was about to begin and the crowds filled the church. I stood before Transparente thinking of the end of my work. Nobody will name it anything other than Transparente—clarity. I also did not engrave the words: "Narciso Tomé—Maestro of the Cathedral in Toledo." What has been engraved is not in keeping with the last will of the cardinal. Before Narciso, I wrote my own name. "Esperanza and Narciso Tomé" sounds more just, here and now. I know one day my name will be removed.

Years of hiding in the skin of my husband, years of mourning for lost love, they were my cocoon, the larva of my life. If I was able to bring the light into this dark cathedral, I will bring it as well into my life. From today, I will be Esperanza Tomé who is telling this story about myself and my husband, Narciso.

This is our story.

We are this story.

*

All that was left was the removal of the ladder, which reached to the skylight where a sheaf depicting rays of sunlight was being painted over for the last time. When the painter was finished, I ordered him to leave the ladder, and I climbed to the top in order to check the paint. On my chest, I felt Narciso's medallion. I had begun to wear it after the first time the redheaded blacksmith from my dream appeared in my house and brought me manchego cheese imprinted with the Cross of Jerusalem. I had never seen these cheeses before. These crosses, also, were usually hidden. I wore this cross as a sign of freedom, my freedom from feelings of anger, jealousy, and sadness, and his freedom, Narciso's, from his feelings of guilt for his affair. I did not know if Narciso lived, and if he lived, where he was. I trusted that if he lived, he would feel my forgiveness.

For a year I wore the medallion, and each month the cheese with the sign arrived at our house. Until finally, a few days ago, this same redhead handed me the cane that he always carried, along with the cheese. In the cane, a sword was hidden. The same sword that struck Narciso?

I am not religious, but I did not want that weapon in my house. I respected the work of the blacksmith, and I did not throw the sword into the Tagus. I decided to use it as a votive, a gift to the altar of Narciso, a gift for him, himself. I had it hidden under my coat.

Nobody was under the ladder, because the church servants had closed the entrance to the ambulatory to preserve order. I was alone. The ladder trembled below me, and fear whirled inside me that with the altar finished I would fall from the ladder to my death, or worse, fall onto a stranger's sword… Fear, superstitious fear, gripped me at the top of the ladder when I pulled the sword from the stick and slid it into the gap behind the metal sheaf of rays, below the Last Supper, in the place where Narciso sat. I knew I had to descend before I fell, but I was so near the window that I could not control myself and I glanced through it quickly.

On the other side, a sea of heads surged, trembling like the rungs below me. All of Toledo had come for the blessing of the altar. I saw them as we are seen from the heavens, and each head was a single world, a single globe, a single Earth. Each of them was a lifetime of looking with hope, or hopeless fatigue, wishing or suffering, lonely, dejected, abandoned, unwanted. And then, on my back, I felt a warm look. A bright beam slipped along my cheek and touched somebody in the crowd and still another and still another, like the finger of a child lifting entire worlds from dead letters. Like a pointer for reading the Torah, which leads the reader to Truth. And from the top of this rickety ladder I saw them all, Tomé Sr. and Maja, the pale boy who no longer bleeds and the fat employee of the Inquisition, Petra with my children and the redheaded blacksmith with a black woman, standing hand in hand, Noah, who was so thin that he seemed to float, and my brothers, their wives and their children. And finally, there, far, at the very end, in a crowd of beggars I saw him.

I saw him very clearly, as though I were seeing him for the first and last time.

# The End

# ACKNOWLEDGEMENTS

I WOULD LIKE TO ACKNOWLEDGE THE WORK OF THE PUBLISHING Team of FriesenPress and especially Christoph Koniczek and Joshua Robinson. I would like to thank my editor and my friends who helped me with bringing this text to the final form. I would like to thank my son, Max Karpinski, who has translated the text from Polish to English. I am also grateful to Hannah Karpinski, who has put finishing touches on my editing. Finally, I would like to express my gratitude to my partner, Eva Karpinski, who has dedicated numerous hours of reading and improving the text in both languages.

9 781525 523694